The Library
Union Street
Wells BA5 2PU

6/25

SOMERSET
COUNTY LIBRARY
CANCELLED

Please return/renew this item by the last date shown on this label, or on your self-service receipt.

To renew this item, visit **www.librarieswest.org.uk** or contact your library

Your borrower number and PIN are required.

LibrariesWest

4 6 0358369 7

DEATH ON WOLF FELL

Also by Nick Oldham from Severn House

The Jessica Raker thriller series

DEATH AT DEAD MAN'S STAKE

The Henry Christie thriller series

CRITICAL THREAT
SCREEN OF DECEIT
CRUNCH TIME
THE NOTHING JOB
SEIZURE
HIDDEN WITNESS
FACING JUSTICE
INSTINCT
FIGHTING FOR THE DEAD
BAD TIDINGS
JUDGEMENT CALL
LOW PROFILE
EDGE
UNFORGIVING
BAD BLOOD
BAD COPS
WILDFIRE
BAD TIMING
SCARRED
TRANSFUSION
DEMOLITION
DEATH RIDE

The Steve Flynn thriller series

ONSLAUGHT
AMBUSH
HEADHUNTER

DEATH ON WOLF FELL

Nick Oldham

SEVERN HOUSE

First world edition published in Great Britain and the USA in 2025
by Severn House, an imprint of Canongate Books Ltd,
14 High Street, Edinburgh EH1 1TE.

severnhouse.com

Copyright © Nick Oldham, 2025

Cover and jacket design by Nick May at bluegecko22.com

All rights reserved including the right of reproduction in whole or in part in any form. The right of Nick Oldham to be identified as the author of this work has been asserted in accordance with the Copyright, Designs & Patents Act 1988.

British Library Cataloguing-in-Publication Data
A CIP catalogue record for this title is available from the British Library.

ISBN-13: 978-1-4483-1442-3 (cased)
ISBN-13: 978-1-4483-1665-6 (e-book)

This is a work of fiction. Names, characters, places and incidents are either the product of the author's imagination or are used fictitiously. Except where actual historical events and characters are being described for the storyline of this novel, all situations in this publication are fictitious and any resemblance to actual persons, living or dead, business establishments, events or locales is purely coincidental.

No part of this book may be used or reproduced in any manner for the purpose of training artificial intelligence technologies or systems. This work is reserved from text and data mining (Article 4(3) Directive (EU) 2019/790).

All Severn House titles are printed on acid-free paper.

MIX
Paper | Supporting responsible forestry
FSC
www.fsc.org FSC® C013056

Typeset by Palimpsest Book Production Ltd.,
Falkirk, Stirlingshire, Scotland.
Printed and bound in Great Britain by
TJ Books, Padstow, Cornwall.

The manufacturer's authorised representative in the EU for product safety is
Authorised Rep Compliance Ltd, 71 Lower Baggot Street,
Dublin D02 P593 Ireland (arccompliance.com)

Praise for Nick Oldham

"Ominous and terrifying . . . Readers who like their police procedurals gritty, violent, twisty, and tense will love it"
Booklist Starred Review of *Death at Dead Man's Stake*

"Suspenseful . . . Oldham heightens the tension"
Kirkus Reviews on *Death Ride*

"A brutal, gut-wrenching read with a roller-coaster ride of a plot"
Booklist on *Death Ride*

"Riveting"
Publishers Weekly on *Death Ride*

"Oldham continues to push the envelope"
Kirkus Reviews on *Death Ride*

"Pulse-pounding action, nail-biting suspense . . . perfect for Ian Rankin fans"
Booklist on *Scarred*

"This edge-of-the seat narrative, with constantly ratcheting tension, features a twist-a-minute plot and a thoroughly unexpected shock ending"
Booklist on *Transfusion*

About the author

Nick Oldham is the author of the acclaimed Henry Christie series and the Steve Flynn thrillers. He is a retired police inspector, who served in the force from the age of nineteen.

@NickOldhamBooks

This one is for Belinda

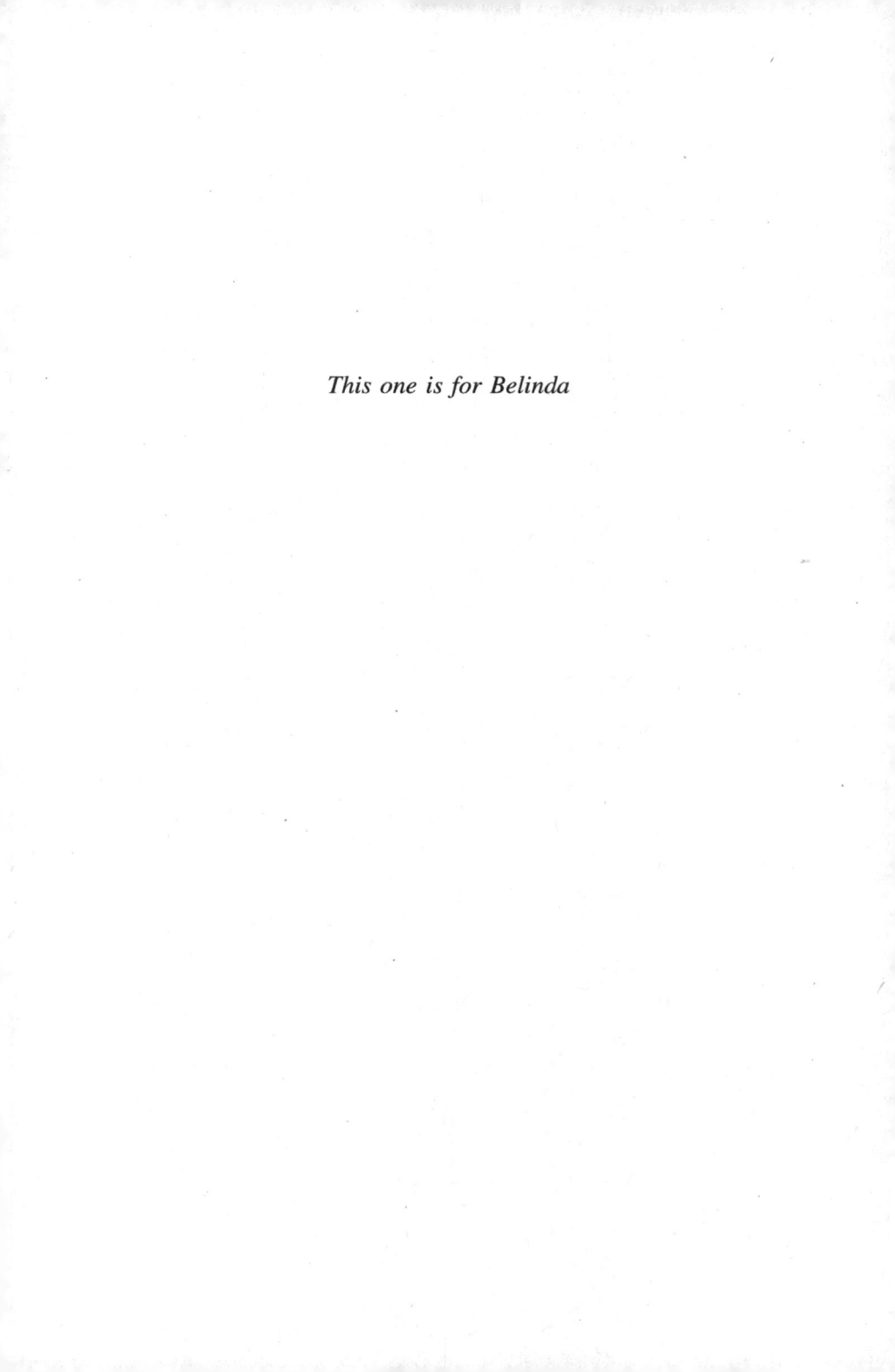

ONE

On a day that Lance Drake should – technically – have been celebrating, he was in fact almost overcome by terror.

To be honest, he had been terrified for the last few months, but it was a kind of subdued terror. Today, when he should have been rejoicing, his level of terror reached new heights.

So he spent that morning in his cell on the remand wing at Preston Prison refusing to come out. He'd been too ill even to go for breakfast, knowing that awful griping pain in the pit of his gut would have resulted in him bringing back anything he tried to swallow. Even the sausages, which weren't bad at all.

Instead, he stayed rooted in his cell, his harsh prison blanket pulled tightly over his head, and even though he hadn't got flu and was quite warm he shivered uncontrollably under the heavy bedding.

And he cried.

Tears streamed down his face, making his pillow soggy.

Pathetic, he knew.

He also knew that he was pretty lucky to have made it through the last few months and be alive, or at least free from any serious injury, and was as surprised as anyone he was still drawing breath.

Because he had truly expected to have been murdered by now.

He would not have been shocked to have been stabbed to death in the showers or hoisted head-first from the top landing or just simply strangled or suffocated in his bunk whilst he slept.

He expected every other prison inmate to be the one to make him meet his maker. He did not trust anyone who caught his eye, which is why he had tried to avoid any eye contact since coming into prison. He was even wary of the screws – didn't trust any one of the bastards as far as he could chuck them.

He fully expected to be leaving prison in a zip-up body bag. And that had been the subject of many a vivid nightmare, images of his mutilated corpse being carried through the jail by black-clad undertakers, along landings, down metallic steps, around tight corners, out into the secure yard to be hefted into the back of a waiting hearse.

That is how Lance Drake thought his life would end: in pain, squalidly.

But not this. Not to be informed quite late the day before that he would be released on conditional bail to be shoved out into a far more dangerous environment beyond the prison walls where the prospect of a brutal death was inevitable and would be much more painful and drawn out than even having a sharpened toothbrush handle skewered repeatedly through his ribs into his heart, lungs and liver. Death on the outside would consist of torture before demise.

'Kill me now, kill me now,' Lance said repeatedly from under the covers. 'Oh, God.' He buried his face into his grubby pillow which stank of sweat.

The cell wasn't locked, the door just slightly ajar. Lance heard it creak further open on hinges that hadn't been oiled for far too long. He recognized the noise and knew who had stepped into the cell because of the metallic clip of the footsteps. It was the prison officer called Drew who had heel protectors nailed on to his boots and had the most identifiable approach of all of them. He was a smart, mature guy, a stickler for the rules, but maintained his authority through fairness, firmness, a decent sense of humour, a touch of empathy and the ability to give a prisoner a dig if necessary.

Actually, Drew was about the only prison officer Lance half-trusted and he was the one who had delivered the news to Lance that he was going to be released and seen his reaction of dismay.

Lance kept his face pressed into his pillow, totally aware of Drew standing in his cell.

'I'm going nowhere,' Lance said, his voice muffled but audible. 'You can't make me, Mr Drew. I'm dead if you do – dead.'

'Sorry, mate, but you can't stay here . . . big waiting list and all that,' Drew told him softly.

'I won't move. I'll be dead before I reach Preston town centre,' Lance sobbed.

'Honestly, mate, I'm sure you'll be fine. You won't even be going to the city centre, OK? I've arranged a taxi for you. It'll take you directly to the bail hostel. It'll be waiting for you outside the door, OK?'

'I can't afford a taxi,' Lance whined.

'It's on the house.'

'And where is that hostel again?' Lance asked. He had been told but wanted reassurance again.

'Accrington.'

'Not Clitheroe? Not the Ribble Valley?'

'Nope. So come on. There's paperwork to sign for your release.'

Lance pushed himself up on to his elbows, still slobbering on his pillow.

'Come on, mate,' Drew said. 'You'll be fine. Hunker down in the hostel, keep a low profile in Accy. You'll have your own room, so lock the door.'

'OK, OK.'

Lance finally sat upright and swung his spindly white legs off the bed and looked up at Drew.

'What if I said I was going to do a runner? That I won't comply with any bail conditions? You couldn't let me out, then, could you?'

'I'll pretend I haven't heard,' Drew said, 'because going off what you've told me about your predicament, I wouldn't actually blame you for legging it if I'm honest.'

Lance's mouth twisted down at the corners and he rubbed his face.

'C'mon, lad, freedom beckons.'

Lance swore and pushed himself to his feet. His legs felt very weak. He purposely took his time getting dressed and stuffing his belongings into a creased carrier bag. He then followed Drew through the prison, dragging his feet like a petulant teenager, to the ground floor section of the old building where his discharge paperwork was dealt with, signed, and he was handed copies. His bail conditions were outlined to him and, very reluctantly, Lance put his signature on this paperwork too. A short while later, after an ankle tag was fitted, he was taken to the area in which prisoners being discharged were usually met by relatives or friends.

No one was waiting for Lance, which was a relief, and he was told to wait for the taxi to arrive which would take him to the bail hostel in Accrington.

When it pulled up outside, Drew helped Lance to his feet as his legs had gone very wobbly, accompanied him out of the prison and deposited him in the back seat of the vehicle. As well as having wobbly legs, Lance was also feeling very, very nauseous, and it was all he could do not to vomit in the footwell. His skin had turned the colour of parchment paper. He smiled wanly up at Drew.

'Thanks, Officer Drew,' Lance managed to splutter. 'Appreciate you lookin' after us.'

'No problem, Lance. Keep your head down. You'll be OK.'

Lance gasped. 'I doubt it, but look, if I get convicted . . . no, when I get convicted, I just hope I get sent down here and you can look after us again.' Lance, like many northerners, used the word 'us' to mean 'me'.

'If you get sent down here, Lance, I will, I promise.'

'Thanks, mate, thanks.'

Drew stood back and closed the back door of the taxi, which moved away from the kerb. He muttered to himself, 'Like hell I will.'

Drew gave a surreptitious wave to a van parked on a small car park opposite. The driver flashed the headlights once and edged out of the parking space, on to the road and slotted in a couple of vehicles behind Lance's taxi.

Drew nodded then retreated back into the prison.

It's all about information, he thought. Information meant cash, and just by passing a snippet of information, an envelope containing one thousand euros had been left for him on the front wheel of his car on his driveway sometime the night before. Not life-changing dosh, but it would mean a nice amount of spending money on his imminent holiday to the Canary Islands.

As Drew waved and smiled at a colleague behind a desk who buzzed him through a steel door into the secure area of the prison – Lance Drake was not even on his mind now.

And in the taxi, now heading out of Preston along New Hall Lane towards the motorway, Lance, whose eyes were unfocused and blank with despair, didn't have a clue he was being followed.

The journey to Accrington took around half an hour. Traffic was fairly light along the motorways – M6, M61 and M65 – finally exiting the latter at junction seven and travelling into the old mill town where traffic did begin to build up along Hyndburn Road, busy and stop-start at several sets of traffic lights along the way.

There had been little conversation between Lance and the taxi driver, a heavily bearded young man whose ID certificate informed Lance he was called Ibrahim who, throughout the journey, had been regularly checking on Lance via his rear-view mirror. Ibrahim could see Lance's obvious discomfort and worry about something affecting him in a big way.

'Are you OK, man?' Ibrahim finally inquired, bringing Lance out of a trance-like state with a sudden jolt.

Lance shook his head forlornly and said, 'I'm a dead man walking.'

'You serious?' Ibrahim asked.

Lance looked at the taxi driver's eyes in the mirror. 'Yeah.'

'Right, OK.'

They had reached a set of traffic lights on the road outside a large Asda superstore which turned to red on their approach. The taxi stopped four vehicles from the front of the queue.

'Thing is, man . . .' Ibrahim said, glancing into the mirror.

'What?' Lance asked suspiciously.

'Back there' – Ibrahim jerked his head backwards – 'and I don't know if this is connected to what you saying, but y'know, pretty unusual, a van's been with us ever since we left the prison.'

'Eh, what?' Lance spun around and looked through the rear window, his head weaving from side to side to get a view. 'Where? What? Which one?'

'Three cars back, a silver van of some sort.'

'All the way from the prison?' Lance's neck stretched as he attempted to look over the tops of the cars behind.

'Yes . . . might be nowt.'

Lance spotted the van, but could only see the top quarter of it and it was impossible to see who was at the wheel or how many were in it.

Yes, Lance knew this could be complete coincidence, that some other person had completely innocently set off at the same time and taken the exact same route from one side of the county to the other. People made that journey all the time, didn't they? But instant panic inflamed and skewered his thinking, and one thought that skittered through his mind was that, maybe, Drew – his trusted prison officer – might have betrayed him somehow, but he didn't have long to dwell on that horrible prospect.

'And you didn't bother to tell me?' Lance demanded.

'Never even thought 'bout it,' Ibrahim admitted.

'Shit!' A word Lance repeated about ten times. He rotated forwards and saw the lights ahead change. 'Gonna bail,' he announced.

As the taxi crawled forwards, Ibrahim keeping it deliberately slow, Lance shuffled along the back seat to the rear nearside door.

Ibrahim jammed his brakes on and shouted, 'Go man! Best of!'

Lance burst out, keeping low as he scuttled across the width of the pavement and vaulted a low barrier over into the car park at the front of the superstore and, keeping his head down, he crabbed his way between parked cars, stopping and peering over a bonnet towards the road to check whether his escape had been clocked.

His heart, which was pretty low in his chest to begin with, sank even lower.

Of course his escape had been spotted.

A young guy with a blond mop of hair and a baby face Lance did not recognize slid out from the passenger side of the van, which looked like a Transit, and jumped easily over the barrier into the car park whilst the van itself swerved out of the line of traffic and, with the driver sounding the horn in anger, accelerated down the wrong side of the road against oncoming traffic, causing vehicles to swerve to avoid a collision. The van then veered sharp-left once it had jumped the lights and sped into the Asda car park to begin a slow prowl along the lines of parked cars, whilst the guy who had jumped out was doing the same, working his way up and down on foot.

Lance slithered terrified on to his backside and leaned against a car.

He was being hunted and the hunters were closing quickly on him.

He scrambled away on all fours, rolled between some parked cars, then slowly raised his face to peer through the windows of a Fiat 500, trying to pinpoint his pursuers.

The van was easy enough to spot and was currently going in the opposite direction but he'd lost sight of the blond guy on foot, which was a worry, but then the blond man's head suddenly popped up from behind the wing of a car. He was obviously getting down low in order to peer underneath cars to try and spot Lance hiding.

Lance ducked back down and his panic grew exponentially as he tried to think of what to do next.

Sprint back to the road and leg it into the wilds of Accrington, a town he did not know well, or head for the superstore and try to do a disappearing act in there, maybe find a way out through a staff or fire exit?

Neither choice filled him with glee. The relative safety of his prison cell seemed a very long way away and he hankered for its tight four walls and harsh blankets.

One thing for sure was that if he stayed here, rooted to the spot, he would be found.

With an immense effort he twisted on his heels and, still keeping his head below the car line, he moved quickly towards the store, his big problem being that he would have to reveal himself on that final sprint across the concrete apron separating the car park and the store entrance, although he might get missed amongst other shoppers who seemed plentiful and possibly able to offer him some cover.

He went for the sprint and a few moments later he was inside, crossing the inner foyer, passing an unmanned security booth, then was through the automatic barriers into the store itself, walking along a fruit and veg aisle, at which point he realized that in his panic he'd forgotten to bring his bag of belongings with him from the taxi.

Not that there was much in it, but it meant he now had nothing, just the clothes he stood up in and twenty-odd quid in his back pocket. He half thought about nicking some clothes whilst he was in-store – he was an experienced and skilful shoplifter – but he dismissed the idea. It would be just his bad luck to get spotted and nabbed by a store detective . . . but that also gave him food for thought: there was a balance to be had. He wanted his freedom but also wanted to stay alive and, as perverted as it might seem, he'd felt safe on remand, so perhaps there was some sense in getting caught brazenly stealing from here to ensure a quick return to stir. But even as he thought that, he knew even inside his time would be limited: the bad guys just hadn't got him yet.

The best way forwards would be to stay out and disappear into the ether.

Decision made. First thing was to keep out the grip of these two guys from the van, then 'do one'.

He upped his pace through the Ready Meals aisle.

Then stopped abruptly.

The blond guy who had been after him on foot from the van was now standing at the end of the aisle with the cheese counter as a background to him. He wasn't a big fella or anything, just a skanky gofer, a bit older than Lance probably, maybe early twenties, but with a mean twisty grin on his baby face under his mop of hair.

He raised his hand and pointed at Lance, whose bowels released a tiny fart.

Lance didn't hesitate.

He pivoted, almost losing his balance, and set off running in the opposite direction, but stopped again because there was another guy at the far end of the aisle, grinning, beckoning Lance to come to him. His mouth moved as he spoke to his companion via Bluetooth. Lance guessed this guy was the van driver. He'd heard the two men talking and now knew their names – this was Deerman, whilst the blond guy was Chapman.

The only thing Lance had in his favour now was speed and dexterity.

He picked up a handful of chapatti breads from the Indian food display and ran at the guy, flinging the goods at him like a wave of Frisbees, then skidding sideways and ducking at the same time in an effort to contort his way past.

But Deerman didn't even flinch or react to the spinning breads. His eyes were set firmly on Lance. He twisted with his prey and reached out to grab him, almost managing it, but Lance slipped through his hands like he'd been greased up. However, the contact Deerman made was enough to put Lance off his stride and he rolled into a display of bananas, which toppled over and he found himself trying to scramble through a sea of the loose and cellophane-packed bunches of fruit which impeded his getaway and held him back just long enough for him to feel two hands clamp on to his shoulder, then the knee in his back as he was slammed face down into the tiled floor, squishing his face.

'Got ya!' Deerman's voice snarled in his ear.

Then a hood – which could have been a schoolkid's pump bag with a drawstring fastener – was pulled over his head and he was manhandled up to an angle of about forty-five degrees and dragged at that incline through the store. He even heard one of the guys say to someone, 'Nothing to see here.'

Not one person challenged them.

The next twenty minutes or so were just a fearful blur of darkness for Lance. He had been hurled into the back of the van where his head connected with something very hard that stunned him momentarily. A door slammed, then another and he felt the lurch as the engine revved and the vehicle moved.

He tried to squirm but was pinned to the floor by a foot planted on his spine and a voice growling, 'You move an inch and I'll stomp your head to mush.'

Lance took the message on board, stayed flat, face down on the hard metal floor, his head still covered by the hood which, ironically, gave him a sense of security because he knew that when it came off, as it would, he would be in big trouble.

Lance sat there, said nothing, unable to stifle the sobs that wracked his chest or stop the tears flowing down his cheeks.

He knew his wrists and ankles had been cable-tied to the arms and legs of a chair he had been finally dumped in. At least he was thankful he hadn't been strung up by his ankles like a pig's carcass such as he'd seen in so many cheap gangster films.

Perhaps that meant that whoever had kidnapped him had some kind of compassion about them.

That said, he had a good idea who had snatched him, knew their compassion was minimal and was probably all squandered on their pet cat if they had one.

Finally he decided he would be getting no kindness because of what he had done to them, maybe cost them over three-hundred grand and been responsible for getting one of them killed, which all meant that, basically, Lance Drake was very, very screwed.

With a heroic effort he stopped sobbing and tried to focus his eyes to see if he could actually make out anything through the dense fabric of the hood and attempt to work out where he was, but he could not see a thing.

He knew he was in a cold place. Maybe a factory unit of some sort.

And it reeked of weed.

Possibly a cannabis farm.

He could do with a spliff himself right now or preferably an overdose of heroin so he could check out in a state of bliss.

He guessed both would be denied him. If he was going to 'check out' it would not be in a state of bliss. Quite the opposite.

Footsteps behind him.

Lance tensed up, waiting for the piano wire around his throat, which was the way in which the man he'd ratted on had been disposed of in an act of collateral damage. This was the level of villain Lance was involved with, had worked for and who had provided him with a meagre living, moving drugs and other items around for them, delivering and supplying them on their orders.

He wondered what it would feel like.

Rumour was that the guy he'd blabbed on had been killed by using the inner cord of a washing line rather than piano wire. Apparently it had cut deep into the guy's neck, sliced through his Adam's apple and windpipe like a hot knife through butter and almost decapitated him. That was what Lance had heard whispered but didn't know how much of that was true.

Suddenly he jerked as he felt a hand, fingers splayed wide, land on the crown of his head like a raw egg bursting.

Lance emitted a pathetic whimper, akin to a kitten being trodden on.

But then the fingers drew together, gripped the hood and drew it slowly off his head.

Lance blinked, feeling his pupils shrink as the blackness was replaced by light, and he saw he was in a warehouse of some sort. Not huge, perhaps a section of an old mill, constructed of brick.

Alongside one wall was a table of some sort, and Lance recognized and his eyes confirmed what his sense of smell had told him: this was a cannabis packaging plant and there was a neat stack of compacted weed in vacuum-packed brick-sized portions at the end of this conveyor belt.

God, he needed some of that!

Because he also saw that the chair on which he was affixed – and Lance's insides almost crumbled to nothing at this – was in the centre of a large sheet of thick polythene, which was a bad sign in anybody's books. This time it was exactly like some of the gangster films he'd seen; ideal for rolling dead bodies up in and disposing of them without leaving a trace. He felt utterly desperate and horror-stricken.

He looked around and for the first time noticed a figure sitting in a dark corner of the warehouse, in shadow. He was also very aware of the person behind him, the one who had removed the hood.

No words were spoken.

Lance kept quiet, kept still. He knew better than to plead for mercy. It would fall on deaf ears and would sound woeful. So he waited.

The person in the corner remained seated, and as Lance focused on them it became clear that they were wearing one of those full-body police-style forensic outfits with pull-on plastic slippers, disposable gloves, a hood pulled over their head – fastened tightly – and a Covid-style face mask.

Lance gulped nosily, even though his throat was dry. He wasn't completely thick, so it took him only a matter of seconds to connect what the person was wearing to the polythene sheet under his chair and for him to realize that, as one of his cell mates in prison had continually bleated, he was 'fucking doomed'.

Maggie Horsefield watched the arrival of Lance at the mill as he'd been dragged from the back of the van then subsequently tied to the chair on the polythene sheet. As soon as she had heard the street snatch had been successful she had prepared herself for this encounter, this face-to-face with Lance which was the culmination of a process, via various layers and intermediaries, that she had engineered, mainly through the employment of her bent solicitor to get a barrister to challenge Lance's bail situation. Her solicitor had been successful against a weak CPS lawyer who was easily swayed by an extra payday to be very laissez-faire and not try very hard to keep Lance Drake in custody whilst on remand.

When Maggie got word Lance had been lifted, she had been in the portable cabin that was the office in the scrapyard known as Primrose Breakers, a business she owned in Clitheroe, checking the books to make certain that when they were inspected by the cops, as they surely would be – again! – they were squeaky clean.

The local cops – led by an increasingly annoying police sergeant called Jess Raker – had given the scrapyard some stick recently as they (and Raker in particular) tried desperately to trace a blue Peugeot that had been stolen from Blackburn and involved in a fatal hit-and-run 'accident'. The car, as Maggie Horsefield knew, had actually come through the yard, been scrapped, crushed and disposed of well before the police came a-nosing around, without any record being made of its appearance, then disappearance.

And strangely, the normally reliable CCTV system that covered the yard seemed to have big chunks of footage missing, which didn't go down well with 'Bitch Cop' as Maggie callously called Jessica Raker.

Maggie, or Mags as she was better known, left the yard in her Range Rover on hearing about Lance's abduction but swapped vehicles en route to the location Lance was being taken to, and arrived driving a bashed-up old Land Rover she owned but which was registered to a non-existent person in Lancaster and could not be traced back to her.

The location was a sectioned-off part of a disused old cotton mill out in the back of beyond, reached by way of a rough track close to the village of West Bradford to the north of Clitheroe. Most of the mill still existed but not many people ever came close other than kids causing damage, so it was an ideal location for a temporary cannabis packaging plant. One day, if Mags had her way, the whole mill would be converted into luxury apartments which would be owned by her, but that idea was a long way from fruition.

On arrival, she'd put on the forensic suit, over-slippers, gloves and face mask before entering the unit, being quite obsessive in her fear of getting nabbed by science. She had personally rolled out the polythene sheet, prepared the chair and cable ties in the centre of the sheet and then assumed her seated position in the shadows to await Lance's arrival.

Down by her side on the floor was a zombie knife which she glanced at occasionally and winced, understanding why the government wanted to ban them because she knew how terrifying they were in the wrong hands – and they were always in the wrong hands.

Even Mags didn't like them.

She much preferred the stiletto she carried in her clutch bag and had used quite recently to good effect to ward off and kill a would-be rapist who had deserved every centimetre of the blade she had plunged up into his heart.

She picked up the zombie knife and laid it flat across her lap, waiting for Lance's arrival. Today, though, the zombie knife was appropriate to the circumstances and her hands were the wrong ones.

When the hood had been whipped off Lance's head, she gave him a few seconds to orientate himself before standing up and approaching him.

TWO

Sergeant Jessica Raker was in her element, mistress of all she surveyed. She loved this environment, the buzz it gave her, that spurt of adrenaline which would continue to be topped up inside her as the show got on the road and things started to happen.

She leaned on the lectern at the front of the parade room at Clitheroe police station, her eyes shining as they played over the assorted rows of police officers in front of her, including one dog – Police Dog Flynn, a gorgeous German Shepherd with a glistening coat – who sat there as attentively as any of the cops she'd just briefed on this morning's operation.

Jess half-grinned as Flynn's ears came to attention when she asked, 'OK, any questions?'

She expected Flynn to bark one, but he didn't, just allowed his pink tongue to loll out of his mouth and drool with slaver.

Jess looked around the room at the dog handler and the half-serial of Support Unit officers – six constables and one sergeant – all kitted out in dark blue overalls and black steel toe-capped boots, highly trained in many things and well equipped and ready for that day's foray into a suspected cannabis-packing factory near West Bradford. These guys – they were all men that morning – were a cool, ultra laid-back crew and, Jess got the feeling, dependable and professional.

It was expected to be a fairly straightforward job with not too much drama.

Some nice information had come from a dog-walking member of the public that there seemed to be suspicious activity going on at an old, supposedly disused mill – some comings and goings, some unusual vehicles to-ing and fro-ing and a few dodgy-looking individuals.

The dog walker hadn't really thought too much about it but it had fermented in her mind for a few days, after which she'd seen fit to report it to the police and the information had eventually filtered through to Jess's desk.

She had then deployed PC Vinnie McKinty to have a bit of a snoop around in an unmarked car, but he had found the place deserted and locked up. The windows were boarded with steel plates and it was impossible for him to peer through, but he had picked up a couple of stray cannabis leaves near to a loading bay and sniffed up the reek of weed itself.

Two-plus-two: this was either a cannabis farm or packaging plant.

A few more discreet drive-bys over the next couple of days didn't uncover any activity and Jess guessed the place might well have been abandoned. However, when it proved impossible to trace any active owners, she decided to mount a small operation, backed by a search warrant, and then if anything came of it to investigate more deeply who actually owned the place. She secretly hoped the trail would lead to the door of Mags Horsefield with whom Jess had much unfinished business, but that was just a pipe dream. Sometimes it was impossible to trace property ownership.

Jess checked her watch. Almost time to hit the road.

She looked at Vinnie McKinty and Police Community Support Officer Samira Patel who would both be coming along for the ride, and also caught the eye of DC Dougie Doolan, the local CID officer who had secured the warrant but would not be turning out with them because he was struggling with a bad back.

He nodded at her.

She looked at the 'troops' and said, 'Let's go, guys.'

Mags dragged her chair over to Lance, flipped it around and, spreading her legs, sat on it backwards, leaning her breasts on the back rest, looked at her trapped prey through the gap formed by her tightly fastened forensic hood and the left-over Covid mask covering the lower part of her face from the bridge of her nose down. It wasn't as though she wanted to hide her identity from Lance – he knew exactly who she was – but apart from the forensic need, there was also the psychological advantage it gave her over the young man. As all serious criminals knew, a hood and a mask always scared victims shitless, even other crims.

Lance's terror was going off the scale as his eyes took her in and his brain continued to digest everything, including the zombie knife dangling freely, enticingly, between Mags' thumb and forefinger.

'You know they know exactly where I am,' Lance blurted.

'Who would that be? And how?'

'The authorities. My probation people or whoever it is that's supposed to be tracking me.'

'Tracking you?'

'Yeah. You know I'm ankle-tagged, don't you?'

Even though he could only see Mags' eyes, Lance could tell there was a wide smile on the face of his kidnapper.

'You're under the illusion that your tag has been activated?' Mags mocked him.

Lance's slightly cocky expression dropped from his face. 'You mean . . .?'

'I mean your tag will get turned on when I say so. At the moment it's suffering a technical fault.'

'You're shitting me?'

'Nope.'

Hurriedly Lance said, 'I'm sorry.'

'Sorry for what, Lance baby?'

Lance heard a glugging noise behind him. Mags raised her eyes to look beyond his shoulder and Lance attempted to twist his head around to see what was happening and saw the blond guy – Chambers – who had nabbed him from Asda working his way around the building, sloshing liquid out of a jerry can around the floor. The reek of fumes invaded Lance's nostrils: petrol.

He looked desperately at Mags who was still letting the zombie knife swing between her fingertips like some sort of deadly pendulum, between her and her victim.

'Sorry for what, Lance?' Mags asked again.

The glugging sound stopped.

Lance looked over his shoulder at the guy who was now placing things down on the floor which looked like mousetraps.

He looked at Mags.

'I'm waiting,' she said.

Lance started to sob. 'I'm so sorry . . . for getting caught and losing all those drugs.'

'Losing? Don't you mean getting them seized by police?'

'Yes, yes, I'm sorry.'

'Do you know how much that cost me?'

'A lot?'

'More than a lot, Lance . . . a fortune.'

'I was just unlucky.'

'Unlucky to be spotted riding a stolen motorbike, unlucky to be carrying almost half a million quid's worth of cocaine stuffed up your jacket?'

Lance nodded. 'Yuh.'

Mags took a proper grip of the handle of the zombie knife and held it pointed upright.

'But that's not all is it, Lance?' Mags probed.

He shook his head despondently.

'You went on to tell the police that you knew where even more of my drugs were being stored *and* some of my cash – why did you do that?' she asked sweetly.

Lance was silent.

'Lance . . . I asked you a simple question. It may well be wise to answer it.'

Mags slowly waved the zombie knife. Lance watched it move from side to side like he was spellbound by the dance of a cobra.

'To get bail,' he answered.

'Well, that went well, didn't it?'

'No.'

Mags said in a very non-threatening, conversational tone, 'I'm going to slit your throat. You know that, don't you?'

He emitted a deep wail. 'I'm so sorry,' he said hoarsely. 'I don't deserve . . .'

'Deserve what, Lance? To have your throat slit and then have your head cut off.'

'Jesus, Jesus!'

'Jesus?'

'No . . . please, God, no.'

'Lance, let me tell you something, mate.' Mags eased herself up to her feet and swished the blade through the air, making Lance jump. 'You don't deserve a damned thing. You get nicked on a stolen bike carrying my gear then, to try and save your own skin, you blab to the cops.' She swished the blade again like a medieval knight brandishing a broadsword. 'Neither is acceptable.'

'I know, I know, I know . . .' His voice trailed off to nothing but helplessness.

Mags walked over to him, then stepped behind him.

He could feel her presence. Then her left hand slid across his forehead and she jerked his head back, exposing his throat. She laid the blade of the knife across his windpipe and he could feel the honed sharpness against his skin and knew it would cut his throat with ease.

'Don't, please,' he gasped.

Then he felt Mags' hot breath at his ear. She had pulled down her face mask. 'Why ever not, Lance? I'm going to slit your throat,' she breathed like a lover. 'Then step back and watch your blood spout like a fountain until you bleed out, writhing in agony, and then I'm going to set fire to you and burn you to fag ash – and the rest of this place with it.'

This was Lance's last-dance gasp, and with it he said, 'I'll do anything . . . anything to make this right.'

'Anything?' Mags growled, her lips still close to his ear, so close they touched his lobe and a strange, almost exciting shimmer ran through him that probably should not have done in the circumstances.

'Boss!' a voice called from the door of the unit. It was Deerman.

Mags closed her eyes in annoyance, took the knife away from Lance's throat and said irritably, 'What?'

'Cops. We gotta move. Now.'

Because of the location of the old mill, Jess decided there wasn't really much point in trying to sneak up on the place. There seemed to be little activity and there was a good possibility the occupants or whoever was using it had moved on. A sneaky-beaky approach was considered, even though it would have been difficult, but was discarded and a direct assault decided on. These Support Unit guys all looked pretty fit and handy to Jess so if anyone was on the premises or tried to do a runner they'd be easily caught. Plus they also had the guided missile with fangs that was PD Flynn.

Jess was in the lead car – the Clitheroe section Land Rover Defender – which was now the main car driven by Vinnie who, by default, had become the most experienced cop on the shift even though he still had less than four years' service; his 'seniority' gave him first dibs on which car he drove. Not that there was much argument because there was usually only him and maybe a couple of others on duty at the same time, both of whom had less service.

But Vinnie was pretty good, despite his inexperience. He was sharp, determined and a bit ambitious. Jess hadn't known him long but she saw potential, and one day, in the not too distant future, Vinnie would get a job in CID and she would be sad to see him go.

'You OK, sarge?' Vinnie had asked when they clambered into the Defender. He asked her every day, concerned still about the traumatic experience she had recently undergone at the hands of a previous senior PC on the shift, Dave Simpson, who had turned out to be corrupt, dangerous and violent.

The incident with Simpson and a contract killer nicknamed The Saint had only been a few months before and the legal ramifications from it still rumbled on uncomfortably, casting a cloud over the whole of the police station which was only now beginning to clear. But Jess was OK and found she could mostly box the whole thing away in her mind, though occasionally an interior door burst open and some of the brutal images of that violent day with Simpson and The Saint would overcome her, but that was not often now. At the moment she was concentrating on her role as a sergeant with responsibility for the Ribble Valley and also her role as a mum for Lily and Jason, her two fast-growing kids . . . but husband Josh still remained in the hard-to-do category mostly.

She smiled at Vinnie. 'Yeah, I'm good, thanks.'

Vinnie headed out towards Waddington, a pretty village north of Clitheroe, then beyond that to West Bradford where the old mill could be found.

Sitting behind Jess and Vinnie on the bench seat of the prisoner compartment was Samira Patel, literally the first person Jess had met on her first day at Clitheroe. She was very fond of her, seeing potential in Samira as well because she hoped to become a fully fledged cop one day, although her recent attempts to get through the application process had been unsuccessful. Still, Samira was not daunted because she knew she would get there one day. She not only wanted to be a good copper, but also show it was possible for a woman of her background to become an effective front-line officer. Both Jess and Dougie Doolan were behind her ambition and were trying to help by mentoring her through that particular labyrinth.

Behind them in an armoured personnel carrier, known as the Battle Bus, was the Support Unit, packed to the gunnels with muscle and he-man equipment such as crowbars, door rams, shields and batons, and behind them in the little convoy was PD Flynn and his handler.

'So not a lot seemed to be going on?' Jess asked Vinnie about his recent drive past to the old mill, even though they had had this discussion before.

'No, nowt, sarge.'

'Gotta be worth a proper look, though?'

'Absolutely – hopefully it'll be connected to Maggie Horsefield, and if we can put the place out of action it'll be a good thing.'

'Fingers crossed.'

'On another, unrelated subject, what's your take on that woman who's still missing?' Jess asked him. She didn't need to explain what she meant: she was referring to a woman who had been reported missing from her home, supposedly having gone walking in the countryside near Dunsop Bridge, and had not been seen for a few months now. Jess knew Vinnie was still looking into the disappearance and had spoken to family members, ex-boyfriends, etc. Jess knew that Vinnie and Dougie Doolan had interviewed her latest known ex under caution but had got nowhere.

Vinnie sucked in air with a hiss. 'My gut says the whole thing isn't right, but gut instinct isn't evidence.'

'True, but keep digging,' Jess encouraged him.

He chuckled darkly. 'Just hope it won't be a shallow grave I have to dig her out of.'

Jess gave him a sideways frown. 'Let's hope not.'

The convoy passed through Waddington, then into West Bradford, slowing down as they reached the turn into the lane leading up to the old mill.

Even though Jess wasn't expecting any problems as such, she switched on her inner full-alert button. Any incident could throw up the unexpected, and as they drove past an old Ford Focus parked up tight to the side of the lane, the young white male on board slumped down low in the driver's seat in dark shadow with the peak of a baseball cap pulled over his face and a mobile phone held at ninety degrees to the side of his head. Jess didn't like it. Not that there was anything overtly suspicious about a lad sitting in a car by himself, it was just one of those things that made her eyes narrow.

'Just pull in, will you, Vin?' She gestured to the side of the lane.

Over the radio she called to the rest of the convoy that she was stopping for a moment. Not a 'brakes-jammed-on' thing, just a slow pull-in. She glanced through the mesh separating the driving cab from the prisoner section. 'Samira, will you hop out and just check out the guy in the Ford? We'll crack on and one of us will pop back and pick you up in a few minutes.'

Samira had also spotted the guy in the car through the back window of the Defender. 'Yep, will do,' she said, getting it immediately.

Vinnie pressed the automatic release for the back door which was on the dashboard. The door clicked open, Samira slid out, waiting whilst the Battle Bus and dog van went past, then began to walk towards the car.

Deerman waved his phone urgently at Mags.

'From Dimbo, down the road,' he said, using the nickname of the lad in the Ford Focus who was on lookout duties. Mags always liked to have prewarning of any potentially unwelcome visitors in such situations, particularly when she was about to slit someone's throat. 'Two cop cars and a carrier just turned into the lane.'

Mags cursed, then said to Lance, '*Anything?*'

'Anything. I'll do anything,' he confirmed desperately. 'Just don't chop me head off.'

Instead, Mags quickly cut the cable ties with the blade of the zombie knife, dragged Lance to his feet and shouted to Deerman, 'Blow this place!'

She shoved Lance out ahead of her and yelled at him to get in the Land Rover as she got into the driver's seat and fired up the engine. 'Keep your head down, don't be seen,' she ordered him.

Inside the mill, Chambers ran swiftly to each of the mousetrap-like devices he had positioned around the floor, and stood on each one to activate the short fuse that gave him a minute to run before it ignited a small, explosive-like firework designed to set fire to the vapour rising from the petrol he'd splashed around, the intention being to destroy anything inside the unit. He sprinted to the door but before he left, picked up two pre-prepared milk bottles, half-full of petrol with petrol-soaked rags stuffed into their necks, lit them both with a cigarette lighter and lobbed them high and long into the centre of the floor, near the chairs. Then he ran.

Samira noticed the exhaust pipe was pumping out obnoxious-looking smoke and the lad was obviously sitting there with the engine ticking over. The lad had turned to look over his right shoulder, watching the police convoy move on, and for a few seconds his face was quite close to the glass in the driver's door window and then his expression on seeing Samira heading in his direction was one of shock and surprise. Samira knew instantly he was going to slam the car into gear and do a getaway.

Which he did.

Samira upped her pace to a jog.

The car's engine revved, making the exhaust pump out a bigger cloud of blue-black smoke and noxious fumes, and the car lurched forwards as the lad let out the clutch, something he did far too quickly and in a panic. The car did a kangaroo hop then stalled.

Samira said a triumphant, '*Yes*,' to herself and increased her pace, coming up alongside the car.

The lad behind the wheel stood on the clutch and twisted the ignition key. The engine turned over unhealthily but refused to fire up.

Samira emitted another, 'Yes!' as she reached the car and yanked open the driver's door, now recognizing the lad for the first time as none other than Dave Dawson, nicknamed Dimbo, one of the Clitheroe town centre denizens suspected of low-level drug dealing around the pubs and clubs. He was someone Samira had stopped and searched a few times without success, it had to be admitted. Dimbo wasn't as dense as his nickname suggested, and he was known to be violent.

As she pulled the door open and the engine failed for the second time, Samira shouted, 'What're you up to?'

She got no reply.

As fast as a twisting snake, Dimbo recoiled out of the car, said nothing, but launched himself at Samira, showering her with punches, from the left and right, to her head and shoulders, beating her down to her knees as she tried to protect herself with her forearms.

Once down, Dimbo unleashed a nasty kick to her ribs, but then spun back into the car. The few seconds of respite for the engine must have allowed it to clear and this time it started instantly. He released the clutch with more care and accelerated away, leaving a plume of foul exhaust smoke behind him.

Samira was shocked, but not too badly hurt. The blows had mostly been glancing. She pushed herself up and watched the car disappear towards Waddington and despite the surprise of being assaulted, she committed the registration number to memory and then spoke on her radio.

Dimbo was now on her 'to-do' list.

With one last very wistful and angry glance over her shoulder as she swung the old Land Rover around in the space outside the warehouse, Mags reached over and shoved Lance further down into the footwell. She had planned to move the stock of packaged cannabis out before setting the premises on fire and now she would have to destroy it because of the approach of the cops, and that annoyed her a lot.

'Keep down!' she screamed, her voice slightly muffled because she had pulled up the face mask. The car rocked around but because of its poor turning circle she had to slam-on, crunch into reverse, back a few yards, then go forwards again, chucking Lance back and forwards in his confined space.

Behind her the two guys who had snatched Lance from Asda were doing the same with the Transit van.

But even as Mags turned the Land Rover around, she knew this was a futile manoeuvre because the lane towards the road, which the cops were now steaming down, was only wide enough for one vehicle. She'd meet them head-on and be trapped. They wouldn't give way and there was no chance of her being able to outrun them in reverse, so she needed to take evasive action.

'Hold on!' she shouted to Lance. He looked up from his position, curled up like a foetus, with nothing to actually hold on to. 'This is gonna get well rough,' she warned him.

The lane ahead curved up and then dropped down to the right and Jess could see the old mill at the bottom, still very identifiable as a mill, built from deep red Accrington brick in the early twentieth century. The chimney had been demolished years ago but the remainder of the mill stood virtually intact, having been divided up into commercial units which had never caught on, but then had fallen in disuse over the years and boarded up. No doubt it would eventually all be demolished to become a housing estate, but at the moment, in itself it was still a magnificent building of its time.

As the Defender turned the corner, Jess was slightly gobsmacked to see another Land Rover coming up towards it, head-to-head, with one person on board behind the wheel but who was difficult to make out because of the angle and glare of the windscreen. And behind that was a van.

'Interesting,' Jess murmured. 'Block the lane,' she ordered Vinnie.

He anchored on, skewing up at a slight angle so there was definitely no way past, but the approaching vehicle veered sharp right and smashed through a rickety wooden five-barred gate and into a field in which a small herd of llamas was grazing peacefully.

They raised their pretty heads on their elegantly long necks, then screamed in panic, sounding like an orchestra of broken trumpets, and scattered as the Land Rover accelerated and bounced towards them across the field.

The van behind the Land Rover followed, but somehow managed to get wedged on one of the gate posts, coming to an instant stop and blocking the entrance.

The doors opened and two lads ran for it.

'Shit,' Jess said as Vinnie brought the Defender up to the van. In his eagerness, he was about to jump out and give chase on foot but Jess grabbed his arm and said, 'A job for Flynn.'

Vinnie smiled conspiratorially. 'Oh, yeah.'

Then Samira's voice came over the radio: 'Sarge, sarge . . . I've been assaulted by the driver of the Ford and he's driven off.'

Jess swore again, this time using much more colourful words from her extensive 'swear word' vocabulary.

In the distance she watched the fleeing Land Rover, now at the far side of the llama field, crash through a gate and bounce on to a track which Jess knew would bring it out on to Bowland Gate Lane near West Bradford reservoir, and realized the chance of grabbing whoever was at the wheel was just about zero and, in the scheme of things, not as important as ensuring that Samira was OK.

And in answer to that thought, Samira continued to transmit over the radio, 'But I'm OK, sarge. I've got the reg number and I'm now making my way up the lane to join you.'

'Roger that,' Jess acknowledged with relief.

At which moment the escaping Land Rover disappeared from view, the driving cab of the Transit van burst into flames and then, from the old mill, came the low boom of an explosion followed by a swirling plume of smoke billowing out of the door and upwards into the air like a mini-nuclear bomb had gone off.

On the plus side, without having to be told, Flynn's handler had already released his keen beast, which had pinpointed one of the lads running from the trapped van – the blond-haired one. The dog had cleared the hedge with one bound and was bearing down on him.

Thirty seconds later, with Flynn's teeth firmly imbedded into the thick muscle at the back of his thigh, the young guy screamed in agony.

In some selfish way Jess was secretly pleased that there was a fire at the mill because it meant she had a legitimate excuse to call out the fire service, then cross her fingers and hope.

It was all a bit pathetic, she realized, but as she waited for the firefighters who had arrived at the scene and were currently inside the mill after having quickly dealt with the flaming van, her little hope had come true as the crew manager stepped out through the pall of smoke still coming through the door, pulled off his mask and walked towards her as though he was some kind of mystical he-man from a sword and sorcery film. He had that cockeyed grin on his lips and despite herself, and everything else going on in her world, her heart definitely skipped a beat and her stomach tightened up a notch.

Such was the aura and allure of Joe Borwick.

With an inner shimmer, Jess pulled herself together, but not before she had exchanged a furtive glance with Samira, who had been slyly observing her with a perceptive purse of her lips. Jess mock-snarled at her for seeing this reaction to Joe. Samira winked and wafted herself with her hand and blew out her cheeks as if she was having a hot flush.

Jess and Samira had become quite good friends since Jess had moved to Clitheroe – not so much as to impinge on their professional relationship, but enough for each to know the other's background and circumstances. Jess had admitted that she found Joe Borwick pretty attractive, but nothing more than that. However, the very insightful Samira could see that, perhaps, Jess liked him more than she let on.

Joe came towards Jess, running his forearm across his sweaty brow.

'Sorted,' he said, 'but interesting.'

He looked her in the eye and she wondered if that last word – interesting – had some kind of double meaning. She managed to find some saliva to moisten her mouth, otherwise she would not have been able to talk, and said, 'Interesting how?'

It transpired that 'interesting' didn't have a double meaning which, from a purely unprofessional point of view, she found slightly disappointing.

Joe jerked his head for her to follow him into the mill.

It stank: a mixture of smoke and petrol and the overpowering stench of burned cannabis; a pall of grey hung just below the ceiling. The walls and floor, though made of brick and concrete, were scorched and black.

Jess covered her nose and mouth with the palm of her hand but Joe held out a spare face mask for her which she gratefully fitted, then stood to one side of him and looked around.

'It's pretty much an empty space,' Joe said. He pointed to four small, burned black objects on the floor about the size of computer mice. 'Explosives,' he said. 'Nothing too fancy but big enough to cause a bang and a spark and ignite petrol vapour which I think had been sloshed around. There are also the remnants of a couple of smashed bottles which look as though they had petrol and rags in their necks.'

'Molotov cocktails,' Jess murmured.

'Yep. Petrol bombs.'

'So whoever did this was determined to destroy anything in here, even that lot.' Jess pointed to where a firefighter was still dousing a pile of what looked like green and black compost against the wall, which smoked continually. 'Cannabis,' she said, and thought. 'Must have hurt leaving that lot behind.'

'Mm,' Joe said. 'This is also interesting.'

He steered her by the elbow across the floor with him – a sensation she liked – towards the skeletal remains of two plastic chairs positioned a few feet apart on what looked like a carpet of some sort, measuring about twelve-foot square.

Joe pointed. 'This was a sheet of polythene laid on the floor, what's left of it.'

'OK,' Jess said.

'Not that it's my job to jump to conclusions, Sergeant Raker,' Joe said mock-formally, 'but I'd say this was some sort of crime scene within a crime scene.' He walked to the edge of the melted sheet and pointed at one of the chair frames.

Jess saw four thin strips of something next to the chair which looked like lengths of shoe laces.

Then she realized what she was looking at: 'Zip ties,' she said. 'Looks like someone might have been tied to this chair.'

'I'd say so,' Joe agreed.

'But it looks like they've been snipped off.'

'Agreed.'

'So, there's a story to tell here,' Jess said, and looked at Joe. 'I assume you've checked for a body?'

He nodded. 'Nothing.'

'OK, good.' Jess pivoted on her heels and looked around the charred room. It was bare, with no remnants of furniture or equipment, other than the chairs and what looked like a table of some sort along a wall which was only just recognizable. Other than the blackened pile of cannabis there was nothing else that might have been used as part of a packaging process, and it looked to Jess as though the villains could have been in the middle of removing everything before setting the place alight and flitting. Equipment that would no doubt be taken to the next location to be used for such an enterprise. On the face of it, this jumping from place to place made no business sense, however the people behind these enterprises didn't pay rent, usually, just moved into places like cuckoos, used them and moved on. Sometimes they did this because they thought they'd been compromised which could possibly have been the case here if they had spotted Vinnie snooping around.

It was a shame they'd had a lookout posted – which was what Jess believed the lad in the car at the end of the lane was – so the police had missed the occupants by a whisper, but at least not all had been lost.

Samira had identified the lookout and got his car registration number.

One of the lads from the van had been nabbed by PD Flynn.

They'd left a stash of valuable cannabis behind which they'd decided to destroy as they fled, saving Jess a job.

The chairs, polythene sheet and the plastic ties were a puzzle, admittedly.

And it would have been very nice to have got the driver of the Land Rover.

Very nice indeed.

THREE

The journey across the llama field was rough to say the least, especially with no seat belt on; more especially if you were stuffed down in the front passenger footwell.

Once Mags realized she was definitely going head-on with a police car, she whipped the steering wheel down and careened through the gate to her right, not at that stage aware she was entering a llama enclosure, which was a surprise to her but not a big enough one for her to hesitate – something she never did when shaking off a cop's tail.

She immediately spotted the gate on the opposite side of the field and aimed mercilessly for it, not really caring if llamas were slow-witted or the fastest creatures on earth.

It they didn't scatter, so be it: crushed llama.

She held on grim-tight to the wheel as the Land Rover bounced across the field, hoping not to smash the crown of her head on the roof, and also seeing the terrified eyes of Lance in the footwell as he peered up between his fingers and whinnied loudly.

A glance in the mirror and she saw the Transit van had followed her into the field but had got stuck between the gateposts somehow and the occupants were legging it across the grass.

She wasn't too concerned that either or both of the lads might get arrested. They were trustworthy, completely unbreakable and would never dob her in when interviewed by the police, otherwise their fates would be well and truly sealed.

The Land Rover lurched sideways over a hump in the field.

Lance smacked his head on the centre console and screamed like a baby.

'Shut it, wimp,' Mags shouted as the vehicle rocked and bucked like a trawler in a storm. It may have been made to deal with rough terrain, but not in a comfortable manner.

Ahead, the llamas reacted more positively to the approaching threat. Each screamed and reared up like a My Little Pony toy, the group split and bounded away like their legs were springs, leaving a gap for Mags to aim for, beyond which was the gate which she gunned towards, then crashed through.

One last twist of her head saw the two lads haring across the field – one going one way, one the other. Also that the Transit was in flames and that a big German Shepherd dog had cleared the hedge and was giving chase. She didn't have the time or inclination to feel sorry for whichever one of them felt its fangs.

Then she was out of sight, speeding down Bowland Gate Lane, smooth in comparison to the field she'd just left.

As she drove, her face became distorted with anger as she ripped off her face mask.

Not just because she had almost been caught with her knickers around her ankles, figuratively speaking, which was a big lesson in that respect, she thought, knowing she would have to have a few harsh words with herself later about that over a single malt whisky, but because in the fleeting glance she'd got, she managed to recognize the face of the cop leading the police charge along the lane to the mill.

So far she had held back from going toe-to-toe with Police Sergeant Jessica Raker, but maybe now it was time to let her know, in no uncertain terms, that Mags Horsefield was not someone to cross swords with. Battle lines needed to be joined.

At the junction with Grindleton Road, Mags braked, stopped and looked down at Lance whose fingers had completely closed over his eyes now, such was his terror. Hesitantly they parted.

'You'd do anything?' Mags demanded.

For a brief moment Lance did not understand. Then it clicked. 'Yeah, yeah, anything – but I do have that tag, you do know that, boss?'

'Fixed, no probs . . . anything?'

'Yeah, anything.'

'Right. Let's make a start, I need to make a statement.' Mags pondered for a moment. 'A subtle but brutal one to begin with, then escalate if necessary.'

Jess watched the section van pull away, driven by one of the other PCs on the early turn at Clitheroe, the prisoner with the punctured leg in the back cage screaming police brutality and demanding a brief and medical attention. Jess had contacted the custody office at Blackburn – where all Ribble Valley prisoners were taken – and been told to ensure he was taken to the A&E department at Blackburn Hospital for treatment and the obligatory tetanus jab before being presented at the station. Samira had been told to go along, too.

PD Flynn was sitting upright next to her with his handler.

Jess scratched the dog's head and said, 'Well done,' and the animal seemed to smile at her. She liked police dogs.

As the van disappeared up the lane another vehicle came down, the CID car driven by DC Dougie Doolan. Jess also liked Dougie, who was the longest-standing detective in Clitheroe and looked upon as part of the furniture. He was also the longest serving cop at the station but also remained one of the most effective despite his years in the job. He could have trod water and got away with it, but he chose to graft.

He pulled in alongside the Defender and rose stiffly out of his car, rotating his hips because of the obvious pain and discomfort he was feeling. Jess had noticed this was getting more regular and pronounced over the last few weeks and she was becoming concerned about him even though she – technically – wasn't his supervisor. His own line manager, a detective sergeant, was based in Blackburn and had only sparse contact with him.

Dougie hobbled towards her.

'Back playing you up?' she asked.

'I'm OK . . . I've OD'd with paracetamol,' he said, wincing with pain and dismissing her concern. 'They should kick in soon. Anyhow, what did we end up with here?' Dougie pointed to the mill which still had smoke wafting out from the open door.

Jess turned and walked with him. 'Looks like we might have walked in on a scene from *The Expendables*,' she said, referencing the loud, violent movie franchise her son Jason was currently wading his way through. She seemed to recall that quite a few characters in that were often tied to chairs and tortured, scenes which made her shiver when she recalled her own, recent experience of such a situation which she'd been lucky to survive.

'My favourite films,' Dougie said with gusto.

'Really?' Jess screwed up her face.

'Oh yes.'

Jess shook her head sadly and said, 'Boys will be boys.' They were standing at the door looking into the mill. 'Might mean nothing,' Jess admitted, 'but it does look like someone was possibly bound to the chair with cable ties which were cut off. Now whether that was done well before we arrived or because we arrived, we don't know at the moment. But whoever was in here fled – presumably once they got word from their lookout down the lane who was so desperate to get away he assaulted Samira.'

'Dave "Dimbo" Dawson,' Dougie said. 'We'll soon find him.' He sounded confident.

'What about the guy in the back of the van with bite marks in his leg?' Jess asked. 'He hasn't told us his name yet and none of us know him.'

'I had a quick glance at him,' Dougie said. 'Don't know him, either.'

'Out of towner?'

'Possibly, but even so, Dawson is connected to the drug trade around the Ribble Valley and maybe the guy arrested and his mate who got away are too and we just don't know them . . . yet. Anything from the Transit van or the Land Rover?'

'The van is registered to someone in Blackburn. The Land Rover is registered to someone in Lancaster, so I don't hold out much hope of much coming from them, actually.'

'And you didn't get a good look at the Land Rover driver?'

'Nope.'

'Pity.'

'Yes, 'tis. At least we managed to corral all the llamas, though.'

'That could have been fun, rounding them up,' Dougie smiled. Then he looked at Jess. 'Maggie Horsefield?'

'I do hope so,' Jess answered fervently, but then her radio came to life, a transmission from HQ Control Room. 'Receiving,' she said.

'Had a report of a vehicle on fire which could be connected to

the incident you are currently involved with,' the comms operator said. 'It's a Land Rover.'
'Location?' Jess asked.
The operator gave this to her. Jess heard it clearly but it didn't quite compute so she asked her to repeat it. Then she turned to Dougie who said, 'Go! Now!'

At Jess's urgent prompting, Vinnie drove the Defender quickly, but he kept silent, picking up on his sergeant's demeanour as she stared trance-like through the windscreen.
He went back to West Bradford, then tore left through the village along Grindleton Road, passing through the actual village of Grindleton, then onwards towards Sawley, but before getting there he went left and to the next village along, which was Bolton-by-Bowland. Where Jess lived.

Mags always kept a couple of vehicles stashed in various locations around Clitheroe, usually dull, middle-aged cars that wouldn't draw attention to themselves.
'You never know when you might need a quick exit under the radar,' she had been heard to say once or twice. They were usually cars that came into Primrose Breakers and were then fitted with new registration plates but which would withstand a cursory inspection and PNC check by a cop who might not know what to look for. The cars were left in places and garages around town and replaced after a few weeks. Mags maintained that each one had to have a can of petrol in the boot plus a box of matches because another of her sayings was, 'You never know how far you might have to travel, nor do you know when or if you might have to set the damn thing on fire.'
Today being a prime example.
After managing to evade the law and avoid llamas she drove at a steady, not over-fast pace to Bolton-by-Bowland and managed to pull in at the exact spot she wanted to, outside a cottage on the main street about a hundred yards before the Coach & Horses, the village pub.
She looked down at the battered, curled up figure of Lance. 'You're good at nicking cars, aren't you?'
He nodded energetically. 'I'm good at nicking anything.'

'In that case, get out and go nick a motor and meet me up at the war memorial opposite the pub in ten minutes or less.'

'Er, what pub, what war memorial?' he asked. 'I don't even know where I am.'

Mags jabbed her finger. 'Up there. You'll see. Now go – do!'

Lance scrambled out of the car and trotted up the main street, getting his bearings. As per usual for this time of day, the village was as good as deserted. Mags watched him for a moment with a sneer of contempt on her face, despising a lad who wouldn't know what loyalty was even if it hit him over the head with a frying pan.

She reached back over her seat and stretched for the petrol can secreted between the front and back seats. She shook the can to ensure there was something in it, then twisted round on her seat and up on to her knees so she faced backwards and sloshed the petrol around. She decided not to do the same on the outside of the car because even in such a quiet location as Bolton-by-Bowland she would surely get spotted dousing a car with petrol.

Once empty, she tossed the can on to the back seat, then holding her breath so as not to inhale any of the fumes, she wriggled out of her suit and boots, balled them up with her mask and threw the lot over her shoulder, then opened the driver's door because she knew she might have to move fast.

Half hanging out of the car, she struck a match and flicked it over her shoulder.

Even before it landed she was walking swiftly up Main Street towards the war memorial, checking all the time to see if anyone had clocked her.

She reached the memorial just as the Land Rover went up with a very satisfying burst of flames. The car seemed to jump on all four wheels as the exploding vapour smashed out each window and the flames licked up around the roof.

Even from where she stood, Mags felt a waft of heat hit and wrap around her like a blanket.

Part of her whimsically thought that she should have been an arsonist. There seemed to be a lot of satisfaction in it.

The explosion and the flaming car did bring people out of their houses and Mags realized she had to get out of the village pretty damn quick.

'C'mon, Lance,' she urged just as an old, very sedate-looking Jaguar stopped in front of her. Lance was at the wheel, grinning.

Mags got in alongside him, sank into the deep leather upholstery and the big car surged away.

The fire service weren't far behind Jess and Vinnie in the shape and personnel of the tender that had attended the fire at the mill, but this time Jess wasn't bothered one way or another if Joe Borwick was part of the crew.

Vinnie stopped the Defender fifty yards short of the burning vehicle on Main Street and closed the road to traffic coming from that direction. Jess hopped out and went on foot past the flaming Land Rover and stood in the middle of the road outside the Coach & Horses to stop traffic coming in from the opposite direction.

She wasn't too worried about the car itself exploding. Over the years she had been to a lot of vehicle fires, whether ignited by accident or design, and had never had one explode spectacularly on her. After the initial boom they burned. Quite intensely sometimes, but burned . . . although she never took it for granted. She knew of some that had exploded, but she was pretty sure this Land Rover had gone past any chance of that happening. It had had its moment and was now just a flaming shell of blackened metal, plastic and rubber.

Down the road, the fire service arrived.

Vinnie waved them through and they quickly began to douse the flames, running their hoses up to Kirk Beck, the fast-flowing stream running through the village by the Coach & Horses.

Jess was content to watch and stop traffic, although there wasn't too much to flag down, and the word 'content' wasn't the right one to reflect the conflicting moods swirling through her brain.

She found herself gritting her teeth as she surveyed the scene, her jaw rotated, her nostrils dilated not very prettily.

She wanted to believe this was simply a coincidence.

That the person who had escaped from her at the mill had got this far, dumped and fired the getaway car right here, right in this position, this exact position.

Right outside her front door.

Once the fire service had extinguished everything, leaving nothing but the coned-off, bleak remains of the Land Rover, Jess reopened the road, radioed Vinnie to do the same and the traffic began to flow again. She then walked back to the wreck which was directly outside the little cottage she and her two children, Lily and Jason, and husband Josh lived.

After relocating from the Metropolitan Police, this is where she and her family had found themselves living. A three-bedroomed, but quite small, rented cottage in a pretty village in the Ribble Valley in Lancashire, and she had moved into the role of a police sergeant basically responsible for almost every aspect of policing in the valley, from rural crime to parish council meetings, sudden deaths to antisocial behaviour. Her job covered everything, and after a particularly difficult first week she had settled well into the role, putting her personal stamp on that 'everything'.

Jess walked around the remains of the Land Rover, which seemed to have fused its chassis to the melted tarmac, and the road, until it was repaired and resurfaced, would bear the scorch marks of the fire.

A deliberate reminder, Jess thought: something she would see every single day.

Or was she reading more into this than it really was? Maybe it was just a coincidence.

'Wow,' Vinnie said, inadvertently exacerbating her bleak thoughts. 'Right outside your house!'

'Tell me about it, Vin.'

'No damage to the house, though?'

'No. House is OK,' Jess said.

Vinnie looked into her eyes searchingly, picking up on something not right. 'You OK, sarge?' he asked, and not for the first time that day.

'Yep, yep,' she said in a clipped way which when translated said, 'Nowhere near.'

But Vinnie didn't press her.

'Get comms to get on to the local authority,' Jess said to him. 'This needs moving and the road needs repairing.'

'Will do.' He turned away to speak into his radio whilst firefighter Joe Borwick sidled up to her, seemingly oblivious to the fact the burned-out car was right outside her house.

Not that he needed to know.

He and Jess had first met at an incident on the first day of her posting to Clitheroe a few months ago, and despite there being an obvious mutual attraction – and Jess did love it when she was at a job and the fire service were there and Joe was amongst the personnel – it had never gone beyond a laugh and a minor flirt. She knew a little bit about him, he knew a little bit about her and that was the sum total.

Jess was still married by a thread, and as much as some sort of liaison with Joe was a guilty fantasy she was determined that as long as Josh was still her husband she would never cheat on him, even though he had cheated on her big style whilst they were living in London.

Her mind drifted as she thought fleetingly about how the past few months had been between her and Josh. After his first tantrums (as Jess called his negative reactions to the move north) they had settled down and tried to make things work, but recently Josh seemed to have made excuses to spend more time in Manchester where his job now was – clients, workload, train delays – all of which seemed quite weak to Jess, though she had to admit she was pretty busy with work and the kids herself.

'Penny for them,' Joe said, interrupting her reverie.

'Oh, they're not worth that,' she said, coming to.

'I'll bet they are.'

She chuckled and as much as she would have liked to chat small talk she said, 'Are you done here?'

'Yeah, I guess.' He actually sounded disappointed and she felt slightly guilty by her sharpness.

'Well, it's all stacking up for me,' she said. 'Needs must, so gotta go.'

'OK, nice seeing you again.'

There was a pause during which they quickly reassessed each other, liking what they saw, then they went their separate ways. He glanced once over his shoulder whilst she watched him walk away for moments longer than she should have done.

Then he turned suddenly and pointed his finger at her and said, 'You know, we should go out for a drink sometime.'

Jess stared at him. 'You do know I'm married, don't you?'

Joe responded with a knowing smile.

Inspector Price, Jess's line manager, was waiting for her in the sergeant's office when she arrived back. He was playing his usual psycho game with her, lounging in *her* chair behind *her* desk, a mug of tea in his hand made in *her* mug, simply to wind *her* up.

He didn't like her and had never made the effort since she had transferred from the Met due to her shooting dead a member of a notoriously dangerous London-based organized crime group, or OCG. He was against the move because it had prevented one of his mates getting the sergeant's job, and despite the fact that particular mate had turned out to be a corrupt, conniving, violent – but now dead – officer, didn't make Price any more welcoming towards Jess.

She was canny enough to play a waiting game with him – picking which battles to fight and which to back away from, even though she knew he was out to get her – knowing that if he overstepped the mark or tripped up in some other way, she would be ready for him. He was based at Blackburn police station, not Clitheroe, despite being her direct supervisor, so she didn't see too much of him and, mostly, he let her get on with her job. But she was also aware that he might be as corrupt as his 'mate' had been – something she always bore in mind when dealing with him.

'Sir,' she acknowledged him, taking off her hi-vis jacket and sitting in the chair opposite. The usual form of address for higher ranking officers was 'boss' but Jess thought that was too informal for her liking with Price. 'Sir' kept him at arm's length.

'So,' he said, looking across the rim of the mug. Her mug. The one she'd got at a Rolling Stones' concert in Hyde Park, the mug she cherished, and he knew it.

'So what?'

'So, another shitshow.'

'You may have to expand on that one, sir.'

'Well, let me see: a warrant executed – no result, except for fires everywhere; two lads leg it from a van, one of which is detained by a police dog, at the moment for no reason whatsoever, so quite likely a claim for false arrest and police brutality will be forthcoming via a no-win no-fee sleazeball outfit, no doubt, and the other lad got away . . . but from what? You can't even put either of them or her in the mill.'

'Her?' Jess frowned. 'Who said, her?'

Price was halfway through sipping a mouthful of tea and Jess's question seemed to throw him sideways, making him choke on the beverage which was partway down his gullet. He brought it all back in a disgusting manner, spluttering into the mug, horrifying Jess who felt no urge to slap him on the back to help him through this event. If he started choking to death in front of her, she would probably have remained a spectator.

Finally he placed the mug down and slobbered whilst wiping his hand across his mouth.

'Went down the wrong hole,' he said.

As if she hadn't heard, Jess said, 'You said, "her"?'

'Well, isn't that who you hoped it would be . . . that woman you've been harassing for the last few months?'

'Who would that be?'

'Maggie Horsefield.'

'Mags Horsefield, is, as you know, suspected of being the main drug dealer, and more, in the Ribble Valley. The number one organized crim.'

'And you have not let up on her and her legitimate businesses, have you?'

'No, we have not let up on her,' came a voice from behind Jess before she could respond as Dougie Doolan entered the office. 'And we are not going to.'

Price's mouth sagged open a tad.

'And I arranged the warrant,' Dougie continued, 'based on legitimate intelligence and if there hadn't been a lookout operation – red flag! – we'd have been successful. Yeah, we don't know for certain if the person in the Land Rover who got away was Horsefield but one thing is for sure: something serious was going on in that mill this morning and quite possibly our arrival looks as though we might have saved someone's life. Boss.'

Price listened gobsmacked to Dougie. 'How do you reach that conclusion?' Price asked.

Jess explained the chair, the cable ties, the polythene sheeting.

'Oh,' Price said, now somewhat lost for words.

'And no, we don't know who was in the getaway Land Rover but it was abandoned and set on fire right outside my house, which is something that Maggie would be eminently capable of doing, trying to warn me off by sticking a middle finger up at me, us; plus the lookout who assaulted PCSO Patel is known, so when we arrest him we may have an "in" to Horsefield's OCG.'

'OCG? Organized Crime Group? Warning! Imaginations seem to be running away with us, don't they?' Price guffawed. He had got back to his equilibrium after Dougie's interruption.

'I don't think so,' Dougie said patiently. 'So, a false arrest – stroke – police brutality complaint will be worth the price. But I'll bet it never happens,' he went on, making it clear he had overheard all the conversation Jess and Price were having before he stepped into the office. 'Whoever that lad is, he has a lot of questions to answer.'

Although Price had recovered it was clear he was intimidated by Dougie, which slightly annoyed Jess, but also pleased her. It was good to have an old lag like Dougie as an ally – and a detective to boot.

'Right, right, fair dos,' Price said, beginning to bumble around now.

'So leave it with us, eh?' Jess suggested to him.

He slapped the mug down on Jess's desktop jotter, the contents of which slopped over on to the blotting paper, pushed himself up to his feet – which was no mean achievement getting his large belly over the edge of the desk – and went to the door.

'Keep me updated,' were his final brusque words before leaving.

Jess and Dougie waited in silence, listening as his footsteps receded, finally waiting for the sound of the back door opening and closing before the both of them exhaled.

'Cheers, Doug, but you didn't have to step in for me,' Jess said. 'I'll fight my own battles.'

'Hey, don't I know it!' the detective said unoffended, 'but a bit of backup's always welcome. Plus, Price is our battle too, Jess. He's not good for the Ribble Valley, particularly since the departure and demise of Dave Simpson. He hasn't got any friends left and the plan for world domination has collapsed, so he's feeling mean and hard done to . . . Oooh!'

Without warning Dougie doubled over, clutching his lower ribs in agony. He gasped.

'Woah, Doug!' Jess shot up from her seat, going to support him. But he flapped her away and manoeuvred himself into the chair. 'What is going on?'

'Nothing, nothing.' He took a few long, deep breaths as the pain subsided. 'Tummy ache, last night's curry.'

'Right, OK,' Jess said, unimpressed by the diagnosis. To her it seemed much more sinister than a bad tikka masala. She'd seen him wince and wave it off far too many times since she'd joined the team.

'I'm fine. It's gone.' He forced a smile.

'Um,' she said.

'So . . .' Dougie changed tack. 'Maggie Horsefield, you reckon?'

'I reckon.'

Maggie Horsefield was at the very top of Jess's to-do hit list. She suspected her of being behind the untimely deaths of two old people, one a resident, the other on the waiting list of the best old people's care home in town; Jess believed they'd been killed on Maggie's orders to bump her own ailing, ageing father up the list to get him in the home sooner. Unfortunately Jess hadn't been able to prove this, but she was never going to let it go.

Mags was also believed to be the number one drug dealer in the valley, peddling her wares through the pubs and clubs she owned or controlled. This had led Jess to 'up' the police presence in and around these premises and organize a number of raids which had not been greatly successful but at least let Maggie know the police were after her.

Jess also believed that Mags had cops on her payroll, one of which had been the late Dave Simpson, but Jess hadn't been able to prove that connection either. Yet.

And another very worrying, sneaking suspicion Jess had was Mags had provided information to the Moss gang, the ultra-dangerous organized crime group in London which had then put a contract killer – The Saint – on to her, which ended in a violent confrontation Jess had been lucky to survive.

So yes, Jess was very happy to admit that while Maggie Horsefield was her number one priority and she would bring her down by whatever legal means possible, there would be some misses along the way.

However, there were slight complications in that scenario that Jess hadn't completely got her head around.

Firstly she and Maggie had a 'history'. They had been teenagers together before Jess had gone to university, and been at loggerheads with each other over a boy, so she didn't want to be accused of making her quest for Maggie's head personal – although, without doubt, some percentage of it was.

The second conundrum was that Maggie's daughter Caitlin and her own, Lily, were best friends at school, a tricky situation Jess wasn't sure how to handle, although she was pretty certain that Maggie was revelling in it, and perhaps getting insights into Jess's home life that were uncomfortable.

As Jess pondered these, her desk phone rang.

It was Samira.

'Hi, sarge . . . I'm at Blackburn custody office with that lad who Flynn bit . . .'

Because Jess's mind had been whirling a little it took a moment to realize what Samira was on about. Flynn being the police dog. With fangs.

'We've been to A&E with him. He's been treated, including a tetanus jab in his bum, which was delightful . . . but now he's here I'm not one hundred per cent what he's been arrested for and the custody sergeant is looking a mite sceptical.'

Jess had the phone on speaker so Dougie could listen in.

She shrugged at the detective.

Without hesitation and honed by years of spouting believable bullshit to custody officers, Doug said, 'Suspicion of being involved in the production and supply of a controlled drug,' loud and confidently enough for Samira to hear.

'OK, that'll do,' Samira said brightly.

'I'll come over and interview him,' Dougie added.

'Who is he, incidentally?' Jess asked.

'Won't say, but he's got a London accent. And he's being very awkward.'

'OK, tell the custody officer I'll be over in half an hour or so,' Dougie said.

'London accent?' Jess said when she hung up.

'Interesting,' Dougie said and stood up, still wincing slightly.

'You sure you're OK?'

'I'll be fine, honest.'

She watched the detective leave her office, not convinced.

FOUR

Although she struggled to get Maggie Horsefield out of her mind – Jess being fully aware the woman was inhabiting her brain space rent free and this was not a healthy thing – she did have many other responsibilities in her role, and after Dougie set off for Blackburn she purged all thoughts of Horsefield for the time being and settled down at her desk to apply herself to other pressing matters.

Firstly she had to prepare for a parish council meeting out at Slaidburn which she knew could be a rough ride. She had done another one already and found the members to be outwardly amicable, but once proceedings commenced they turned into ferocious gremlin-like critters akin to Jack Russell terriers shaking a rat, the rat being Jess, and she emerged feeling as though she'd been in a tumble dryer. Then she had been unprepared – it had been her first ever parish council meeting – but was determined it would not happen again, so she spent a good deal of time reviewing police incidents, crimes and responses over the last month and, in her mind, practising her measured tone of voice, her best reassuring level, that the police would always be there to address their needs – even if it was a teeny white lie.

In the end she had a bullet-point list prepared and was happy enough she could tackle any issues that were lobbed at her, even the low balls.

That took over an hour after which she leaned back in her chair and sent a text to Dougie over in Blackburn to check on his progress with the dog-bitten prisoner, but her concentration on typing this was rudely interrupted by what seemed to be the sound of an explosion on the street outside the station.

Vinnie McKinty stood back, holding a hand to shade his eyes in a fairly useless attempt to protect himself from the heat of the flames rising from the burning vehicle on King Street.

Jess rushed out of the front door of the station and was

momentarily assaulted by the same invisible blanket of heat which took her breath away but which she managed to step through to stand alongside Vinnie.

The car in front of them was well alight, flames rising high.

'Shut the road off and evacuate nearby shops for the time being,' Jess said, 'and get the fire bobbies here.'

'Geoff's diverting traffic up there,' Vinnie said, referring to one of the other PC's who had already started to keep traffic away. 'I'll divert 'em from the bottom of King Street,' he said, gesturing towards the end of the road. 'Another burning car, eh? It's a pandemic,' he chuckled as he strode away.

'It's something all right,' Jess said to herself. 'I'll try and get some shops evacuated, just in case. Have you PNC'd the car?' she called to Vinnie.

'No, not yet.'

Jess went quickly to the front of the car.

Knowing cars as well as she did – knowledge that came with being a street cop for many years – she knew it was an old Jaguar XJ6. It was a deep maroon colour and not many minutes before had been a well-maintained model from 1976. Jess knew this because she also recognized the personalized number plate immediately.

'It's from Bolton-by-Bowland,' she called to Vinnie.

'How do you know that?'

She sighed, shielding her face from the heat. 'I just do,' she said, not particularly wanting to explain to Vinnie that for the protection of her family she had made it her business to go to the extreme of being able to know every locally owned vehicle in the village (not that there were too many to remember in such a small space), plus all the regular delivery and farm vehicles so that she could spot a stranger and, hence, a possible threat. Having once been the target of a contract killer made you do things like this, although she knew it wasn't a great way to live.

So she knew this Jaguar, this once pristine example, belonged to an old guy in the village who had the bearing of an old-fashioned colonel or wing commander with his thick, bristly moustache who spent his time renovating old cars. Jess had seen him pottering around the village occasionally in the Jag, probably not going anywhere, just keeping the engine turning over.

He always waved when he drove past and Jess also knew him from the Coach & Horses.
Jess hoped he was well insured.
Her personal mobile phone rang and she answered it. The screen showed the call was from a withheld number.
'Hi, Jess Raker,' she said. There was silence at the other end, maybe a rustling noise, then the call was disconnected. Jess glared at the phone with annoyance, thinking it was just one of the numerous scam calls she, like thousands of other people, received all too often.
Then it rang again, still no number shown.
'Jess Raker,' she said.
Silence, then a harsh laugh, then disconnection.
Jess stared at the phone again.
In the distance was the wail of fire brigade two-tones.

Like an oversized Artful Dodger, Lance Drake mingled amongst the crowd of onlookers gathered to watch the Jaguar go up in flames.
The Jaguar he had set fire to.
Standing partly behind other people, he was holding the mobile phone he'd been given by Mags as discreetly as possible at chest height, videoing the burning Jaguar and the figure of PS Jess Raker as she received one phone call, then another. From him.
Lance had a nasty, victorious smirk on his chiselled, rat-thin face for more than one reason.
First, he loathed Jess Raker with a vengeance. As far as he was concerned she had done the dirty on him by going back on her word following his arrest for possession and supply of drugs: how in hell was he supposed to have known that the guy he fingered would be dead before the cops managed to close in on him? That was so not his fault.
The smirk was also that he was still alive, hadn't had his head severed from his body by a vicious woman – the one who bore him a deadly grudge for blabbing to the police and potentially screwing up her multi-million pound drug operation.
Not that at the time of his initial arrest had he known who the boss of the drugs operation was. He'd been so low down the chain – in the dregs of the gene pool – that he hadn't even got a clue who he was skivvying for. All he did was carry out instructions and

deliver stuff around the valley. At that time he didn't even care who the drug lord was. Or 'lady' as it transpired. So long as he got paid was all that mattered.

But as he lounged around on remand he did find out who the boss was.

And now he knew how lucky he was not to have watched his head roll across that polythene sheet because it turned out he could still be useful to her and he intended to be so and do whatever he was bid. It would also mean that much-needed cash would be coming in his direction, although no figure had been put on it yet.

His first task, after stealing the Jaguar – although Mags had screamed at him why the hell could he not have chosen something less conspicuous to nick rather than a huge, classic motor – was to abandon the car outside Clitheroe police station and set it alight. Just as another warning for Raker, in case the first one – a blazing car outside her home – wasn't quite clear enough. However, the logistics of that had somewhat troubled him. There were double yellow lines outside the nick and to have parked up there, then set fire to the car would have been an attention-grabber. So he had decided to set it on fire *before* leaving it, which was a tense few minutes for him.

He had fired the car on the railway car park then driven like a demon the couple of hundred yards or so to the cop shop with a fire blazing on the back seat. The flames had started to rage within moments of him dropping a lighted match on the petrol he'd sluiced over the back seat. The flames grew within seconds, licking at the back of his neck. He'd driven, leaning forwards with his face almost between the spokes of the huge steering wheel, and slewed to a stop and piled out before he was cremated.

It had worked pretty well.

He had legged it smartly across the street – unobserved, he thought, because there weren't many other pedestrians knocking around at that time – and slunk into a shop doorway as people quickly gathered to gawk at the fire, then a cop raised the alarm as the flames rose nicely, engulfing the car, and then Raker rushed out – all of a dither, Lance thought – which is when he started filming her on his phone and ghost calling her as Mags had instructed him.

It wasn't as though he was the only one using a phone, so he didn't stand out in that respect, but as Raker took the calls he made to her she started looking around at the watchers, at which moment, possibly by an act of God, the folk in front of Lance stepped apart in a choreographed move and exposed him to the woman's direct line of sight.

Jess looked up from her dead phone, surveyed the crowd.

As ever, quite a few of them had their phones out and were taking videos. Par for the course, these days. That wasn't the issue. Cops simply had to tolerate being filmed at incidents – it was an unpleasant part of the job and most officers did not let it stop them doing what was necessary.

Then two people who were standing next to each other stepped apart, revealing the guy standing behind them who was also using a phone.

Jess did an almost comical double-take on this particular individual because for a very brief moment she did not recognize him.

Then she did!

Lance Drake was in the crowd.

He was glancing at the screen of his phone as he filmed her but at the exact moment she recognized him and a look of astonishment came across her face, he realized he'd been clocked.

For what seemed an eon, their eyes locked, although this was only a millisecond, and nothing happened, neither responded.

But like the feral animal he was, Lance moved first and a second later Jess launched herself across the street, because even if she was wrong about Lance and his connection to the blazing Jaguar she did not like the coincidence of it, not least because she was under the impression he should still be locked up on remand.

Lance slammed his free hand into the back of a woman standing just to one side of him and sent her staggering to her knees, spun on the spot and sprinted away into Railway View, up through Church Walk, through the car park behind the council offices, under the archway and out on to York Street, with Clitheroe library to his left.

He didn't pause, and dashed across the main street, zig-zagging between moving traffic into Wellgate.

Jess was no slouch. Having been a firearms officer in the Met, which required a high degree of personal fitness which she had managed to more or less maintain since her move north with daily runs and gym membership (although she didn't visit as often as she should), she knew she should have outpaced Lance, but by the time she emerged through the archway on to the main street he was nowhere to be seen.

Fact was, she knew he could have – and probably had – been released from remand legitimately for a variety of reasons, which wasn't a great problem for Jess. Annoying things like that happened in the legal system.

What triggered her was his presence there in the first place.

His link to a burning stolen car outside the police station, then thinking backwards, making possible connections: maybe a link to a burning stolen car outside her house; and maybe a link to a drugs packaging factory that had been swiftly abandoned and set alight.

OK, she accepted that the last two trains of thought were simply speculation, but in terms of being a cop that was often the point at which seemingly unconnected circumstances started to mesh together and lead to actual evidence.

However, one thing was certain as she stood on York Street and caught her breath: she needed to have a word with Lance Drake. She looked up Castle Street towards the castle itself and watched as a fire tender slowed and turned into King Street to tackle the blaze down at the nick.

Jess was busy for the remainder of the day and could easily have gone on working until midnight. But her tour of duty was 8 a.m. to 4 p.m., though she had come on at 7 a.m. to prepare for the mill raid and she wanted to finish work on time to be able to pick up Lily and Jason from school and also see if Mags Horsefield would pick up her own daughter, Caitlin, from the same school.

Jess and Mags hadn't actually spoken for a few months, though they'd passed each other a few times at the school gates where Jess had been highly amused at Mags' stuck-up nose-in-the-air shunning of Jess, who she knew was out to get her.

Jess grabbed her civvy jacket and raced to the school in her battered Citroën Picasso.

She was disappointed. There was no sign of Mags at the school gates but when Lily came out of the door she was with Caitlin, with whom she was far too friendly with for Jess's comfort.

Jess watched them approach. Two girly mates, walking shoulder to shoulder, checking each other's phones, giggling conspiratorially, looking very similar to each other from hairstyles and make-up downwards. They did break apart at one point as Caitlin took a phone call, short and sweet by the looks of it, at the end of which she looked annoyed and exasperated.

The two girls had a rushed head-to-head discussion and from the gestures and glances in her direction, Jess could see she was the subject.

At the school door behind them, Jason came out, grubby, mucky, still in his rugby kit, spinning a rugby ball with the expertise of a juggler.

Lily and Caitlin crossed the road to Jess and stood by her window, which she lowered.

'Muuum,' Lily whined, alerting Jess there was going to be some sort of request coming.

Jess smiled at Caitlin, then said to Lily, 'Yes, dear?'

'Mum, Caitlin's mum can't come and pick her up so, so, she's told her to get a taxi home, but that'll mean, like, waiting here for another twenty minutes, so I was wondering, like . . . can we take her home, give her a lift?'

Jess didn't hesitate. 'That is absolutely no problem but' – here she looked at Caitlin – 'you need to check with your mum that it's OK . . . in fact, call her now and I'll speak to her.'

'OK.' Caitlin handed Jess her phone. 'Last call received. Just press call back.'

Jess took the phone and dialled.

The phone rang out, not immediately answered, but then Mags came on the line. 'The hell d'you want, you little bitch?'

'Mags, I'm touched. How did you know it was me?' Jess cooed sweetly.

'Who is this?' Mags demanded, then it clicked. 'Oh, it's you. What're you doing with Caitlin's mobile?'

'Calling you, my love.'

'Why?'

'Caitlin wants to know if you'd let me run her home. She doesn't want to wait for a taxi . . . gosh, you must be extremely busy today not to be able to come and pick her up. Everything OK?'

'I'm in a meeting.'

'Well, whatever . . . yes or no?'

The heavy reluctance in Mags' 'Whatev' drew a wide smile across Jess's face.

Jess handed the phone back to Caitlin. 'Hop in, love.'

Jason – muddy and needing a shower desperately – had already bagged the front passenger seat but the girls were happy to slide into the back.

'You'll have to remind me where you live,' Jess fibbed to Caitlin, looking at her in the rear-view mirror. In fact she knew exactly where she lived, but decided to play dumb.

Caitlin gave her the address.

The meeting Mags was in was more of a personal thing than business, although there was a bit of the latter involved. It was taking place in a very large bedroom in a sixteenth-century former coaching inn set above the River Hodder called the Inn at Whitewell. It was the best room in the place with an immense double bed, a large seating area and a view overlooking the curve of the river. It cost a pretty penny but was worth it.

Particularly as the man she was in bed with – who had once again brought her to an outstanding climax, followed by his own earth-shattering orgasm during which Mags thought she was going to be pounded through the headboard – rolled slowly off her, gasping, out of breath from a bout of lovemaking that had lasted just over eight minutes, but which had exhausted them both.

'Out-effing-standing,' the man said, echoing Mags' thoughts.

'I second that,' she agreed with an extra shimmer of delight.

She rolled in close to him and laid a leg across his thighs.

It was at that moment that Mags' mobile phone rang, displaying Caitlin's number. Mags had to clamber over the man to reach the phone on the bedside cabinet.

'Shit – is that the time?' she said, having completely forgotten the existence of her daughter. 'I'd better get this,' she said to the man.

'No probs,' he said. He didn't mind having Mags straddling him, a sight he found quite exceptional.

Mags answered the call. 'What . . . in a meeting . . . get a taxi. Not hard, is it?' she said curtly to Caitlin. They exchanged one or two more brusque words, then Mags hung up.

The man squeezed her rump and slid a hand between her bum cheeks. Just as they were about to start on round two, which Mags knew would be more considered than the first one which had been quite bonkers, her phone rang again.

She swept it up and answered, very annoyed now.

The call, however, wasn't from her daughter as the man between Mags' thighs soon worked out as Mags became stiff and intense as the short conversation progressed.

When the call ended, Mags lobbed the phone on to a bedside chair on top of her discarded clothing.

'Not your daughter, then?' the man guessed.

'How perceptive,' Mags answered feeling some of the sexual desire leave her.

'Who, then?'

'Police Sergeant Jessica Raker.'

'You're taking the piss!' the man said, shocked on hearing that name.

'Her daughter goes to school with mine, same class. They're mates. Not much I can do about it,' Mags confessed.

'And you didn't ever tell me?'

Mags shrugged her naked shoulders.

'Wouldn't be an issue if Raker was dead, would it?' the man pointed out.

'Yeah, well, that didn't quite work out for you, did it?' She sagged a little over the man and her breasts brushed his chest. 'And now she's hounding me from pillar to post, so I could still do with her six feet under to be honest. So much for your contract killer, eh?'

The man chuckled mirthlessly. 'Didn't end well for him, did it?'

'No,' Mags said, beginning to grind herself against the man. 'But as it happens I'm in the process of warning her off . . . by various methods.'

'Maybe that's something we could get involved in . . . we have unfinished business with her . . . ahh,' he gasped as something delightful began to happen to him. 'At least my dad has – me, I'm not so sure to be honest . . . not least because the cops are all over us like a rash now, even though they can't prove a thing . . . Jeepers, jeepers,' he said, clenching his teeth as Mags rotated her hips.

'Cops haven't followed you up here, have they?' Her lips formed a perfect 'O' shape as something delightful also began to affect her.

'No, I'm too careful.'

'What about your wife? Did she follow you?'

'Like I said, I'm too careful to be followed.'

'Let's hope so,' Mags said and set about screwing the man underneath her towards another amazing finale for them both.

At the end with both sweating profusely, lying side by side, catching their breath, Mags asked, 'Did you bring your shotguns?'

'I think you know the answer to that,' he snickered.

'It wasn't supposed to have a double meaning.'

'I know, I know . . . and yes, I've brought two of the best shotguns money can buy. Two Purdeys.'

'I look forward to putting them to good use.'

'Me too. Should be fun.'

Mags rolled sideways and looked at the profile of the man with whom she was having an affair which gave her serious misgivings but the fact was, that despite herself, she couldn't stop seeing him, although this was only the third time in four months. Even so, any tryst with him was fraught with danger. From the cops, definitely, but maybe even more so from his wife Leanora who suspected the affair and who was very dangerous, as Mags had once discovered.

Mags, normally blasé about men, and could take or leave them and use them simply for her own pleasure, was completely overwhelmed by this one who, somehow, didn't even need to try and impress her, even in bed. He just did.

He also ran one of the most powerful organized crime gangs in London which supplied a lot of Mags' street products, and meeting him in the capacity as a drugs wholesaler was how their relationship had started, evolved and continued.

Now Mags wanted more. She wanted everything this man had to offer.

His name was Tommy Moss and he ran a multi-billion-pound OCG called, simply, the Moss gang, and nicknamed Moss Bros.

Jess continued to play dim and asked Caitlin for directions to the very, very (Jess could easily keep adding the word 'very' here) nice detached house in a small, exclusive gated community near Hurst

Green, a village situated between Clitheroe and Longridge, known for the internationally renowned school that was Stonyhurst College. It was well out of Jess's way but she didn't mind because it was a good excuse to get a close look at the place she was very interested in from a police perspective.

The journey took them over the River Hodder, giving Jess a glimpse of Cromwell's Bridge, the old footbridge over which Oliver Cromwell marched his troops to the Battle of Preston in 1648. It was also the place where the previous sergeant had supposedly taken his own life by throwing himself from the bridge, although Jess had actually unearthed the truth of the matter a few months earlier: not suicide, murder.

She hadn't known the sergeant personally but had come face-to-face with his killer and as she drove over the current bridge – Lower Hodder Bridge – she couldn't help but shiver inwardly a little at the memory.

Caitlin directed Jess to the exclusive estate consisting of eight homes, all of which commanded stunning views over the River Ribble at that point. The small community was protected by high walls and electronic gates. Caitlin had a remote control which she pointed at one of the gate posts and the high, ornate, wrought iron gates opened smoothly to allow entry.

Jess had to grin a little at two prominent signs. One said, NO COLD CALLERS and the other warned the estate had a neighbourhood watch scheme, which Jess knew was untrue. Another, slightly less prominent sign, told of twenty-four-hour surveillance cameras and a regular security patrol with dogs, which was true. Jess knew this because of her research into Mags.

'The one in the corner.' Caitlin pointed out the largest house. Jess had done some online house price checks and the estimate was just over two million. Jess also knew that a building company linked to Mags had bought the land and built the houses.

So, round figure guess, Jess estimated the properties in front of her were probably touching the sixteen-mill mark.

'That's a lovely house,' Jess said, pulling on to the curved driveway as if she'd never seen the place before.

'Just a house,' Caitlin said snottily, like a teenager.

'Oh, it's nice. Trust me,' Jess confirmed.

She wanted to keep up the pretence of not knowing much because she wasn't too sure how much Caitlin knew about her mother's personal and professional relationships with Jess, both of which were pretty unpleasant.

'Thanks Mrs Raker, appreciate it.' Caitlin hopped out of the car after giving Lily a big hug. Jess watched her walk to the front door and go in before leaving and keeping on the back roads all the way home to Bolton-by-Bowland.

FIVE

The first thing Jess did on arriving home and managing to park outside the cottage – the burned-out wreck of the Land Rover had been removed by a recovery garage – was to nip around to the house of the old guy who owned the stolen Jaguar which had turned up in flames outside Clitheroe police station.

He lived in a detached house surrounded by an ancient, high stone wall on the edge of the village and had a couple more restored Jaguars in his wide driveway, one being an instantly recognizable E-Type, one of the few cars Jess coveted because of its beautiful, ageless lines. She especially liked red ones, as was this.

His name was Walter Grindlestone. He was in his late eighties and lived alone in the house following the recent death of his wife. Jess had bumped into Walter and his wife a few times in the Coach & Horses and knew him well enough to address him by his first name. He was usually smartly dressed, rarely seen without a tweed jacket, corduroy trousers and brogues, and had a stunning handlebar moustache. As Jess walked up to his house she spotted him in his big, four-car garage leaning under the bonnet working on the engine of another sports car, the make of which she didn't know. He was wearing oily blue overalls.

He looked up with a spanner in his hand.

'Jess,' he said.

'Hi, Walter.' She gave a wave.

Wiping his hands on a rag he approached her, just as Jess recognized the make of car he was working on, a Jensen Interceptor.

'You come about the XJ6? Have you found it?' he asked hopefully.

This took her aback slightly. 'You haven't been told?'

'Told what, Jess?'

Shit. She bit her lip. She was sure she'd asked someone to inform him. Maybe she was going crazy.

'Oh, I'm really sorry, Walter, my mistake. You might want to sit down.'

Walter leaned on the Jensen instead and took the news stoically, although he was clearly affected by it.

'Sorry,' Jess found herself apologizing.

'Not your fault, eh? Lovely car but to be honest it was the runt of the litter and I'll get insurance money for it, though it wasn't worth all that much. I presume it was stolen by the scumbags who left that burning Land Rover outside your cottage?'

'Probably . . . now this one's a beaut,' Jess said appreciatively as they walked past the E-Type on her way out.

'Now that is worth a small fortune. You can have a go in it if you like?'

'Seriously?'

'Course. I love 'em and cherish 'em but I don't mollycoddle 'em. They need to get on the road occasionally.'

'I'll take you up on that one day soon,' Jess promised him.

Back at the cottage, Jess's mother, Marj, had arrived and the place was in a mini-form of chaos. Marj, who was widowed, had followed Jess north after her transfer to Lancashire and was currently also living in rented accommodation in the village but was close to signing up for a new-build house nearby. Jess had been delighted by her decision to come north if only for the sake of Lily and Jason who adored their grandmother who in turn spoiled them rotten.

It was also a great help for Jess in terms of childcare. With Josh working long hours commuting by early train into Manchester each day and frequently staying overnight when meeting clients, looking after the children had fallen to Jess who was often close to pulling her hair out juggling school runs and their expanding social activities and her own job. Her mum gladly stepped in to help.

Another facet of her mum's move north was that somewhere

along the way she had acquired a rescue dog, or 'pre-loved' as she called it. Why she picked the one she did, Jess would never understand. She could have chosen something the size of a Yorkshire Terrier, but Mum being Mum she plumped for a Weimaraner.

'It was her eyes,' her mum had cooed with her head tilted sideways. 'She looked at me, batted her eyelids and I was hooked.'

Fortunately the dog, rather like buying a used car, did have some sort of service history which Marj had diligently checked out. The dog was four years old, very beautiful, had been well trained by her previous owners but the unexpected arrival of human twins had made it impossible to give her the attention needed – and she needed a lot, hence turning up at the used-dog lot.

But Marj was up for it, as were Lily and Jason; Jess less so.

The dog had a lovely nature, thrived within the family, but had a strong, wilful streak which required someone with a firm nature to deal with.

Now at the cottage, Marj had arrived with the dog – named Luna – and it and the kids were involved in a crazy chase around the furniture, but as soon as Luna saw Jess come in she went for her in a manic show of affection which was difficult not to respond to and soon four humans were haring around, chasing and being chased by a barmy dog.

Finally things calmed down.

Luna curled up on a specially bought dog-pouf, the kids retreated to their rooms and Jess and her mother went into the tiny kitchen to prepare tea. Jess had left a beef casserole in the slow cooker which was just about done to perfection. Potatoes and carrots were now required.

Mother and daughter stood side by side peeling their respective vegetables. 'You made any decision yet?' Marj asked bluntly.

Jess knew exactly what she meant, but went around the houses anyway. 'About what, Mother dear?'

'That so-called husband of yours. Your marriage,' she said, staying blunt.

'We're working on it, not that it's any of your business.'

'It involves you, it involves my amazing grandchildren, so it is my business I'll have you know.'

Jess didn't really have an answer. Things were not great, to say the least. But she truly wanted the marriage to survive. Josh had hurt her badly in London, seeing a younger work colleague, but he assured her it was over and he hadn't dragged that baggage north. Jess wanted to believe him but was finding it hard to trust him.

A very hard task after everything that had happened.

'Yeah, maybe you're right.' Jess finished peeling her spuds, rinsed them and sliced them into quarters with a heavy kitchen knife. Once the potatoes and carrots were in separate pans and starting to bubble, Jess made herself a mug of tea and went to sit on the wall out front for a bit of self-reflection.

Although the Citroën was parked directly outside, she could still see the charred marks on the road surface where the Land Rover had been set alight. Her mouth twisted at the thought, wondering if this really had been a direct middle-finger warning at her, or just a coincidence. She would have liked to write it off as the latter, but it didn't sit easily with her.

The problem was that if it was directed at her then it was too close for comfort with regards to the kids and now her mum, because deliberately dumping the car right outside the cottage put her family in danger and that wasn't acceptable on any level.

Deep down she knew Mags was behind it.

Had to be.

She must have been at the wheel of the Land Rover that had managed to get away that morning. Jess hadn't been able to identify the driver but there were some things in her favour.

First there was the lad in custody who'd been chewed on by PD Flynn.

Then the sighting of Lance Drake.

And there was also the fact the lad who was on lookout duties who had assaulted Samira had been identified and he'd be locked up sooner rather than later if Jess had her way.

All three had questions to face and the answers might just point to Mags.

Jess mulled all this over, trying to get things in order for the next day, when all of a sudden her shoulders sagged wearily and she couldn't stop the wave of misgiving about dragging the kids away from London. Yes, her own life had been under immediate threat after the shooting when she had learned that a contract had been put out on her, but she somehow couldn't shake the feeling that she'd jumped out of the frying pan into the furnace and it had all been selfish of her.

But then something happened that flipped those dark thoughts on their head, something that would never have happened in London and which affected each member of her family that day. It all began with a terrible scream, the likes of which Jess had never heard before.

It came from inside the cottage and Jess recognized it as coming from Lily.

Jess hurled her remaining tea out of the mug and, fearing the worst-case scenario and with her heart in her mouth, she sprinted inside where her mother greeted her with, 'Kitchen! Kitchen! In the kitchen! In the kitchen!'

'Oh, my God,' Jess uttered, her imagination churning.

From the kitchen, Lily screamed again.

Jason, looking terrified, shot down the stairs. 'What's happening?'

'Don't know.'

Jess barged across the living room and burst through the kitchen door where she discovered the terrible, awful reason for Lily's screams of terror.

Her daughter was standing on a kitchen stool, horror etched across her pretty face.

Luna the Weimaraner stood perfectly still almost in the pose of a Pointer dog, with just the slightest quivering of her muscles giving it away that she was actually a living, breathing beast, and she was staring intently at the gap between the cooker and a kitchen unit.

Lily was pointing too, her right finger jabbing at the floor and the gap on which Luna's canine eyes were transfixed.

'It's in there, it's in there!' Lily screamed. She sounded as though she had seen a demon of some sort, one that was obviously a shape-shifter that could spirit its way into narrow gaps.

Jess pulled up short, assessing the dramatic tableau in front of her. 'What's in there?'

'A mouse, a mouse!' Lily cried.

The corner of Jess's mouth cracked into a half-smile. 'A mouse?'

'Yes, a mouse. Get it! Get it!'

Jess wasn't exactly fond of the little critters and had a certain dislike of them, but not to the musophobic level now being displayed by Lily and probably her mother.

Before she could speak to bring down Lily from the heights of terror, the mouse's head appeared between the cooker and cabinet. Jess had no idea what type it was – house, field or even a vole – but such consideration didn't matter to Luna who moved like lightning, jabbed her head forwards and suddenly the poor rodent was in the dog's mouth. Luna turned proudly to Jess who could see the back legs and tail sticking out between Luna's jaws. The shoelace-like tail flicked back and forth and the back legs scrambled in mid-air.

Jess held out a hand. 'Give.'

Luna seemed to assess this instruction. Jess could see the hesitation in the dog's whole demeanour and her eyes.

'*Give*,' she said again, more firmly.

But there was no way she was going to hand the mouse over willingly. She almost seemed to smile at Jess.

Jess lunged, hoping to grab Luna's collar.

Luna ducked, Jess missed.

The dog very neatly sidestepped and tore past Jess into the living room with no intention of forfeiting her squirming prize.

Jess spun to give chase.

Her mum and Jason leapt aside as the dog raced around the settee with Jess in pursuit, skittering on the concrete floor, as did Luna, her claws clattering, which is why she opened her mouth just a tad too far and the mouse spun out on to the hearth and instantly disappeared behind the log burner.

Luna went for it but Jess grabbed her collar this time and yanked her away and said to Marj, 'Kitchen, please.'

She dragged the unwilling dog out of the living room.

Jess turned to Jason who was standing there with a huge grin plastered across his face, loving every moment of it. 'Get me the hand shovel and brush,' Jess ordered him, 'and let's see if we can't capture this little beast.'

They took up their positions.

Lily and Marj peeked through a crack in the kitchen door, holding Luna back with some difficulty. The dog whined for freedom.

Jason was ready with the sweeping brush at one side of the log burner.

Jess was ready at the other side. She knew this was going to be a brutal affair. It had to be. Such was life in the countryside.

She glanced at the eyes at the kitchen door – Lily's terrified, her mother's slightly less so, and the dog with murderous intent plastered across her face.

'Right, with the end of the brush handle, you go in from that side, Jase,' she briefed her son. 'Do a bit of poking around at the back of the fire and see if you can get the little blighter to run in my direction.'

Jason looked worriedly at the shovel being wielded in his mum's hand. 'And what are you going to do?' he gulped.

'Flatten it.'

He weighed this up for a moment then said, 'OK.' He started to probe around the back of the fire as best he could. Jess set herself up in a position from which she could spring instantly into action.

The end of the broomstick rattled the back of the fire.

Behind them, Luna howled desperately, wanting to be part of the hunt.

Jess focused on the hearth.

Then the mouse appeared running at full pelt towards Jess.

Her reactions were good. On the firearms range Jess was often the fastest and most accurate shooter on the team, so getting a mouse should not have been much of a problem as the back of the shovel whooshed downwards. The mouse must have seen death coming from above and swerved – but not fast enough.

The shovel smashed down hard on to the small creature, flattening it as promised, in one deadly, traumatic blow.

The beast disintegrated under the shovel and Jess felt bad for it.

She kept the shovel in place, did not move, but looked at Jason who stood there, suddenly ashen-faced.

'You may not want to see what's under here,' Jess warned him. 'Maybe you should join the others in the kitchen.'

Jason didn't need any more encouragement to leave.

Jess waited for the kitchen door to close before slowly lifting the shovel and revealing the pathetic crushed body underneath.

She didn't feel very triumphant as she scooped up the remains and took the body to the front door intending to put it down a drain.

As she opened the door, Dougie Doolan was about to knock.

Jess stood there with the dead mouse on the shovel. 'Hi, Doug.'

* * *

'Sorry 'bout that,' Jess said, settling down at a table in the bar of the Coach & Horses opposite Dougie and a lady Jess assumed to be his wife. It was an hour and a half later. Jess had done tea for her mum and the kids whilst Dougie and his lady had been for a meal at the pub. 'Life in the countryside,' Jess apologized.

'No problem, though I didn't expect a blood bath.' Dougie grinned. 'I was just popping by to bring you up to date with stuff and we were going to eat here anyway.'

'So are you going to introduce us?' Jess prompted.

'Oh, yeah of course. Jess, this is my partner, Helen; Helen, this is Jess Raker.'

They shook hands and Helen said, 'Ah yes, I've heard a lot about you.'

Jess looked queryingly at Dougie who quickly said, 'All good, I promise you.'

They sipped their drinks. Dougie and Helen were on red wine having just finished their meal; Jess was on a pint of the now ironically named, as far as Jess was concerned, 4 Mice lager, brewed in the pub itself, a tipple she had very quickly grown to savour and appreciate.

'So, where are we up to, Dougie?' Jess wiped her lips.

'As regards the lad PD Flynn arrested, not far at all,' he said, referring to the individual who had been picked up legging it from the Transit van. 'He tells us there's no offence running away from a cop and that the other lad, the one who got away, was the driver and he was just getting a lift from him and he must have been the one who set fire to the van. Claims he knew nothing about the mill.'

'I presume he claims he doesn't even know the other lad?' Jess guessed.

'Same old, same old,' Dougie said. 'All we do know is that he's from London, which in itself should be an offence,' he smiled. 'Turns out he's called Liam Chambers. Ring a bell?'

Jess shook her head. 'London? Really?' She didn't like the sound of that.

'Looks like he could have OCG connections from the intel, but he has nothing pending such as warrants or anything, not wanted, not circulated.'

'But he's up here?'

Dougie nodded.

'I don't like that,' Jess admitted. 'Linked to Mags, you think?'

'Anything's possible with her.'

Jess certainly did not like that – a Londoner on her patch. Because of what had happened to her previously, any mention of the place made her jumpy.

'Which OCGs is the lad linked to?' she asked. Dougie knew all about Jess, her background and why she had left the Met.

'Don't know yet, still digging,' Dougie said.

'The Moss gang?'

'Like I said, I don't know, Jess. Sorry.'

'OK, OK.' She took a nervy gulp of lager.

'There was nothing on the van, either . . . so we had to let him go,' Dougie said delicately, expecting a strong reaction from Jess. 'There was nothing to hold him for.'

Jess kept it under control and just said, 'Bugger.'

'But there is something,' Dougie went on.

'Go on.' She glanced at Helen who seemed to have zoned out of the work-related dialogue and was looking at her phone.

'Lance Drake. I checked, like you asked.'

'And?'

'He got bail from remand. It's conditional – he has to wear an ankle tag and reside in a bail hostel in Accrington.'

'He'll disappear,' Jess predicted.

'Well, so be it,' Dougie said philosophically. 'Seems his brief caught the CPS with their thumbs up their arses,' he added colourfully.

'No change there.'

'Anyway, he got bail first thing this morning . . .'

'And by this afternoon he was in the audience watching a stolen car burn outside the nick, one stolen to replace the Land Rover that burned brightly outside my house,' Jess said, working all this backwards again, 'a vehicle which evaded us as we were about to close down a suspected drug factory. So was he the driver I couldn't ID? Or was he the one tied to a chair?'

Dougie shrugged. 'He'd've had to move PDQ to get there from Preston Prison.'

'True, but doable.'

'However, however . . . what I was about to say before I got rudely interrupted was' – he grinned at Jess who mouthed the word 'sorry' – 'the solicitor who briefed his barrister for the bail hearing in judge's chambers is also the one who does civil and criminal grunt work for Maggie Horsefield.' He sat back, folded his arms smugly and let that little gem of information trickle into Jess's brain, which it did.

'Circle of life,' she said.

'Question, though – why would Mags do that? Go to all that trouble to get a low-life like Lance out of jail?'

'To kill him?'

'Quite possibly. She is very extreme. Anyway, I need to pee.' Dougie used the chair arms to raise himself to his feet, then headed towards the loos.

Helen raised her eyes from her phone and watched him go, then leaned across to Jess and looked earnestly at her. 'I think he's poorly,' she said. 'And he's not telling me. Can you do anything?'

Jess strolled the short distance home after meeting Dougie, reflecting on Mags Horsefield (again), what he'd updated her on workwise and also what Helen had said to her – in confidence, she had stressed.

Jess's assault on Mags had yielded some successes, but more failures.

Sure, some of the drug raids Jess had led had disrupted trade a little around the Valley but none had taken her to Mags' doormat. The woman had remained untouched, which was frustrating. No one arrested had ever pointed to her and she seemed to rule by fear and intimidation, and because of this lack of success Jess was beginning to think that maybe Mags should be put on the back burner for a while. She would just have to keep hoping Mags would do something incredibly stupid that would give Jess and the cops an 'in'.

Plus, Jess also had a day job and could not allow herself to be totally consumed by Mags. She had the whole of the Ribble Valley to police. She wasn't a proactive detective able to allocate time and effort into just one criminal. Jess had people to supervise and lead. Staff performance targets to set and review, which all took time if done properly. The more she pondered it, the more she thought that stepping back from Mags would be a good thing and make her own life less stressful.

What Helen had said about Dougie also concerned her. Although

Dougie wasn't a member of her team, she saw it as her responsibility as a sergeant, colleague and friend to find out what was going on with him. If he told her to mind her own business, which she thought he might, that was fine but at least she must try.

What she could not have foreseen was that, without trying, Maggie Horsefield would come raging back into her life and Dougie's health situation would take a dark turn indeed.

SIX

As she reached her front doorstep, her mobile phone rang: Josh, her husband.

'Hi, how's it going?' he asked sweetly.

She really wanted to share the 'dog and mouse' story but the tone of his voice warned her off. It would have been great to have a joint belly laugh at the incident, one of those something and nothing things, but which was really important for the family despite the horror and violent death.

'Yeah, good. Where are you?' she asked. 'I can't hear the clatter of a train in the background.' She tried to sound light-hearted but struggled with it.

'Er, look, love,' he began.

Three words that should have come with a trigger warning.

'Let me guess,' Jess interrupted abruptly. 'Office? Clients? Meetings? Overnight in Manchester?'

'Pretty much sums it up,' he admitted flatly.

'Just make sure it doesn't involve a secretary,' she warned him bluntly and hung up, very peed-off at him.

'You really don't have much experience of goats, do you? It's plainly obvious.'

The accusation came from the mouth of what Jess – in her head only – called an 'older man'. She knew he was called Fred Beetson and was the reigning chair of the Newton, Slaidburn & Stocks Parish Council, also known as the NSSPC, which was having its regular monthly meeting at the Hark to Bounty pub in Slaidburn village.

Because most members were of a certain age, the meetings had a start time of 11 a.m. and a strictly enforced finish time of 12.30 p.m., so members could retire, business done, go to the toilet and then head into the bar to continue any discussions over beer, wine and subsidized steak-and-ale pie.

This was Jess's first ever NSSPC meeting and although she had done the prep work, she was regretting not having boned-up on goats. Who knew?

She thought the meeting went well, generally. She'd had her slot and updated everyone on local crime, public disorder and other police-related incidents and figures, but somehow the talk had veered off to complaints about a local goat breeder who had allowed his animals to stray and damage residents' gardens – and now they were up in arms about it.

Jess was half-tempted to respond with a facetious reply but she was far too professional for that, even though the question had been posed in quite a patronizing manner. A quick glance around the table in the meeting room at the half-dozen or so other council members, all of whom seemed to be hanging on her reply with bated breath, plus a quick glance at Joe Borwick who was there to answer questions about fire safety and carbon monoxide alarms, made Jess realize the question was of high importance.

'You have me there,' she conceded and confessed, 'I have no goat experience.'

'Well let me tell you,' a lady called Mrs Robbie piped up. 'They are an absolute menace and a blight on the village.'

'And that . . . that . . . bastard needs fettling,' another man added vehemently. His name was Croker.

'Mr Croker! Language,' Fred rebuked him with the wave of a gnarled, arthritic finger. Fred looked sideways at an old woman on his left who was scribbling down the minutes of the meeting. 'Miss Jones,' Fred said – almost making Jess crack up – 'please ensure the minutes record my verbal admonition of Eric Croker for continued use of bad language which will not be tolerated, no matter how emotive the subject of straying goats is.' He turned back to Jess. 'And believe me, sergeant, goats are very emotive.'

Croker looked miffed but took the hit with just a mutter of dissent.

'They ate my best knickers off my washing line,' a lady called Mrs Dane whinged. 'And a bedsheet.'

'A whole bedsheet?' Jess asked, wide-eyed.

'Between three of them, yes.'

Jess explained this was probably not a police matter but she would be quite happy to go and speak to the goat breeder if supplied with his details and warn him to keep his animals under control. This seemed to satisfy the meeting, which after a lengthy discussion about the wording on a headstone in the local cemetery – also an emotive subject, it transpired – was concluded after Joe spoke to them about smoke alarms and such-like which, even though Jess had an interest in Joe that was not purely professional, she found dull as ditchwater.

Jess had come to the meeting with Samira Patel and they were invited to the lunch after but kindly refused. Jess needed to get back to Clitheroe to tackle the many things piling up in her tray.

However, she did want a moment or two with Joe before getting back, just to tell him how interesting and informative his talk had been. A complete lie, obviously, but after last night's phone call from Josh she was feeling a bit teary and unloved, so she fancied a little bit of flirting and a few appreciative glances from a good-looking guy might go some way to building back her self-esteem.

'Your talk was hugely interesting,' Jess said. Out of the corner of her eye, she saw Samira smirk.

'You're being kind,' Joe replied, 'but it's nice to have an appreciative audience.' He held her gaze and despite herself something crumbled just a little inside her. Possibly her resolve.

'Thanks for yesterday,' she said. 'Vehicles on fire all over the show.'

'Same offenders, you think?'

'I'd say so.'

'Names in mind?'

'One or two people may be getting knocks on their doors in the near future.'

The short conversation was stilted in the way such dialogue often is between two people clearly attracted to each other as they slowly began to ease a path through the long grass, even though at this moment nothing was going to come of it. For now it was just very pleasant to have someone look at her with a twinkle in his eye. She was almost on the verge of making little circles on the floor with the tip of her toes, looking up at him and batting her eyes.

You are so pathetic, her inner critical voice reproved her.

'So, busy day ahead?' she asked Joe, clearly a deep, incisive question.

'Hopefully. Apparently there's an arsonist on the loose,' he grinned, 'or maybe there'll be a huge industrial fire that'll keep us going?'

'What about a kitten stuck up a tree?'

'I'll be there! What about you?'

'Well, beat up a few prisoners, take a few bribes, that sort of thing.'

They both laughed, each sensing what the other felt and the tension that was bringing to their interaction.

Jess's radio was on mute from the meeting but she saw Samira turn away to speak into hers.

'Best get back, then,' Joe said. 'Got a pole to slide down.'

Despite herself, Jess guffawed at the double entendre and she said, 'Isn't that my line?'

'It could be.' Joe waggled his dark eyebrows.

'Sorry to butt in, sarge,' Samira said, fully aware of what was going on between the two. She almost said, 'Sorry to interrupt the love-in,' but knew better.

Jess broke away from looking into Joe's eyes, though it was a wrench. 'What is it?' she asked Samira, her voice much testier than she wanted it to be.

'Er . . .' Samira tapped her radio. 'Problem at Wolf Fell Hall. It's all kicking off between the Hooray Henrys.'

'Wolf Fell Hall? Where's that?' Jess asked as she got in beside Samira in the somewhat bedraggled police car the PCSO was allowed to drive, the one with no two-tone horns and a blue light that was at best temperamental.

'Err . . . Wolf Fell,' Samira said.

'Well, obviously Wolf Fell . . . so where's Wolf Fell?'

'Chipping way,' Samira said, referring to the pretty village of Chipping situated east of Clitheroe, about halfway between that town and Garstang.

Jess knew Chipping, a quaint village nestling under Parlick Hill and quite close to Beacon Fell, though she had never heard of Wolf Fell before. But there were so many fells and moors with individual names in the Ribble Valley it would be almost impossible for anyone to know them all. She wasn't aware of Wolf Fell Hall, either.

'Hang on to your hat,' Samira said and fired up the engine and set off out of Slaidburn, firstly towards Dunsop Bridge.

'Do we know what's happening?' Jess asked.

'Not as such. Comms took a treble-nine from a mobile number and a shrieking lady said there was going to be a murder, get up here quick.' She looked at Jess. 'That's about it.'

'OK, pedal to the metal, lass.'

Whilst en route Jess radioed comms to ask for any updates but there was nothing since the first call, despite a number of unanswered callbacks from comms.

She fished her mobile phone out and did an internet search for Wolf Fell Hall, but out in the wilds the signal was terrible and she couldn't find anything.

She did radio through to Vinnie just to confirm he was also on his way – he was, ETA fifteen minutes.

Dougie Doolan also called up. 'I can be making if you like?' he offered.

Jess considered this a moment. 'Do you know anything about the place?'

'That's why I want to go,' he said. 'Shooting 'n' fishing parties, and other sorts of parties,' he said mysteriously.

'What other sorts?'

'Orgies.'

Jess looked sideways at Samira who almost swerved into the River Hodder.

'Orgies? Did I hear that right?' Jess asked.

'Notorious for them,' Dougie said. 'Which is why . . .'

'Well, it might be best to satisfy your curiosity, Dougie,' Jess said.

'Absolutely. I'm turning out from the station. I'll bring up the rear.'

'Oh, more importantly, the shooting party stuff? Is that likely to be an issue for us, Doug? Do we need an ARV to make way?' Jess asked, answering her own question really. Hooray Henrys (a phrase she hadn't heard for a long time) armed with shotguns, fuelled by champagne could be a lethal combination, and a few unarmed cops could well be a good substitute for grouse and Jess did not fancy having her bum peppered with shotgun pellets.

She called the control room and asked for an ARV to be making its way. Better safe than sorry.

At Dunsop Bridge they bore left, keeping on the road to Whitewell. Samira had recovered from her little blip at the mention of an orgy and was concentrating on driving fast but safe as she crossed the bridge over Langden Brook, a tributary of the Hodder which ran on their left-hand side.

'How's the application going?' Jess asked Samira, knowing she was in the process of applying to become a police constable again.

'Next stages upcoming. Psychometric tests and a physical.' She said the last word despondently. She was excellent with the brain stuff but the physical was one of the areas that Jess had spent extra time with Samira. She wasn't unfit as such but was a touch overweight, so Jess had embarked on a training and diet schedule with her to improve her overall fitness and hopefully drop a few pounds. She'd also done some psychometric tests with her and was certain Samira would give it a great shot this time round. Jess had seen so much potential in her that she thought it would be a shame for her not to be an actual cop.

'You'll be ace,' Jess assured her.

Samira exhaled a long, unsteady breath.

'Panicking not allowed,' Jess said.

'I know, I know.'

Jess's radio chirped up: HQ comms room. 'Receiving; go ahead.'

'We've just had that caller on again from Wolf Fell Hall. Now telling us that all is fine there and no need for police attendance.'

'Received. What's your take?' Jess asked the operator.

'Not happy.'

'OK, me neither. We'll still attend and keep the ARV coming,' Jess instructed.

Jess couldn't even begin to conceive of any situation in which she would not attend an incident based on a second call asking for the police not to come. It often meant someone had been put under pressure and that, in fact, nothing was fine.

Samira veered right and was suddenly on a very narrow, steep road signposted to Chipping. The surface was pitted and pot-holed. Because of the gradient she dropped a gear but the little car struggled on some sections until it finally levelled out at Long Knots and then there was a sharp left which Samira almost drifted around.

For a moment Jess was stunned, not by the driving, but because there, in the middle of nowhere, stood a lone red telephone box.

'Fancy that,' she said.

'I know, odd, eh?'

'Like this whole bloomin' valley,' she muttered. 'Not least because we've just driven past a wild boar park and a telephone box.'

Samira chuckled.

The car began its descent into Chipping.

'Not far now.'

As they drove through the narrow streets of Chipping, they met Vinnie coming into the village in the Defender from the direction of Longridge, and with him leading the way they drove along Fellbrow Rake, then bore right, passing a sign for Wolfen Hall.

Jess did a double-take. 'Is that where we're going?'

'No, that's Wolfen Hall,' Samira said. 'Straight on a bit more then we get to the entrance to Wolf Fell Hall. Completely different.'

Jess nodded. Into her radio she said to Vinnie, 'Blue light, please.'

'Roger that.'

'Why?' Samira asked.

'Sometimes it's best to announce an arrival and a statement of intent.'

The road ahead narrowed, but was still tarmac.

To be honest Jess usually preferred to arrive by surprise to incidents when possible, but she doubted that trying to sneak up to Wolf Fell Hall would be possible at any time, especially when the two police cars whizzed between a pair of huge stone gates into the land surrounding the hall. After about a hundred yards of a leafy, tree-lined drive, a whole impressive vista opened up as the drive swept down through a beautiful landscaped area towards the hall nestling at the bottom of the drive, set against the backdrop and magnificence of the actual Wolf Fell, which rose steeply behind the building. It was a view that took Jess's breath away on what was a clear, almost perfect day and she couldn't help making the comparison in her mind that she often did now between the Ribble Valley and London.

Obviously London was London, jam-packed with iconic buildings old and new, and stunning open spaces . . . but this . . . *this* . . . her brain could hardly find the thoughts to do justice to what she

Death on Wolf Fell   69

was seeing in front of her and she realized just how lucky she was to be working in such a jaw-dropping environment.

Just a pity her family didn't completely feel that, too.

However, she gave herself a mental pinch.

'Now that's one heck of a pad – at least from a distance,' she commented appreciatively.

'Certainly is,' Samira agreed.

The house was approached by the great, curving, descending driveway culminating in a huge, circular gravel parking area at the front. In Jess's opinion it wasn't quite as spectacular as the house used for *Downton Abbey*. This one seemed quite a bit smaller, although 'quite a bit' still meant huge. She didn't know much about historic houses, or even history come to that, but she guessed the place was probably a few hundred years old and throughout its existence had probably undergone many renovations, extensions and changes in ownership.

What did interest her most, though, rather than trying to guess the history of the place, was the here and now and the large number of vehicles parked in the turning circle at the front of the house, mostly of the four-wheeled variety such as Range Rovers, Shoguns and other big SUVs and some flat back pick-up trucks such as Ford Raptors.

All those plus the number of people milling about, maybe over two dozen men and women, and as she got closer she could see most were in traditional-looking shooting gear: tweeds, breeches, flat caps and Sherlock Holmes' style deerstalkers; there were a lot of shotguns visible, some held broken over people's shoulders or in the crooks of their elbows, others propped up against the cars. There were also plenty of drinks in hands, bottles of Champagne perched on car roofs, plus lots of wicker hamper baskets visible as folk tucked into chicken legs and vol-au-vents; several waitresses clad in tiny black mini-skirts swished between people with trays of drinks and food. A few dogs were also in evidence, spaniels and Labrador types.

Also noticeable, and sad, were the hundreds of dead birds and rabbits laid out forlornly on plastic groundsheets.

This was obviously the social gathering at the conclusion of a shoot-up on the moors.

'Look at all those dead birds,' Samira cried in anguish as she pulled up behind the Defender, which had looped in a wide arc to stop near the main entrance to the hall.

'The aristocracy,' Jess said, tight-lipped, 'seem to enjoy killing defenceless creatures.'

'Which might include us at the moment,' Samira pointed out, 'until the ARV arrives.'

'Hopefully they won't be that stupid,' Jess said with uncertainty. Her eyes criss-crossed the assembled shooting party, none of whom seemed remotely interested or concerned by their arrival. That was with the exception of two men standing at the top of the steps outside the front door. This pair were different: dressed in black jeans, black T-shirts and black trainers. Both were probably mid-thirties, not stocky but looked like quite fit, muscular guys and as far as Jess was concerned seemed to have stepped right out of central casting. If these individuals weren't bodyguards or some sort of security detail, Jess decided she would pack up and go home right now. Ex-cops, or former military, she wasn't certain. But they were the only ones interested in her and her colleagues, and their faces were serious.

Jess got out of the car and gave Vinnie a slash-throat gesture for him to shut off the blue lights now.

She walked towards the hall, the gravel crunching satisfyingly under the soles of her Doc Martens shoes, her favourite footwear, even off duty. Samira and Vinnie were in her slipstream.

It was no surprise when the two guys she ID'd as security (or whatever) exchanged a quick word between themselves and lurched towards her.

'Heading us off at the pass,' Jess muttered to herself.

She nodded at a couple of the post-shoot attendees but they were clearly uninterested in the three cops. The Champers and canapés were very much flowing and being quaffed. Lots of laughter and jollity, Jess guessed, was about to ensue.

Then she was face to face with the two guys, one of whom – the slightly older one, the boss maybe – held up a hand, gesturing for her to stop right there.

'Afternoon, sarge,' he said, trying to be affable in just those two words. And failing. Jess detected a southern accent, also just in those two words.

She stopped.

'No need for you to be here,' the younger one snapped, drawing a quick look of irritation from his older colleague.

The older one then forced a smile. Jess frowned and thought there was something vaguely familiar about him.

He said, 'Everything's sorted.' He twirled his forefinger. 'You can about-face now, if you like, guys. Literally, nothing to see.'

'Nah,' Jess said, drawing out the word with a touch of steel. 'I'll be the judge of that,' she said firmly. 'What's gone on?'

'Just a bit of a disagreement, all sorted now,' he promised her with a deadpan face. 'So, yeah, you can go.'

Jess shook her head. 'I want to speak to whoever phoned in on the treble-nine system.'

'You don't have a name?' the guy sneered.

'No, but you obviously know all about it,' she said, 'so take me to whoever called. Let me speak to them and I'll decide if I stay or go.' She was already getting angry by this point. 'And I'm definitely not going until I do.'

'Like I said, you need to go,' the guy insisted. He took a threatening step towards her, holding up his hand as a barrier in front of her chest.

The younger guy adopted a threatening, ready-to-move stance just behind him.

'I want to speak to the owner of this property,' Jess said.

'You can want all you want.' The guy smirked. 'Not gonna happen.'

A tiny spurt of adrenaline entered Jess's system and her heartbeat upped a notch. But she felt calm and controlled, not remotely intimidated by this man and his running mate.

'If you touch me, you're under arrest,' she warned him.

He sniggered mirthlessly and looked derisively at her, then at Samira and then Vinnie, weighing up his odds, obviously anticipating a confrontation. 'I don't think so, love.'

'Let me go past, or get me the owner – your choice,' Jess said.

Jess saw the guy's jaw roll, then he hacked up and spat on the gravel, at which moment two vehicles appeared at the top of the driveway, heading towards the house. One was Dougie Doolan's CID car and the other a liveried ARV Ford Galaxy.

'Firearms cops, boss,' the younger guy hissed into the other's ear.

The man sneered at Jess and said, 'Stay here, I'll get you the owner.' He spun and disappeared into the hall, leaving his subordinate to stand between Jess and the entrance, his legs shoulder width apart, chest out, his head doing that 'bobbing' thing she'd seen so many tough guys do when pushing for a confrontation with the cops.

The two cars pulled up behind Jess.

Dougie got out of his and walked stiffly up to her. The two ARV officers also got out of their vehicle and Jess gestured for them to hang fire.

'No orgy so far, Dougie,' Jess informed the detective.

'Time yet.' He grinned.

'Dirty old man,' she ribbed him.

'Comes with the territory and I'm pretty much past caring,' he said.

At first Jess took the remark as a bit of a joke until she looked at Dougie's face and saw a pained expression coupled by a wistful, lost look she found slightly confusing. She wondered if this had any connection with what Helen, Dougie's partner, had confessed to her about her worries regarding his health.

Jess logged it. She would speak later.

She cast her eyes over the security man who was staring at her; she gave him a nice smile and then, as she waited for the return of 'Guy One' as she'd named him, she looked at the shooting party again, not expecting to recognize any of them, even if in fact they were local people, as she was still pretty new to the area despite having grown up in the Ribble Valley.

'That one there,' Samira said, sidling up alongside Jess and pointing discreetly to a rotund, middle-aged bloke scoffing half a meat pie, 'owns a chain of baker's shops, two in the town centre. Rich dude, as well as a chubster.'

Jess nodded. She knew Samira, who'd worked diligently as a PCSO around the town centre for a few years, had a good knowledge of its denizens. 'So not all Hooray Henrys,' Jess said.

'Wannabees, more like,' Samira said. 'Minted, though.'

Vinnie had sidled up to her other ear. 'And that guy' – he pointed out another middle-aged man of similar proportions to the baker – 'owns a car dealership in Whalley.'

'Yeah, I think I've seen him before,' Jess said, having been around to a few car sales places to try and offload her Citroën Picasso, which with over 130,000 miles on the clock was well past its best before date, although it was still reliable. 'Dougie?' She turned to the detective. 'Do you know some of this lot?'

'A few.'

Jess was still looking at mostly ruddy, male faces with a smattering of women when she spotted the back of someone who looked very familiar, a woman mostly blocked out by the back end of a black Range Rover, which Jess did recognize.

Jess saw this woman was talking to a man, a very handsome, alley-cat looking guy, maybe early forties. They were face to face, touching. She was laying her left hand on the lapel of his shooting jacket, but had a glass of Champagne in her right. There was obviously something intimate going on, the man was smiling, nodding, looking into this woman's eyes (Jess guessed), although there was one moment when the man looked up past the woman, straight at Jess and mouthed something to his companion which caused the woman to become completely still and turn her head slowly to look at Jess . . . who swore inwardly.

But the moment was interrupted by the reappearance of Guy One followed by an oldish woman, dressed in countrified clothes, right down to her expensive-looking Wellington boots.

'Lady of the house,' Dougie said.

Guy One had a look of rage on his face, aimed squarely at Jess as he stood aside to allow the woman to come past him.

'Sergeant,' the woman said.

'Sergeant Jess Raker from Clitheroe police station. May I ask who you are?'

'I am Carolynne, Duchess of Dunsop and Newton,' the woman stated regally.

'Duchess?' Jess said, trying to keep her amusement hidden. 'Dunsop and Newton?' she said, naming two villages which were close by.

'Correct, but you may call me Carolynne.'

'OK,' Jess said, 'Carolynne. Did you make the emergency call?'

'Yes, but I cancelled you. So why, pray tell, are you here?'

'Because I always like to check up on a job, even if I'm told we are no longer needed, Carolynne. I assume this is your property?'

'It is. It has been in my late husband's family for hundreds of years.'

'Oh, very good.'

'And we own thousands of acres of Wolf Fell.'

Jess nodded. 'Used for shooting?' she guessed.

'And fishing, as you can see.' The duchess did a sweep of her arm.

Jess was trying to work out how old this woman was. She was heavily made-up, everything plastered on thickly with false eyelashes that could have caused high winds. Her hair was a strange shade of blue and was clearly a wig. Her skin sagged and she had a neck as scrawny as a gecko.

Possibly fifty years old. Maybe seventy. Or more.

'Anyway, as I said, there is no reason for you to be here. The incident is over, everyone is safe and calm. There is hardly any damage to speak of, so if it's all right with you – off you go!' She made a shooing gesture as though dismissing a pleb – or just a working-class cop.

'Who was involved in this incident?' Jess asked, thinking that better people had shooed her away before now, including a home secretary and, once, she was pleased to say, Prince Philip, and the latter was something that stirred a memory. She looked quickly at Guy One, imprinted his features on to the Rolodex at the back of her mind, then back at the duchess.

'What was the incident?' Jess asked. She wasn't being shooed anywhere.

'Oh nothing. Boisterous boys and their toys.' The duchess giggled.

'What toys?'

She saw the duchess glance around now with an anxious expression on her face.

'Guns?' Jess guessed. 'Shotguns?'

The duchess looked at Jess and sighed. Her thin shoulders dropped in defeat. 'Look, an argument happened, a shotgun was discharged into a ceiling inside the hall. It wasn't aimed at anyone and I'm sure it went off accidentally. That's it! Done, dusted. Over with. Hands shaken, friends again. Brothers. Royalty.' The last word was uttered with a low, warning growl to it.

Jess loved it when even the slightest pressure got people to blab. 'Perhaps I should see these brothers and check they are OK, please. I take it they are inside the hall, not any of this lot out here?' She wafted her fingers at the shooting party in a way she hoped was as dismissive as the duchess's 'shooing' gesture had been to her.

Guy One stepped forwards and whispered something urgently into the duchess's ear, cupping his hand over his mouth to prevent Jess either hearing or lip-reading. All the while his angry eyes were on her. He stepped back, having delivered his message.

'I'm afraid I cannot allow you to see the brothers,' the duchess informed Jess.

'In which case I will enter your house, hall or whatever it is, using lawful powers which give me the authority to enter any property in which I believe there is a threat to life,' Jess quickly lectured the duchess. 'Much better if you take me in and show me, then things don't get . . . unpleasant.'

'I know the chief constable, you know?' the duchess said snootily. 'I know him well.'

Words and a claim, Jess thought, designed to impress but didn't, not least because the chief constable was a woman.

'Right, Carolynne, the time for this bullshit is over. Me and my officers are going to enter the premises, so please make this easy, but I'm not bothered if you don't.' She eyed the security guards, still trying to get a line on them. They had started bouncing on the balls of their feet, getting excited. 'Come on, Carolynne, let's get moving.'

Jess took a few steps forwards.

Guy One and the now-named Guy Two moved into a shoulder-to-shoulder position to block her way.

'Don't be silly,' she said.

The duchess waved the two men down. 'Let's just do this,' she relented.

She turned and went towards the front door.

Jess followed, tailed by her crew, the two security guys bringing up the rear.

Once through the front entrance of the hall they entered a huge, circular, tiled foyer with various rooms and corridors off it. The duchess led them along a long ground floor hallway, and as soon as Jess entered she could hear two raised, angry male voices from a room somewhere up ahead. They were obviously having a go at each other – 'verbals', Jess would describe the exchange. At first no words were discernible but snippets could be made out the closer they got.

'You complete dickhead,' one voice was saying. 'Damned, damned fool . . . you can't just decide that . . . a frickin' waitress for God's sake!'

'I— I—' the second one responded.

'All of us put in danger . . . all of us . . . right up to the top, to the king, you imbecile.'

'She was only a waitress. She knew stuff . . .'

The duchess stopped by an open door, beyond which this argument was taking place.

She gestured to Jess – *after you*.

As Jess stepped into the room, what she imagined was probably called a drawing room, though in her world it was just a big living room, she saw overturned furniture – two large leather armchairs, a dark wooden coffee table with its contents scattered across the carpeted floor, a glass-fronted display case and a broken old writing bureau. It looked as though a very angry elephant had rampaged through, followed by a hurricane. It was complete chaos, made worse by the two youngish men who had probably caused it all, now at each other's throats.

They were both mid-twenties and one had the other pinned to a wall by his throat, their noses almost touching and giving a view of their silhouettes. The one pinned to the wall was trying to struggle free, trying ineffectually to prise the other man's forearm from his windpipe, using fingers that could not get a proper grip. He gasped for air whilst the other one screamed into his face.

Just from the silhouettes Jess saw the resemblance between them. Though both were of a similar age the one doing the pinning looked to be the older one and was bulkier and stronger, hence his position of dominance.

'She . . . was . . . nothing,' the one against the wall gasped, hardly able to speak.

'Idiot! Idiot!' the other one said.

Jess went towards them, feeling like she was walking through a thin, white dust cloud or mist, then realizing what it was when she looked up: plaster drifting down from the ceiling which had been peppered with blasts from two shotgun cartridges; at the same time she noticed a shotgun discarded on a rug, but these were things she was only spatially aware of. She shouted, 'Enough, enough,' as she strode towards the grappling men, intervened forcefully and yanked them apart, immediately aware of the reek of alcohol on their breaths and the stench of weed on their clothing. She shoved the dominant one roughly away and he staggered backwards, caught the back of his knees on an occasional table and went flat on his backside. The other one slithered down the wall, clutching his throat, moaning and snivelling at the same time.

'Oi, bitch!' the one who had fallen shouted at Jess. 'You're not allowed to touch me.' He scrambled on all fours towards the shotgun at which point Vinnie stepped in and placed a foot down on the stock of the weapon.

'You back off,' Jess warned him. 'What the hell's going on here?'

She wafted away the plaster cloud particles and got a proper look at the ceiling in which two main holes plus countless pellet holes had been drilled by the shotgun.

'Sarge, sarge, sarge,' a man called from behind her: Guy One. He put himself between Jess and the man on the carpet. 'You're the one who needs to back off here. These two young men are members of the royal family and you do not, a) speak to them like that, or b) think you can even touch or take them into custody. All is peaceful now, all is under control. Just leave it with me and my colleague to deal with, OK? Minor argument, nothing else.'

'And you are who, exactly?'

'Jack Harker. My colleague and I are personal bodyguards to these two gentlemen.'

'Gentlemen?' Jess said, screwing up her nose.

The one on the floor slumped back on to his bottom and wiped his slavering mouth and snotty nose with the back of his hand.

'So like I said, outside,' Harker – Guy One – reiterated, 'nothing to see here.'

'Shotgun blasts through the ceiling, furniture overturned and damaged' – she noticed a broken window for the first time – 'plus that, not to mention broken vases and cups and a violent altercation right in front of me! Nothing to see! Bollocks, I say to that, Mr Harker.' Jess peered at him through narrowed eyes. Then, 'Do I know you?'

'I very much doubt it,' Harker said a little unsurely, suddenly unable to look her directly in the eye.

'Anyway, bottom line, we are not leaving until I say there's nothing to see here, understand?'

SEVEN

Jess finally brought some semblance of order to proceedings by getting the two alleged members of the royal family out of the smashed-up drawing room and into another room further along the hallway that had not been trashed. It was a large dining room with a big, oval mahogany table and matching chairs and other furniture including display cabinets containing what looked like very rare and expensive silverware, jewellery and pottery. The walls were clad with equally expensive-looking art. A couple looked like framed Constables and others of that sort of era; some looked more modern, maybe Impressionists. *All very nice*, Jess thought in passing, knowing the extent of her knowledge of art would leave room even on a postcard. Her only interest was in mass-produced stuff that she would occasionally buy from a garden centre or supermarket.

The two royals had been separated and plonked down on opposite ends of the dining table, both nursing their wounds, dabbing at abrasions and bloody noses with tissues.

Vinnie had taken possession of the shotgun, broken it and taken out two recently fired cartridges.

Samira was on door duty in the hallway, having been instructed to allow no one into the room, including the duchess who was hovering around like a spirit, but in particular the two security guys, Harker and the other one who was called Leighton.

The other people not being allowed entry were the girlfriends of the royals, two painfully pencil-thin ladies dressed in tightly tailored riding jackets and breeches who had apparently just returned from a canter in the hills. Jess assumed they meant horse rides.

The ARV crew remained on standby outside the hall.

Jess looked pitifully at the two bashed-up royals.

Not that their lineage or position in society mattered to her. They were just two half-pissed guys who had imbibed weed and had an argument which included discharging a shotgun and had escalated enough for someone to call the police on them. But she was also not naïve enough to know they would probably pull social and hierarchical rank on her to keep themselves out of trouble.

Their names were Edward and Bruce Armstrong-Bentley, a surname which did not roll easily off the tongue, but when they spoke their own name they seemed to relish it. To Jess, their double-barrelled surname sounded more like a long defunct British car manufacturer and, even though she had a passing interest in the royal family, their moniker did not mean anything to her.

She was on her feet, keeping up the psychological advantage over them.

Dougie Doolan stood by the large bay window, arms folded.

As the discussion progressed, Jess realized the two men had retreated into self-preservation mode as though now appreciating their fallout and the subject of it was unwise, maybe dangerous, to share.

She could see it in their eyes and regretted not separating them into different rooms, but by the time she realized this it was too late.

'Are you going to tell me what this is about?' she asked, and not for the first time. She saw the look pass between them along the length of the table, the 'say nothing' glare.

'Look,' the older one said – this was Edward – 'it was just a jolly old, brotherly tiff that got out of hand, no harm done.' He was trying to sound reasonable.

'But so much so one of you blew a hole in the ceiling?' Jess asked.

'OK, it did get a bit out of hand, admittedly,' Bruce said. 'But no one was ever in danger, it was just high spirits.'

'So let's draw a line in the sand under this,' Edward said. 'And move on.'

'And we promise to be good,' Bruce added, putting his hands together under his chin as if he was praying and beseeching Jess – a gesture she thought was pretty pathetic under any circumstances.

'I don't know,' Jess said. She looked at them and said, 'Stay there, don't move.' To Dougie she said, 'Hallway.'

Outside, out of earshot, Jess and Dougie walked up and down the hallway in which the two bodyguards and the duchess hung around nervously.

'What do you think? Drag 'em in?' she asked the detective.

Before he could answer, Samira edged up to them with her mobile phone in her hand. 'Sarge?' She handed it to Jess. 'This is them.'

Jess looked at the screen on which Samira had found an entry on some website relating to British royalty about the Armstrong-Bentley brothers. Jess skim-read it, seeing they were twenty-eighth and twenty-nineth in line for the throne respectively, a figure dependent on births and deaths. They had a big, shared pile of their own in Sussex inherited from their parents who had perished in a light plane crash in Kenya some years ago. A lot of their money was tied up in properties in Mayfair and Knightsbridge. A quick read of the entry about their lifestyle showed that both guys were out of control socially, off the rails, probably snorting their fortune away in white powder. They had got to know the duchess and her late husband through their parents who were once part of a big London social scene involving lower ranking members of the royal family.

She nodded at Samira, handed the phone back, then turned to Dougie who had managed to peer over her shoulder at the phone. She arched her eyebrows. 'Well?'

'Too much like a ton of hard work for little result,' he said philosophically. 'There's enough to take 'em in but all they'd get is a polite bollocking and probably the chuck wagons would circle the royal family. You could seize the shotgun, but there's fifty others around here. For me, and I know it's your decision, give 'em that bollocking now and don't make it polite; tell the duchess you're not impressed and if we are called back, arrests will be made, royalty or not.'

Frustratingly his point made sense.

Arresting them would generate a lot of work for nothing, but Jess wasn't happy about it.

Yet she nodded at Dougie then whispered, 'What about the orgies?'

'They're tonight.' He grinned. 'Looks like there's a ball on or something – I just peeked into the big hall down there. All set out, silver service and all that, some sort of band setting up on the stage.'

'Hm . . . and did you see who was lounging about outside like Lady Muck?'

'Our very own drugs queen.'

Death on Wolf Fell   81

'So what's she doing here? Moved up in the world?'
'If I could guess,' Dougie said, 'I'd venture providing nose candy to the hoi polloi.'
'My thoughts, too,' Jess said. 'Anyhow, I'm going back in there and rollock the two royals up hill and down dale, then offer words of advice to the duchess.'

For Jess, after all that excitement, the remainder of the day was spent chasing a cop's worst nightmare – paperwork. She did her best to get as much of it out of the way as possible, concentrating hard and trying not to let her mind slip back to the things that were gnawing away at her.

First, was the burning Land Rover outside her house and the burning Jag outside the station a warning to her and to other cops? One thing was certain, Jess would confront Mags about the incidents, and bluster her way through even though there was no direct evidence to link Mags to the fires. She would have done that at Wolf Fell Hall if she'd had time after laying down the law to the royal family, but when she emerged from the hall Mags and the mystery man she was consorting with were nowhere to be seen. Jess wondered if the poor guy knew he was doing a dance of death with a black widow spider. Jess also wondered evilly if she should warn him off, tell him what a dangerous woman Mags was, just for the spite.

Those thoughts brought a cruel smile to Jess's face. They weren't really serious but the mischief-maker in her was sorely tempted to try and screw up whatever the relationship was.

'Oh yeah,' Jess said to herself, 'what fun that would be.'

Her other recurring thought was whether or not she had done her job properly at Wolf Fell Hall by not making arrests, at least for a breach of the peace. Something inside her hated to see wrongdoers get away with anything.

There was something deeply unsettling about leaving the situation unresolved but sometimes common sense was the best option.

Her desk phone rang.

It was Inspector Price. Without any foreplay, he said, 'There's a complaint been made about you. I mean, jeez, trouble follows you everywhere like a bad smell, doesn't it, Sergeant Raker? Who the hell else could have had a complaint made against them by two members of the royal family and a duchess about the disgusting way in which you spoke to them? You're just a continuous shitshow, Raker – and, yeah, I am gunning for you.'

'I hadn't realized you were,' Jess fibbed as her face flushed up red, all the way from her chest. Her heart began to pound.

'You took my mate's job. That sergeant's role should have been his and now he's dead.'

Jess gulped and controlled her breathing. 'First bit, yep – I got his job, just by accident, though. Second bit has nothing to do with the first, so if you'll pardon my expression, stick it where the sun don't shine. And as regards to the complaint, get it down on paper formally and bring it on. And not only that,' she concluded dramatically, 'your so-called mate was a corrupt git who got everything he deserved.'

She hung up, slamming the phone down hard, hoping the crash of it burst his eardrums.

Then she calmed herself down. Deep breaths. Focus on reducing heartbeat. More deep breaths. Calm. 'I'm quietly gunning for you, too, Inspector Price,' she whispered to herself.

At least she was off out tonight to chill a bit. Not on a bender because she was driving, but a chance to relax, eat a decent meal, chat with some people she'd grown to like very much over the last few months.

She stuck two fingers up at the phone, then stood up. Lily and Jason needed picking up from school.

Mags had obviously seen the arrival of the police at Wolf Fell Hall, although at the time she wasn't sure what was going on or what they were responding to.

Like most of the other guests on the shoot, she had only just returned from the moor and was celebrating the success by lining up their kill, which consisted of numerous game birds and rabbits. She herself had blasted the life out of four pheasants using Tommy's precious shotguns, and Tommy had bagged an even dozen.

Then they were on Champagne and hors d'oeuvres being served on trays by the waitresses prior to the big slap-up meal later at which a selected number of guests (she and Tommy had been invited to the dinner, but they had declined) would attend and be packed with local dignitaries who were all usually up for snorting a few lines of world-class coke at exorbitant prices. They all liked weed too, which was supplied by Mags, plus the catering was done by a company she part-owned, so it was all easy money which she would obviously donate to local charities. She giggled at that thought.

But although having decided not to attend the meal that evening, she and Tommy had arrived very early at the hall, well before any shooting took place, in order to have a slow mooch around the inside, arm in arm, to take in and appreciate the artwork and other valuable items on display in the hallways and rooms. At the conclusion of this tour, Mags – who had been around the place several times in the past – had turned to Tommy with a smirk on her face, slid her arms around his waist and looked up lovingly at him and asked, 'Well? What do you think of all these treasures?'

He'd grinned and replied, 'I like them a lot, babe. A lot.'

The arrival of the cops did unsettle her a bit, although Tommy was fascinated by them, especially when Mags recognized Jess getting out of the lead police car and turned quickly away to take some cover provided by her Range Rover.

'That's her!' she said to Tommy. 'In the flesh.'

Tommy hadn't attempted to take cover. He said, 'I know,' and watched Jess as she scanned the scene in front of her.

This was literally the first time he had seen Jess in the flesh, but he knew who she was: the woman firearms cop who whilst in the Met had gunned down his little brother Terry following a robbery in Greenwich. This had resulted in Tommy's father, Billy Moss, putting out a contract on Jess but that had gone sour: she had survived, and the hitman had ended up in prison minus an ear. Even though there wasn't a direct link to the Moss crime gang it was well known they had initiated the contract, and a very high-ranking detective had made it clear that the Moss family was being scrutinized and one misstep would result in a very heavy law-and-order boulder rolling on them.

The Moss gang immediately backed off. There was far too much money at stake to jeopardize, legit or otherwise, and the Moss gang was not a foolish entity.

Tommy had warned his father that putting a contract on a cop was a fool's errand under any circumstances, but there was no doubt that now, seeing this woman in the flesh, Tommy experienced a terrible inner reaction, suddenly seething with hatred towards her and the thought that he would actually like to put his hands around

Raker's slim neck and throttle the life out of her was very strong. Terry may have been a wayward nutter, but as the saying goes, he was Tommy's wayward nutter.

Mags watched Tommy's whole demeanour change as he looked at Jess. She could see, sense, feel the hatred welling within him.

And she liked it.

She had been instrumental in directing the Moss gang in Jess's direction and it would have suited her to have Jess taken care of just from the point of her own business in the Ribble Valley. It hadn't happened but she liked to keep her options open. And now with Jess having basically declared war on her it was a real pain in the backside and the thought of pushing Jess under a real bus was very appealing. But for the moment the less than subtle warnings would have to do, except what she now felt inside Tommy, that rage ignited by just seeing Raker, made her think differently.

'You'd like to kill her, wouldn't you?' Mags egged on Tommy as he glared at Jess.

Tommy's nostrils dilated. 'Setting a contract killer on her was always a bad plan,' he said almost without moving his lips. 'But deep down, that doesn't mean to say I don't want her wiped off the face of the planet. Terry was a fool and he got what was coming to him, but at the end of the day I loved him and I still grieve for him.'

'So that's a yes?' Mags probed naughtily, even though what Tommy had said seemed a long way off saying yes. She sipped her champers and bit into a prawn vol-au-vent whilst looking up at him, her mind working overtime, churning with violent ideas. 'We make a good team, you and me,' she said.

'We do.' Tommy's eyes stayed fixed on Jess.

Mags snuck a look and saw Jess was now talking to the duchess.

'Wonder what's going on?' she pondered.

Tommy shrugged. 'Dunno.'

Mags looked at him again, knowing that she had really fallen for this guy, Tommy the London-based hoodlum and hard man who ran the Moss OCG now on behalf of his father. Tommy the gangster who Mags saw perhaps four times a year at most for eagerly anticipated sex.

Tommy the married man who had a wife, Leanora, a dangerous woman.

And the ideas churning around in Mags' brain were two-fold. They concerned death and marriage.

'Sarge.'
Jess looked up from the screen of her computer.
Dougie stood at the office door.
'Hey, Doug, come on in. I'm just about to log off for the day.' She beckoned him in and he sat with a long, exhalation of breath.
'Are you really OK?' Jess asked.
'Yeah, yeah, course.'
'OK,' she said, unconvinced. 'What can I do for you, love?' Jess almost winced at calling him 'love', a particularly northern way of addressing folk which she always thought was pleasant and unthreatening but which was now under fire from certain quarters of society, and to be honest she was always careful who she spoke to in such a (nice) way just in case they were offended. She peered closely at Dougie to judge any signs of illness. He just looked weary.

He had a folder in his hand. He tapped it. 'The guy Maggie Horsefield was cosying up to at Wolf Fell Hall?'

'The hunk? Yeah. I didn't get a great view of him even though I toyed with the idea of letting him know she was likely to devour him after the mating ritual.'

'You really don't like her, do you?'

'On so many levels, Dougie, as you know,' Jess admitted. She had told him about hers and Mags' intertwined personal histories that went way back to their teenage years around Clitheroe and the torrid dispute over a dim-witted but well-endowed lad which culminated in a sordid scenario involving fights, damage and threats.

That had been during the summer before Jess went to university in York, where she met Josh, and Jess had been happy to leave that situation well behind and basically never set foot in the town again.

On her return to the Ribble Valley as a cop, Jess had encountered Mags at the school gates to find that their loathing for each other had reignited, especially when Jess learned how big and sprawling a criminal enterprise Mags controlled.

'Anyway, don't blame you,' Dougie said. 'However – that guy?'
'Go on.'
'This is him, isn't it?' He slid an A5-sized photograph out of the folder and placed it on the desk, a grainy black-and-white photo of

the man sitting at a table at a pavement café, talking to another guy whose face was pixellated out. Jess recognized the shot for what it was – a surveillance photo, probably taken from a moving car. There was a Metropolitan Police stamp in one corner of the picture. Even in the photo, which wasn't great, he was definitely a good-looking guy and Jess kind of thought she recognized him, but couldn't quite place him.

'That's him,' she confirmed.

Dougie said, 'Familiar? Think hard.'

'Don't tease me, Doug, I've had a hard day.' However she looked at the photo again and demanded her brain do some legwork. Who was he? What was it that made him familiar?

Then suddenly, she had the sudden intake of breath and instantly she was back in Greenwich in London, shouting instructions and warnings at a young man she was pointing a gun at. 'Stop! Police! Put down your weapon or I'll shoot!' Those kind of instructions, designed to ensure that every person in the scenario came out alive.

As it happened, the young man did not want to listen.

Instead he turned and tried to shoot Jess.

But Jess was quicker and did what had to be done, a moment in time, mere nanoseconds, that would live with her forever. And in that flash of time, as the lad pivoted, she saw his face, the exact features of which were on the photograph of the guy that Dougie was showing her.

'This could easily be an older version of Terry Moss, the lad I . . .' she hesitated. 'The lad I . . . shot and killed in London.'

'That's because it is,' Dougie said. 'Tommy Moss, eldest brother, now in his early forties, last arrested about twenty years ago for a nothing job, really. Kept out of the limelight since, but regularly under surveillance, hence this picture which I managed to get from a contact in the NCA, who were actually following the other guy in the photo.'

'How did you manage to ID him?' Jess said, amazed.

'Almost thirty years of being a jack has some positives.' Dougie tapped his nose mysteriously.

Jess wiped her hand nervously across her features. Even though she had been under threat from the Moss gang she had never spent a lot of time poring over them, which was perhaps remiss but she hadn't wanted to fill her head with them. She had seen photos of all the brothers, Tommy included, and the father, but had never seen him in the flesh before which is perhaps why, she defended herself, she hadn't made the connection. She would have done at some stage, but Dougie – bless him – had beaten her to it.

'This is very interesting,' Jess said, keeping her voice level, trying to keep a quaver out of it.

'Understatement . . .' He hesitated and Jess picked up on it.

'What?'

'My contact says the word is that Tommy is the one who personally contracted the hitman on behalf of Billy Moss, the daddy.'

'Right, so he ordered my assassination,' Jess said. 'And now he's up here, knocking around with Mags.'

'He is. Look, let's not panic. It doesn't necessarily mean anything in relation to you and the Moss gang,' Dougie said, reading her mind and trying to comfort her. 'It's good we know about this relationship, though, whatever the nature of it.'

'Understatement,' Jess said, 'but thanks for this.'

'I'll feed it into our intel system.'

Jess nodded, her eyes still glued to the photograph.

'Anyway,' Doug said more brightly, 'you still up for tonight?'

'Absolutely, can't wait.'

'In that case I'll see you at the Nick o' Pendle at seven thirty p.m.'

'Ooh, just one more thing popped into my mind to do,' Jess said.

For once Jess was slightly early at the school gates. Her mother had been due to pick up Lily and Jason but Jess cancelled her for a couple of reasons, the main one being that she wanted to be the one who picked them up, the second that she hoped Mags would be there to pick up Caitlin.

Jess wanted to have a word in Mags' ear, off the record, although in all honesty she didn't really expect Mags to be there, suspecting she and her beau would still be at Wolf Fell Hall, partaking in whatever event was happening there this evening. If that was the case, Jess was determined she wasn't going to get roped into running Caitlin home again because she saw that as being the thin end of the wedge, and from a cop's perspective it would not be a good look becoming the taxi service for a drug dealer's daughter. Questions would eventually be asked and rightly so.

Vehicles began to gather outside the school with the usual glut of four-wheel drive beasts which made Jess's battered old Picasso look very out of place. That said, she quite liked the difference. Much as she loved nice cars she wasn't envious of anyone who drove one.

She kept a check on her mirrors as well as what was going on in front of her just in case she missed Mags pulling up.

Then she gave what she thought – in her own self-made legend – was her infamous crooked half-grin as she spotted Mags' arrival in the rear-view mirror, slotting the Range Rover into the line of mummies' cars behind.

Although the kids were due to be let out in less than five minutes, Jess wasn't going to let this opportunity slip through her fingers. She got out and walked swiftly up the pavement, coming up to Mags' car, the one with darkened windows which Jess knew were illegal, though that was something she would bust Mags' arse over if all else failed. Petty, she realized, but it was a nice little thing to have up her sleeve just to cause inconvenience.

However, she could still see two people sitting in the front seats of the Range Rover. Because Mags had had to swerve across the road to park, she was sitting on the pavement side. Jess rapped on the window.

Mags' face turned towards her but the window did not open.

Jess knuckled the glass again.

After a pause, the window slowly opened.

Mags looked up squarely at Jess who bent her knees ever so slightly to bring her eyeline level with Mags'. Tommy Moss was in the passenger seat, staring forwards, not looking at Jess.

'Still in your hunting and killing gear, I see,' Jess mocked her slightly. They were both in their jackets with padded shoulders and elbows. 'How come you were up at Wolf Fell Hall?'

Mags' lips pursed. 'I'm royalty, don't you know?'

Jess chuckled. 'You're about as far away from royalty as it's possible to get, Mags, though in your imaginary world I guess this fella must be your knight in shining armour.' She jerked her head towards the passenger, and although her insides were knotted with fear at being in such close proximity to the man who might have ordered her to be killed, she intended not to show it but to keep fronting this out. 'Sir Tommy Moss, no less.'

'Oh, do you know each other?' Mags cut in.

Tommy's head rotated slowly towards Jess, a twitch or two of his nostrils and a pursing of his lips. He eyed her with a steel-cold gaze which sent an extra shiver all the way down her body. He was a good-looking bastard, Jess had to admit. A cruel smile twisted his mouth and Jess felt her knees go a bit saggy, not because of Tommy's looks but because of the violence that seemed to stem from him. Jess could imagine his fingers around her windpipe, squeezing the life out of her.

She got a grip and turned her attention to Mags who said, 'Good of you to run Caitlin home yesterday.' Mags let her left hand drift across and rest tantalisingly close to Tommy's crotch. 'Tommy and I were having a rather heated meeting, weren't we, darling?' She turned and blew him a sweet kiss.

'Shagging instead of picking up your daughter?' Jess sneered. 'You're all class, Mags, true royalty.'

Mags gave her a very thin smile. 'What can I do for you?'

'I'll come straight to the point.'

'That being?'

'All you are doing with your burning cars and ghost phone calls is ensuring that I'm more determined than ever to pull every brick out of your sordid little empire.' Jess lowered her voice. 'Every. Fucking. Brick. And if you dare bring any of it to my family, Mags, then you'd better strap yourself in tight because it's going to be one fucking bumpy ride.'

Mags kept her face bland and simply countered, 'Up yours, Jess.'

Jess ignored that, leaned in the car slightly. 'And yes, Tommy, I know who you are, but here's a warning: tough as you are, Maggie Horsefield is much tougher and will spit you out like a ball of phlegm once she's had her fill of you, so beware, Tommy.'

Jess returned her close-up glare to Mags, slowly unfurled her middle finger, then stalked back to the Citroën, seething with ire. Once behind the wheel, she exhaled and tried to calm down again, but the moment she spotted Lily and Jason coming out of the school side by side, jostling each other and laughing, with Jason as ever balancing a rugby ball on his fingertip, Jess became a mum again, the best thing she had ever been.

Jason even allowed Lily to get into the front seat without the usual punching and scratching and arguing about whose turn it was.

When would they ever grow out of that, Jess wondered. Never, she hoped.

'Hi, guys. You seem happy teddys.'

'Are you still going out tonight?' Lily asked.

'Yeah, why?'

'Yay!' Jason said from the rear.

'Yeah – yay!' Lily agreed. 'That means gran is babysitting us – not that we need it – and so, even though it's a week day, it's pizza, pizza, pizza and the Barbie film.'

'Not too sure about the Barbie thing,' Jason muttered, 'But I'm up for pizza, pizza, pizza.'

EIGHT

Mags closed the window and watched Jess walk away in her door mirror before turning abruptly to face Tommy.

'See! That's the crap I have to put up with, Tommy, darling.'

'She's a bit in your face,' he agreed. 'Got to admire that, but at the same time don't be intimidated, just keep your wits about you and don't get caught out. The plus side of it is that, very obviously the cops don't have anything on you and they don't have any resources. She doesn't have a whole lot of manpower to chuck at you other than having the screaming heebie-jeebies. I wouldn't worry about her; however, that said . . .'

'What?' Mags said, pretending to be hanging on to his every word.

'Now that I've met her in the flesh, I really would like to put a bullet in her brain even though it would be a silly thing to do in the present circumstances.'

'I would very much like to see her dead,' Mags stated.

A mobile phone began to ring. For a few moments there was uncertainty as to its whereabouts until it dawned on Mags. 'Glovebox,' she said to Tommy, who flipped it open and picked out one of the four cheap throwaway phones in there, the one that was ringing and vibrating, obviously. He passed it into her wriggling fingers, a very basic device, just capable of making and receiving calls and texts. Each phone was assigned to a particular individual and when it had been used twice, it was destroyed.

Mags knew who had the number of this phone.

She pressed the answer-call button. 'Yes . . . yes, I know who you are, you divot . . . depends how much I think it's worth . . . OK, that's interesting . . . something else . . . a time and a location? Go on, worth £250. No, no more.'

She ended the call, split open the phone and fished out the SIM card with her fingernail, snapped it in half, then took out the battery and handed the two halves of the phone to Tommy.

'Break 'em.'

She opened her window half an inch and shoved one half of the SIM out through the crack. The other she would lose somewhere on the journey.

Then she looked at Tommy and said, 'Well, well, well.'

'Huh?'

'Your appearance up here is now on a Lancashire Constabulary intelligence bulletin.'

'Shit,' he said.

'But on the plus side, Sergeant Raker could be dead sooner rather than later.'

Jess's mother was already at the cottage with Luna when Jess landed with Lily and Jason.

The kids were ecstatic to see her even though they saw her almost every day now, but the prospect of pizza and a film made them hyper.

Jess laid down the law so everyone, including her mum, knew where they stood.

'Schoolwork first,' she said. She had them all lined up for this briefing, including Luna who was sitting upright and whose tail thrashed left and right and whacked on the floor tiles like a drum. 'Only then do you order pizza . . .'

'Two pizzas,' Jason corrected her.

Jess frowned at him but immediately conceded weakly, 'Whatever.'

That was the briefing over with and the troops dismissed. Lily disappeared into her room and Jason grabbed the dog's lead and was out of the door with Luna seconds later leaving Jess and her mum open-mouthed, staring at each other.

'You're still going out tonight?' Marj asked Jess.

'Yes. Looking forward to it.'

'The Wellsprings?'

Jess nodded. 'On the Nick o' Pendle. Years since I've been up there. It's a Mexican restaurant now.'

'Oh, how awful,' her mother said. She was not one for spices or anything oriental, just a basic pie, chips and peas sort of woman, and Jess knew the pizza she would order for herself that evening would only be as exotic as pineapple chunks and ham. Even then she would pick off the pineapple.

'It's got great reviews and it'll be good to spend some time with my team off duty. We haven't really had much chance yet.'

'Well that should be nice,' her mum agreed, then cheekily raised her favourite bugbear. Again. 'And what about you and Josh? Wouldn't the time be better spent with you two having a heads-together?' She went serious then. 'I see cracks, lots of them.'

Jess bristled, then blinked, trying to hold back the tears at this stiletto into her heart, and wished her mum would just let it go for once.

'Come on, dear, you've got time for a brew, haven't you, before you put your glad rags on?'

Jess nodded. 'And a Hobnob.'

They sat out in the titchy backyard. There was an old wrought-iron table and matching, rusting chairs to sit on. They were comfortable enough but Jess would have preferred her own garden furniture, and as the cottage was rented she didn't feel inclined to fork out.

'What are you going to do, darling?' her mum asked more sweetly as she came out of the kitchen with the brews and placed Jess's mug on the table. She sat down with her hands wrapped around hers. 'You can't go on like this,' she said, getting a sharp look of rebuke from Jess. 'No! I'm going to say how it is, Jessica. Don't think you can hide this because it's all too obvious for comfort. You never know when he's coming home, you're always on pins . . . you seem very uncomfortable in each other's company . . . I mean, when did you last have sex?'

'Mum! For fuck's sake!'

'No, you're right. None of my business – but mark my words, lady, no sex eventually leads to no relationship and then no marriage.

If it's all going wrong, nip it in the bud now!' Marj made an uncomfortable scissors gesture with her first and second fingers. 'And anyway, how do you think me and your dad lasted so long and were so happy – good hard sex, that's how!'

Jess was in the bath. It was about the largest single piece of anything in the cottage and Jess often wondered what possessed the owner to install such a huge standalone bath into such a small bathroom which also had a minuscule walk-in shower cubicle in the corner of the room. *How the hell had it even been manoeuvred up the stairs?* she wondered. Jess rarely had baths, didn't have time for them, but decided to have a long soak before going out tonight. She wanted to pamper herself a bit, smell nice and be ultra chilled, particularly after her mother's marital advice intervention and the uncomfortable revelation about her own sex life which sent a shiver down Jess's spine. Parents having sex was one thing; having good hard sex was off the scale of decency. But the main thing was that her mum had single-handedly trashed the façade Jess had erected concerning the state of her marriage to Josh.

Not that Jess was averse to dealing head-on with issues, but for certain the marriage had gone on to the too hard to-do pile, although she knew this had to be only temporarily. Sooner or later it had to be dealt with. She didn't want to reach old age with any lingering regrets on the subject, however tough it might be.

But would it be a regret moving up north? Dragging everyone with her? She tried to convince herself it had been a necessity, one that Josh should have embraced and supported, but Jess knew it had all come at a bad time for him with his affair and all.

And although he'd easily found a new job in Manchester, Jess knew the commute was horrible. Going by train was not a reliable way to get there and part of her understood why he couldn't be arsed to travel all the way back at the end of a long day.

She sighed, watching the bubbles and water ebb and flow off her chest as she inhaled and exhaled.

And sex.

Oh, God, she thought. *I think I've forgotten how to do it!*

And in a stream of consciousness thing her mind (and body) made the leap to Joe Borwick, and as she closed her eyes the thoughts she began to have about him sent her into a little dreamworld from which she snapped out of and sat up guiltily with the water sloshing off her.

None of that, she remonstrated with herself.

Bad lass.

There was a loud knock on the door: Lily. 'Mum? How long are you going to be in there? I need to pee, like urgently.'

'Just a minute.'

And with that, she slithered deep into the suds feeling guilty about her thoughts, but also with a wicked smile on her face.

'Mum, I just wanna go home,' Caitlin had moaned as Mags drove into Clitheroe and then towards Whalley and not in the direction of Hurst Green after picking her up from school. 'I've got homework and stuff to do.'

'I need to make a detour,' Mags told her. 'Be patient, dear.' She glanced at Tommy and rolled her eyes. 'Kids, eh?'

Tommy arched his eyebrows. 'I wouldn't know.' He and Leanora hadn't had any offspring and were unlikely to do so now. The only experience Tommy had of bringing up a youngster was his little bro, Terry, who turned out to be a complete failure and ended up dead under the shadow of the *Cutty Sark*.

He looked in the rear-view mirror on his side of the windscreen and saw Caitlin's eyes glowering back at him. He wasn't comfortable with her, nor she with him.

He knew enough about Mags to realize that despite their shared lust for each other which was now verging on something deeper, he was the latest in a long line of used and discarded men – 'uncles' no doubt to Caitlin, and he understood Caitlin's wariness and distrust of him. He did wonder where the relationship with Mags was heading and if there was any longevity in it and if they had the necessary wherewithal to stand the nasty flack that would come from Leanora's direction. She had already set a drunken man on Mags who had intended to rape her, a misstep that had resulted in the guy's death. Tommy had disposed of the body and nothing, so far, had come of it, either from the authorities or, indeed, Leanora. Not one word had been spoken, but knowing her as he did he expected to be blindsided by her bubbling rage. He knew she knew about the affair he was having with Mags, so Leanora's silence on the matter was, as they say, deafening. He suspected she was up to something that would be revealed when she was good and ready, so he too would have to be prepared for the worst.

As tough and hard as he was, he didn't relish what this might be.

On the outskirts of Clitheroe, Mags turned into a side road and drove to Primrose Breakers, the main business she had inherited from her father. That had been the springboard for a car-ringing operation which led on to other diverse activities throughout the Ribble Valley and beyond, which in turn led to a lot of wealth.

The gates slid open electronically and she drew in alongside the office. The gates closed and only then were the two XL pit bull dogs released. They ran to the car, circling it, growling and sniffing.

'Jesus,' Tommy said. He'd met them before and they didn't like him much.

'They're good boys,' Mags assured him. 'Licensed, tagged and insured in case they rip anyone's throat out.' She got out, as did Caitlin, and the dogs suddenly became like puppies, vying for attention from the two ladies.

Tommy stayed put. There were various nasty dogs owned in and around the Moss family, but Tommy had never really taken to any of them. He had no great affinity with canines unless they were of the toy variety he could crush underfoot.

Mags beckoned him out of the car.

Reluctantly he complied and suddenly the dogs reverted to type, their hackles rising as they spotted him.

'Spike! Bullseye! Down!' Caitlin snapped.

For a moment the order seemed to go unheeded but then Mags also shouted, 'Down, boys!' and the dogs relaxed.

'Caitlin, love, you stay here with them, please,' Mags asked. 'Tommy – with me.'

Although Jess and other cops had visited Primrose Breakers on a number of occasions recently, their searches and the checking of business books could only go so far and wandering around the yard failed to discover the hidden compartment in the floor of the office underneath the old desk. Mags and the yard manager, Steve Burns, always welcomed the cops with courtesy and patience and on the face of it allowed them to access everything and anything. Mags had been there on one occasion when Jess Raker had come unannounced into the yard, as police were entitled to do, together with her risible entourage of the skinny male cop and the chubby Asian PCSO. Mags had found Jess's obvious frustration from finding sod-all highly amusing. Maybe if she'd turned up with a proper search warrant and a fully fledged search team she might have found the hidden panel which when opened revealed a deep, steel-lined box in which Mags kept various items. Having said that, Mags was smug enough to know that the box would have been empty if the police had landed with a search warrant because she would have been prewarned about the raid from her new source who was eager to please and always on the lookout for a cash-bung.

So today the box did have something in it, of the 'ready to go' variety as Mags called it.

Followed by Tommy, Mags went into the office where two young men and Steve were lounging.

The younger guys were smoking weed and its pungent reek could be smelled across the yard. This irked Mags no end. So, having inhaled the aroma on getting out of the car, she didn't just enter the office, she burst in like a tigress.

Steve was at the desk, but the two younger lads were man-splayed out on an old settee.

Lance Drake and Dave 'Dimbo' Dawson. Two of Mags' employees on zero-hours contracts.

'You fricking imbeciles,' she screamed. 'I can smell weed all the way down to Clitheroe town centre, I can almost see the trail like a fricking Bisto advert. And if I can, that means any cop with half a sense of smell can too. Put them out.'

The lads leapt to their feet, scrambling to extinguish their spliffs under Mags' glare and behind her, Tommy's brutal gaze.

'Jack-arses,' Mags said contemptuously.

Steve looked quite brassed off. 'I told 'em, boss.'

She nodded. 'They should know better.'

By now the spliffs were out, although the reek still clung to the two lads and hung in the air. Mags hated it. Weed was not her personal scene. It was purely a business commodity, and apart from one minor try-out in her teens, which had made her vomit over the lad she was screwing, she'd never inhaled it willingly since. Just grew it, packaged it, sold it. Profited from it.

She spoke to Lance. 'Any probs with that Jag?'
'No, went up like a treat.' He hesitated. 'Just that . . .'
'Just that, what?'
'Er, that cop, Raker, saw me in the crowd, watching.'
'Saw you in the crowd? What exactly does that mean?'
'I . . . I watched it burn.'

Mags studied him as though she had found something completely beyond comprehension. Maybe an alien. 'Go on.'

'She ran after me.'

'You are an idiot, and even now I'm thinking about tying you to a chair again, probably cutting your fingers off, then your throat. What say, eh?' Mags challenged him.

'I'm sorry,' Lance said quietly. He lost his balance slightly due to the drug in his system and Mags couldn't resist smashing the flat of her hand across the side of his face to send him sprawling across the old settee.

Where he cowered.

Next to him, Dimbo smirked, but that didn't stop Mags doing the same to him, knocking him to the floor but in the opposite direction.

'And you – assaulting a cop instead of just head-down and driving away!'

'A PCSO, I think,' Dimbo stupidly corrected her, then realized what he'd done when the sole of one of Mags' riding boots smashed into his face. 'Shit, shit, shit,' he bleated.

'I should feed you both to the dogs . . . however . . . both of you get outside and wait for me. Go on! Fuck off out!'

They scrambled past her, leaving just her, Tommy and Steve in the office.

She exhaled a very long, pissed-off sigh. 'Thank God they're not all like that.' She turned to Steve who had worked for her and her father before her for many years. 'Did you package up the goods like I asked?'

He nodded. 'Like tiny little presents of After Eight mints.'

Mags grinned, imagining the mints Steve was referring to, the small, supposedly sophisticated after-dinner chocolates passed around, allegedly, by high society after a fancy meal to women wearing sparkling ball gowns and men in tuxedos. In reality they were usually scoffed by kids who were then sick.

In this case, though, the little teabag-sized packages were sealed and the contents were somewhat different than dark chocolate and mint.

Tonight's bags contained cocaine.

Steve reached down and unlocked the hidden sliding mechanism on which his desk was fitted to, which in turn was screwed to the floor, making it seem on a cursory glance that the desk was also screwed into the floor of the cabin and immoveable. He pushed the desk. It slid smoothly away from him on a runner, revealing the cover of the compartment underneath a footstool. This cover was locked by screws with Allen key heads which Steve quickly unlocked to reveal the contents of the compartment suspended under the cabin.

In it were a couple of neat stacks of bank notes, sterling and euros, in sealed vacuum storage bags. Next to them was a slim rectangular box, like a shoebox, in which were the neatly arranged packages containing the cocaine, each with enough for just one nice line of it to be tapped out.

Steve picked up the box, which was sitting on top of a nine-millimetre pistol and a couple of fully loaded magazines, which were themselves on four false passports and a fake driving licence, plus several genuine bank cards, all with Mags' photo or fake ID on them, with the exception of one of the passports and bank cards, which was for Caitlin. These items were what Mags thought of as her 'just-in-case-the-shit-hits-the-fan shit'. The 'just in case' being if everything went very, very wrong and the only option she had was to flee. They were things she hoped she would never have to grab and go.

Steve handed Mags the box which she placed on the desk and removed the lid, running her eyes over the contents.

'Nice.' She nodded appreciatively. 'Just like the little pressies you get given at weddings. What are they called?' She turned to Tommy, noticing that he quickly diverted his eyes away from the hidden compartment, which Steve was just re-covering. 'You're married, you'll know,' she said cuttingly. 'Oh no, don't bother, it's come to me – favours. They're called favours.'

Tommy shrugged, unimpressed to be reminded of his faltering marriage.

Steve tightened up the screws and slid everything back into place.

Mags thanked him and went out to Lance and Dimbo who were

Death on Wolf Fell

skulking by a car which looked ready for the crusher, both watching Caitlin as she played with the two XL pit bulls.

Mags sneered at the car. 'Is this your transport?' she asked in disbelief.

'Yeah,' Dimbo answered sullenly. 'Steve scrapped me other cos the cops had the number an' saw us in it.'

'I take it you're referring to the car you were driving when you assaulted that cop?'

'PCSO,' he corrected her.

This time the word had only just come out of his mouth when Tommy stepped forwards and dug a fist into Dimbo's lower gut. Just once, but doubling him over with a whoosh of expelled air and an accompanying groan. Tommy leaned over so his mouth was close to Dimbo's ear. 'Don't ever be smart again,' he warned him.

'OK, boss,' he hissed, painfully through gritted teeth.

Mags stood back watching the display of manhood with a cynical twist to her mouth. She waited for Dimbo to stand up.

Lance hovered to one side, swallowing a tiny bit of terror. One thing he had learned about on remand was the reputation of the Moss gang. He hadn't known exactly who Tommy was but Dimbo had brought him up to speed and that the two guys who'd snatched him from Asda were Moss employees, which meant Mags was deep in with one of the most fearsome gangs in the country.

Lance was suddenly very afraid. Being a low-level drugs runner for Mags was a sort of OK thing, but this link with the Moss lot made his guts quake. A whole different league. Not that Mags wasn't a fearsome bitch, but the Moss crew operated on a different level.

'So you're using this heap of crap?' Mags indicated the car, a battered, rusting Honda Civic which looked as though it had already been crushed.

'Steve give it us,' Dimbo said.

'Steve!' Mags called.

He appeared at the office door. 'Boss?'

'Get these idiots something better, will you? And make sure it's road legal.'

Steve frowned for a moment, then said, 'Will do.'

Mags returned her attention to the lads. Lance with fearful eyes, Dimbo still recovering from the punch in the belly.

She handed the box of drugs to Lance with some specific delivery instructions. These were drugs destined for the pleasure of the lovely people attending the fancy slap-up meal that evening at Wolf Fell Hall. She then gave them both some further very detailed instructions for something else she wanted to be done that night based on information she had received – something that would lead to a particular problem that was bothering her being eliminated once and for all.

NINE

The meal at the Wellsprings was excellent. That, coupled with the amazing view from the top of Pendle Hill and some excellent company, made Jess feel warmly happy. There was no drink flowing, as such: debauched and drunken police dos were pretty much consigned to the past, which was mostly a good thing, Jess thought, although occasionally they were a necessity and helped cops deal with some of the bleaker things the job threw at them. Everyone tonight, except for Vinnie, was on non-alcoholic drinks or coffee, but that didn't make the conversation or laughter flow any less. It was just all very pleasant and the first proper social get-together her shift had had since she had arrived in the valley.

Jess found herself seated next to Dougie Doolan for the meal, and she asked him about Wolf Fell Hall and wasn't surprised to discover that his encyclopaedic knowledge of the Ribble Valley extended to that.

'Apparently goes back to Jacobean times,' he said, picking at a fajita but noticeably not eating much, 'when Catholics were fair game and hunted down pretty ruthlessly. The family who owned the hall were called Bottomcole back then and the place is a rat run of priest holes.'

'Priest holes?'

'Hiding places, escape routes for priests, under floors, in walls, tunnels, et cetera.'

'Ah yeah,' Jess said, vaguely recalling some history lessons.

'The place is a Grade 1 listed building of architectural importance,

Death on Wolf Fell 101

apparently. It's been sold several times over the centuries and is now in the hands of the duchess, who you met. She and her now late husband also own huge swathes of Wolf Fell, rather like other aristocrats such as the king and Duke of Westminster who also own huge tracts of land in Lancashire.'

Jess nodded.

'The duchess's hubby died of the usual things associated with the ruling class – booze, liver disease, fags, syphilis – and left her holding a baby with spiralling debt. He was apparently broke when he turned his toes. And even though there's lots of valuable art around, there's no cash, no income and her business plan was to open up the grouse moor to all and sundry – local riff-raff but with money, if you will. And to provide entertainment in the form of hunt and charity balls which, I hear, have degenerated into coke-snorting free-for-alls and, allegedly, orgies.' Dougie gave Jess a lecherous look which he could not maintain. 'I'm told the money now flows in by the bucketload but the duchess has expensive habits which don't extend to painting and decorating and renovating the place, which if you look closely is a crumbling mess. She does have a draw with some minor royals, as we've seen today, who are also cash-strapped and apparently get paid appearance money and free board and lodgings. Tickets available, I hear.'

'Well I never,' Jess said, sounding like her mum. 'Sounds a shame.'

'A damned shame.'

'And who supplies the drugs, or don't I need to ask?'

'*Allegedly* supplies,' Dougie corrected her. 'And, I've heard on the grapevine, women too.'

'Oooh – while I remember, Dougie. Those two bodyguards, Harker and Leighton?' Jess said and Dougie waited. 'That one, Harker, I thought I kind of recognized him, so after you'd gone earlier I made a couple of hush-hush phone calls down south to some Met mates, and guess what?'

'I couldn't begin,' Dougie admitted, intrigued.

'Harker was in the Met and I recalled him being on royal protection duties, aligned with Prince Harry a while back. But he got busted – all hushed up, obviously, as you do,' Jess said with a trace of annoyance. 'Anyhow, that's why his face rang a bell.'

'Busted for what?' Dougie asked.

'Found in bed with a footman and a groom when he should have been sitting outside Harry's room.'

'Ooh, tasty,' Dougie said.

'Yep, hushed up – he lost his job PDQ but obviously his contacts kept him in work, as we saw today.'

'So he should fit right in up at Wolf Fell Hall and all the shenanigans allegedly going on up there.'

'A perfect fit.'

The meal progressed. Lots of courses and Jess made time to talk to each member of her team, chatting about all and everything. She did keep a wary eye out for Inspector Price who had been invited as a matter of courtesy, but much to Jess's relief hadn't shown up. She wasn't ready to socialize with him in any shape or form. The prospect of making small talk with him made her feel queasy.

At the end of the meal they sat around a table in the bar.

Vinnie McKinty seemed intent on slowly making his way around to sit next to Jess, finally sidling up when someone else moved away.

'Hi, sarge.'

'Vinnie.' She nodded. 'How are you?' It wasn't such a long time ago that he'd been knocked unconscious by a fleeing villain but had recovered quickly. Jess knew such blows could have sneaky, long-term effects and she had been keeping a sly eye on him, but he seemed to be doing fine. She also knew his wife was pregnant.

'All good. Been a good bit of scran and a chat, hasn't it?' he said gesturing around the premises. 'We never did owt like this before you landed.'

'It's the sort of low-key thing we should do now and then.'

'I agree. Good for the team.'

Jess sensed he wanted to tell or ask her something but wasn't sure how to go about it. So she said, 'What's eating you, Vin?'

He winced as though someone had stood on his big toe. 'You know I'm dealing with that missing woman?'

Jess said she did. It was a case Vinnie had been trying to resolve one way or the other since before Jess had taken up the role as sergeant. The story being that a woman in her early thirties had apparently gone missing on a walk up on the moors near Dunsop Bridge and not been seen since. Jess hadn't had much direct contact with the case other than to keep updating the file and looking at further angles for investigation. She knew it was always on Vinnie's mind and every chance he had he revisited aspects of it, reinterviewed relatives, but it seemed to have stuttered to a dead end.

Jess had dealt with many missing-from-home enquiries over the years. The truth was that most mispers, as they were called by the police, turned up safe and well. A few unfortunate ones didn't, either by design – such as suicide, or purposely disappearing – or accident, or as victims of unlawful acts.

It was rare that people never turned up, though, such as those who had planned their own disappearance or those in shallow graves or weighed down in reservoirs.

Vinnie pouted thoughtfully. 'Well, I dunno . . . but that kick-off at Wolf Fell Hall got me thinking, especially hearing those two daft royals having a go at each other. Surprising what gets said accidentally in the heat of the moment.'

'OK,' Jess said. 'Go on.'

'I mean, it never entered my head . . . and why should it?'

Jess waited patiently.

'Well, those parties at Wolf Fell Hall . . .'

'The ones I've only just learned about?' Jess intercut.

'Me too . . . but they must bring in staff, catering, waitresses and the like and . . .' he hesitated again, this time with a clearing of his throat, 'maybe sex workers?'

Jess had one of those bum-clenching moments, one of those cop feelings when something maybe starts to come together, the pieces of a jigsaw, possibly.

'Seems to be a lot of sordid goings-on at the hall,' Vinnie said, 'the kind of thing you expect in London or big cities.'

'Where are you going with this?' Jess said.

'The misper woman, I've dug and dug into her life over the past few months and – headlines, here – she's divorced, lived alone in Clitheroe, ex-hubby down south and not on my radar for any wrongdoing re her disappearance; no kids, but she was on benefits and I've just recently found out from one of her friends that she supplemented her income by waitressing on the side, as folk do.'

'You can say women, Vinnie.'

'Yeah, yeah . . . so, so . . . apparently she got contracts ad hoc, like, and got paid maybe fifty quid for a night's work, cash in hand, and did it maybe three or four times a month for various catering firms, so money not to be sneezed at, I suppose. She did it for a few local companies, none of which really knew her that well, but that's par for the course. Hired help.'

'I get it,' Jess said.

'But . . . what if she did more than wait on?' Vinnie suggested.

'What are you suggesting?'

'Sex. Prostitution.'

'And what makes you think that, Vin?'

He took a long draw of his pint. He was the only one of the team drinking because he was being picked up later by his wife. 'Again, because of what one of her friends told me, and digging into her past, and to be fair this is a while ago, but leopards don't change their spots, do they? She was rounded up in a raid in Blackburn twelve years ago when she would have been twenty. A brothel was shut down and the owner was prosecuted for living off immoral earnings and all that, but none of the women were charged or even cautioned with anything.'

'Not unusual,' Jess said, 'but have you ever thought she could have changed her spots? That she could just have been a vulnerable woman working in a job where she was targeted, abused and maybe assaulted by men with power and one or more of them went too far?' She shrugged.

Vinnie listened, then said, 'You mean men like the Armstrong-Bentleys? Yeah, absolutely . . .'

Jess could see he was trying to get his thoughts in order. The few pints he'd consumed probably didn't help this process. 'I've discovered that she worked for a company which provided food and drink and waiting-on, if you will, for several events that took place at Wolf Fell Hall. I had a look through that glossy magazine called *North West Life, Society and Property*.'

Jess knew of it – a very glossy magazine listing all the very expensive properties for sale in the region, plus photos of attendees at the poshest of functions. She'd flicked through the pages whilst sitting at the dentist's recently.

She took a sip of her non-alcoholic gin and tonic.

'There are some functions listed at Wolf Fell Hall,' Vinnie said.

'Right, OK.'

'With the usual accompanying photos,' he went on. 'Probably four fancy charity dos in the last year or so, a couple of which featuring our two arguing royals and various people hobnobbing with them.'

'As folk do.'

'As folk do,' Vinnie agreed. 'One of the photos from a do about six months ago showed the Armstrong-Bentleys being arse-licked by a few of our own social butterflies, if you'll pardon my French.'

Jess could tell he was getting excited as he got to the point.

'Right, right,' he said again. 'First off, the company that provided the food and drink and waiting-on staff is called Castle Catering and Events. They're a limited company, so I nosed into the Companies House website and looked them up, just out of interest, like. It's run by a woman called Angela Dart. She's the CEO, whatever that means. But . . . interesting bit coming up now,' he promised Jess. 'The website also lists previous officers of the company, those who have retired or resigned.'

He paused.

Jess blinked.

'Does the name Margaret Goss mean anything to you?' he teased her.

'Not sure,' Jess teased him back.

He fell for it. 'Margaret Goss . . . Goss being the maiden name of Maggie Horsefield, who resigned as a director a couple of years back, but which doesn't mean to say she has nothing to do with the business, does it?'

'No, it doesn't.'

'So, not jumping to any conclusions or anything, but our number-one target happens to be connected to the company providing catering services to the duchess at Wolf Fell Hall.'

'And maybe other services too?' Jess speculated. 'Such as drugs?'

'Exactly!' Vinnie picked up his pint and took a long swig from it, then wiped his mouth. 'Which, maybe, is where our two royals come into the scenario. Also, when we were walking towards them along that hallway, one was shouting about a waitress and stuff.'

'And the other was talking about a danger to us all,' Jess added.

'I know it's only a bit of a hypothesis, but just supposing one of them forced himself on our missing woman and she, quite rightly, turned the screw on him, saying she was going to the police . . .'

'And the media, if she knew who he was,' Jess said.

'Exactly!' Vinnie said. 'Exposing what some figures in high

society are really like.' This time he fully drained his pint. Jess assumed the beer was going straight down into his legs. 'Murder. A shit-storm – excuse my French again, sarge – that the whole of the royal family could well do without, even if it only involves this pair of low-ranking tosspots.'

Jess thought it over for a moment, then said, 'Follow it up, Vinnie. Maybe tomorrow we can get our heads together and see how we can take this forward.'

'But I don't want to miss nabbing them if they've buggered off.'

'If necessary, we'll go and knock on their palace door, wherever that may be,' Jess promised him.

'OK, sarge. I'm not nuts, then?'

'Far from it, Vinnie. You have the makings of a good detective. You just need to unjumble things a bit before spouting stuff.' Jess grinned. 'So let's have a look at your misper's timeline tomorrow and see if that helps.'

Jess glanced around the bar, which was quite busy. Her eyes lit on Samira, the PCSO, who was standing at the bar with Dougie. Jess gave her a little wave and Samira gestured with a 'Can I come over?' motion. Jess waved and she came across and sat on the other side of Jess to Vinnie who stood up with his empty glass, belched softly and announced, 'Need another pint.' He headed unsteadily to the bar.

Jess and Samira watched him, amused.

'Good job his wife is picking him up,' Samira said.

'Certainly is,' Jess said, turning to Samira. 'How's it going, love?'

'All right. Just thought I'd let you know I got an address for David "Dimbo" Dawson.'

'Oh, excellent. How did you manage that?'

'Asked around,' she shrugged modestly.

'Just like that? Old-fashioned coppering?'

'Guess so.'

Jess sipped her drink but held the rim of the glass close to her lips as she saw a couple enter the bar. The woman stepped in ahead of the man who touched the small of her back intimately, then slid his arm around her waist as they walked to the bar. The appearance of this pair distracted Jess's attention momentarily away from Samira and, vexed, she forced herself to look at Samira who had also spotted the couple and was aware Jess had seen them too.

'I'd like to go and see if I can arrest him tomorrow,' Samira said, though was canny enough to realize that Jess wasn't totally focused on what she was saying.

'Yeah, yeah, why not,' Jess said. Rather like the eyes in an Action Man figure, Jess's kept flicking sideways, trying not to look at the couple and also trying not to let her emotions boil over even though she knew she should not be affected by what she was seeing: the man leaning side-on on the bar, his attention riveted to the woman who was, Jess wanted to spit like venom, undeniably pretty.

'What time will you be on duty, sarge?'

'After dropping Lily and Jason off at school. Just after eight thirty.'

'That's good.'

'You don't need me along,' Jess said. 'Vinnie's on earlies – why not take him along if he's sober enough?' she joked.

'Yeah, I will.'

At the bar, alongside the couple, Vinnie had just secured his new pint. He turned slightly woozily and noticed the newly arrived pair for the first time. His face lit up and he patted the man on the back and following a brief exchange he looked over at Jess and Samira, as did the man. Vinnie waved and pointed to the man, making a daft face. The man, suddenly, did not look all that happy. He pushed himself away from the bar, whispered something into his lady friend's ear and walked over to Jess who watched his approach with a degree of trepidation.

He stood on the opposite side of the table at which Jess and Samira were seated.

'Hello, sarge,' he said, attempting to make it sound light. In his eyes was fear.

'Hiya, Joe.'

Joe Borwick nodded at Samira who sat there quietly with her hands clasped on her lap.

'Fancy meeting you here,' Joe said inadequately.

'Fancy. Small world, I guess.' Jess took a shaky drink of her mock G&T, wishing it were the real thing. 'Who are you here with?' Jess looked past him to the lady at the bar who was chatting to Vinnie. 'The pretty lady,' she couldn't help herself utter, regretting the words immediately.

'My . . .' Joe started to say.

'Sister?' Jess blurted.
'No, my . . .'
'Auntie?'
'No . . . fiancée,' he was finally able to reveal.
'Ahh, right. Congratulations.' *Fuck it*, Jess remonstrated to her inner self, for sounding too bitter. She had no right.
'It's not new, but thanks,' Joe said shamefacedly.
'You're welcome.'
Jess stood up, totally unable to make any eye contact with him. She swept by him, snatching up her coat from the back of a chair and strode regally to the exit, desperately trying to keep herself in check at least before getting to her car. The short walk was just a blur of disappointment and wrecked hope before she found herself at the Citroën, fumbling in her handbag for the key, her eyes having misted over with tears.
Her fingers found the key, pulled it out and dropped it on to the gravel of the car park. She cursed fiercely and bent down to pick it up, and when she came upright all her energy sapped out of her and she sagged – pathetically she thought, even then – against her car, furious on so many levels but mainly with her own stupid sense of entitlement as regards Joe Borwick.
'Jess!'
She turned towards the approaching footsteps crunching on the gravel.
She said nothing. She had no right on this earth to say anything and though she knew that, it didn't make her feel any better.
'What?' she snapped.
'You OK?' Joe looked very concerned in the fading evening light.
'I will be,' she said. 'I just . . . I mean, "We should go for a drink?"' she mimicked him. 'What the hell was that about?' She shook her head and her mouth before anything more infantile spewed out. 'I just . . .'
'Just what?'
'Don't, Joe, just don't, eh?'
The Citroën was old enough that it could only be opened with use of the key in the door. She managed to insert it in one go but as she opened the driver's door she was totally aware that Joe had come up close behind her.
'Jess,' he whispered.

She didn't turn. She knew if she did she would have folded into his arms in desperation and that would have plunged them both into an intolerable situation. She clambered into the old car and fired up the noisy diesel engine. Before slamming the door on him, she said, 'See you at the next fire, maybe.'

He looked deflated as she reversed out of her spot, crunched it into first gear and swung the car off the car park and accelerated away with a gush of black smoke from the exhaust.

Joe watched, hardly noticing the other car which pulled off the car park just moments after Jess, and went in the same direction. He was too concentrated on Jess and his growing feelings for her which would probably never be reciprocated, especially now.

He sighed heavily, was about to walk back into the restaurant when he saw something on the ground where Jess's car had been parked. He paused, then hurried inside.

Jess was talking to herself, out loud.

'I know, I know. I have no right to expect anything from him. I KNOW!' she reprimanded herself as she sped off the car park, her eyes fixed firmly ahead, willing herself not to turn and look at Joe who she knew was still there, watching her drive off. There had literally been nothing between them. Nothing said, nothing done. The only thing had been coy eye contact, the obvious body language, and maybe his off-the-cuff remark about going for a drink. But none of that mattered because she was married and he – it turned out, quelle surprise! – was fucking engaged to a lass who was far prettier than her. 'I have *no right*!' she said again. 'Silly fuckwit.'

She ran her sleeve over her eyes to clear them of the tears and to try and see where she was actually going – down the narrow, steep road from the Wellsprings on the Nick o' Pendle, down towards Clitheroe and the A59, which plummeted down the side of the huge hill. She glanced briefly in her rear-view mirror at the headlights on main beam of the car right behind her.

'Get off my chuffer!' she shouted at a driver who could not possibly hear.

He – or she – didn't back off, which added to Jess's fury. People driving right up her backside irritated her beyond comprehension and even more tonight when she was already emotionally supercharged.

She put her foot down.

The Citroën, though not the fastest car in the world and despite being a diesel, did have a reasonable turn of speed, and when coaxed could pick up its skirts. So as she plunged down the slope of Pendle Hill, the car sped up yet, annoyingly, the car behind did the same and stayed almost affixed to her back bumper.

She swore, yet at the back of her mind she knew that racing down that hill, particularly in the dark, on a road she had known well in her youth but not so much now, was risky. However, her mood told her to be reckless. She was an advanced police driver, highly trained and in control of what her colleagues in London had called a donkey, which wasn't too far from the truth. It was designed to carry five people in relative comfort, plus luggage and shopping. Its suspension ensured it rolled and swayed on corners and certainly wasn't designed to be hurled along a twisty-turning road whatever the time of day.

As the car hurtled down, Jess remembered there was a cattle grid ahead, followed by a tight right-hand dog-leg. She'd driven up Pendle by the same route earlier to get to the Wellsprings and also remembered it from olden days. So in spite of the tear-blurred vision and annoyance, verging on road rage, directed at the car behind, she was ready for the cattle grid and the turn.

She pressed the brake pedal to reduce speed slightly.

There was some pressure in it as she pushed it down, but not much. And the car did not slow. She pushed the brake again and this time her foot went right down to the floor without any resistance whatsoever. And again, the car did not slow.

She pumped the pedal, suddenly feeling desperate, looking down at it as if a dirty look would make it respond.

Nothing.

Shit!

She yanked up the handbrake and it seemed to come all the way up in her hand and had no effect on the speed.

Then she hit the cattle grid and rattled across it, shaking the old car's chassis like driving across an old-fashioned washboard.

Foot brake pumped again: nothing.

Handbrake: nothing.

Shit: again.

She tried to drop a gear, but crunched the cogs.

Everything was now happening really, really slowly, with no coherent logic to it.

The realization she was going far too quickly to negotiate the right bend coming up.

Her anger at the innocent Joe Borwick had clouded her judgement so badly she had completely forgotten the basics of driving a car, and that when you go down a hill it gets faster and faster and more difficult to control and can bite you on the backside even if the brakes work.

The car behind, headlights blinding her eyes in the mirrors. Why? What was he up to?

Not that long since her car had been tested and the brakes had been fine.

Which meant tampering. Cables cut, brake fluid lines severed. The only explanation.

The car behind: too close.

And the fact that almost immediately after the cattle grid there was that sharp right, then a sharp left with hedges, drainage dykes and fields either side.

By the time she'd reached the cattle grid and managed to get down to third gear, she then had to haul the steering wheel to the right. The car wallowed like a hippo, but she thought she'd made it intact but then felt the rear wheels skitter on the road, still aware that the car following was way too close and then she felt the impact as the vehicle rammed the back corner of the Citroën.

What followed was a perfect storm of physics.

Velocity, plus instability, plus cornering, plus gravity, plus crap suspension, plus tyres not properly gripping the road, plus the tup from behind – and next thing Jess knew her car was completely out of control, that it had flipped over, that she was rolling directly towards a gate, which the car slammed side-on. Although the gate was made of steel, the force of the impact bashed it off its hinges with a terrible tearing, rending noise and then Jess was in the field beyond. The car flipped again and bounced down the slope and she was completely powerless, just thankful somewhere in her mind that she'd put her seat belt on.

Her grip on the steering wheel was ripped away – was that her thumb breaking? – as the car flipped again and she was tossed around in her seat like a mad muppet, rolled twice more and then finally, with a slow, painful roll, it came to rest on its crushed roof. Jess slithered mostly out of the support of the seat belt, drawn by gravity. She slumped loosely, banging her head on the roof and somehow found herself wedged between her seat, the steering wheel and the gearstick. Blackness enveloped her and then there was nothing as she passed out and did not know if she was dead or alive.

Up on the road, the car that had followed her waited for a few moments until the Citroën came to rest after its final roll, then sped away down the hill.

TEN

She knew she hadn't died because she stirred from unconsciousness what seemed hours later, or was it only seconds, maybe minutes . . . yes, it had to be minutes to give time for blue lights to arrive, to have torch beams shone into her face, to be able to hear urgent shouting, orders being given and finally what sounded like an angle grinder as someone, presumably from the Fire & Rescue service (*could that be Joe Borwick*, she thought) began to slice open the crumpled side door of the Citroën and then heave it away with suction pads; then another cut as the seat belt was severed just to get it out of the way; then the sensation of pairs of hands and the sounds of reassuring voices as she felt herself being lifted carefully out, laid on a stretcher, strapped to it and carried up through the field to an ambulance which was reversed up to the gate she had destroyed. It seemed a rough, bouncy old journey up to heaven and she fully expected to be tipped off the stretcher, but then she was slid into the ambulance – not heaven – without further incident.

'I'm OK,' she remembered saying before passing out again.

Inspector Price stood by the bed in the cubicle at A&E.

Jess opened her eyes, saw him and wondered if this was what real nightmares were like, nightmares induced by injuries and drugs, the ones that came bearing demons.

She would have preferred it to have been a bad dream but knew this was real life.

No nightmare could have been depraved enough to feature this monster.

She had been in Blackburn hospital for over twelve hours, having been conveyed from the scene on Pendle Hill to the A&E department. She didn't clearly recall much of the journey, twenty-odd minutes that felt both instantaneous and yet everlasting, making her realize the crack to her skull had made her lose all concept of passing time.

As a road accident victim she had been seen immediately, no waiting about in pesky queues, or left on a stretcher in a corridor, just straight from the back of the ambulance into an emergency treatment room to be surrounded by doctors and nurses and attached to various machines that measured various vital signs.

They seemed mostly concerned about the possibility of a brain injury. Apparently her head had thumped many things during the roll down the hill although she didn't recall any of that. Her airbag had prevented serious head injury, she had been told.

X-rays were done but were inconclusive and she was being kept in for twenty-four-hour monitoring, the first few hours of which had been spent mostly blacked-out, sedated and filled with pain relief, but as she looked at Price standing there at the end of her bed, the agony inside her cranium was almost intolerable as the effect of painkillers wore off and more were required. Urgently.

She thumbed the button to summon a nurse and started to ease herself up into a sitting position, realizing she was now wearing an unflattering hospital gown.

Other than the battered head, though, she seemed to have been lucky. Mostly just swelling, bangs and bruising with a harsh line like a tyre skid track across her right shoulder and across her chest to her left hip caused by the seat belt which had apparently saved her life. One thing that did hurt like hell was her right boob, which must have taken the brunt of the seat belt during the accident. She'd thought her thumb had been broken but apparently wasn't. But it hurt anyway.

All in all, she knew she had been fortunate to say the least. The seat belt and the deployment of the airbag had probably saved her life, but she also knew that there was no hard and fast rule about surviving such accidents. As a cop she had attended several similar ones, some where people had walked away totally unscathed and others where they had been smashed to death. She was in the former category and, as bad as she felt, she was very grateful to be more or less in one piece.

'Inspector,' Jess said to Price.

'I've done you a big favour,' he told her. Not, 'How are you feeling?' which she would have expected from a boss. Or, 'Anything you need?'

'How's that?' Her mouth felt thick, lacking moisture. She needed a drink.

'Ensured that the reporting officer didn't take a blood sample from you for drinking and driving.'

Jess snorted a short laugh. 'I hadn't been drinking.'

'You were seen.'

'I was seen with non-alcoholic gin and tonic, so actually you've done me no favours whatsoever. My blood should have been taken for analysis. Now there will always be that question, that rumour that I am, was, a drink driver.'

'No, there won't.' A face appeared at a gap in the curtains and Dougie Doolan stepped into the cubicle; behind him like a backup squad hovered Samira and Vinnie almost hopping on the balls of their feet.

Price's smug, confident expression dropped immediately.

'We can all confirm that Sergeant Raker drank only non-alcoholic drinks,' Dougie stated. 'In fact we were the only ones who bought her drinks, she didn't even have to buy one for herself.'

'Maybe someone spiked the drinks,' Price said, unwilling to back off.

Dougie gave him a pitying look, not remotely intimidated by the man or his rank but very annoyed by his obvious dislike of Jess. 'B/S,' he said.

Price sniffed up, knowing he was on a loser. Without a word but with a sour, sullen look, he sidestepped through a gap in the curtain and disappeared like the villain in a pantomime.

Jess smiled weakly at Dougie. 'Thanks for that. Always nice to get a welfare visit from your boss.' She adjusted herself on the bed, wincing with pain as she did so.

Her trio of officers trooped in. Dougie remained at the foot of the bed whilst Samira and Vinnie took a side each. Vinnie pulled up a plastic chair and dropped into it, looking the worse for wear from his drinking session last night. Jess grinned at him.

'I presume you have a headache too?' Jess asked him.

'Self-inflicted,' he admitted and shook his face so his cheeks wobbled. He looked pale and rough.

'How are you feeling?' Samira asked Jess, deeply concerned.

'Grog. Sore and bashed about. The experience is not to be recommended. I was lucky.' She looked at Dougie. 'What happened? Nobody's told me much yet.'

'Mm . . .'

'What does that mean?'

'Even though you've been bashed about, you're lucky it wasn't much worse, Jess. It's a good job we managed to get the emergency services on the scene PDQ, otherwise there's every chance you could have been undiscovered in that field until dawn.'

Jess shivered at the thought. 'How come you were so quick, then?'

'Joe Borwick, firefighter guy,' Samira said.

'What about him?'

'Um, well, he saw you drive away from the Wellsprings and then noticed a stain on the ground where your car had been. He recognized it for what it was and alerted us.'

'Brake fluid?' Jess guessed.

'Yep,' Dougie said. 'I've had the road policing department look at your car . . . it's at a repair garage at the moment, by the way, though it looks more like a heap of mangled metal and will be a write-off. The traffic guy said the brake pipes had been cut and the handbrake cable sawn through.'

'Someone tried to kill you,' Samira said with a tremor of fear in her voice.

Tampering with someone's brakes, was a brutal, evil and very premeditated way of attempting to kill anyone.

Jess thought about this after everyone had gone, leaving her alone in the cubicle for the moment, although the noise from the hospital corridor outside was horrendous and concentrating was not easy as she tried to recall the details.

Everything that happened leading up to her getting into her car was clear. The meal out, the chats with her colleagues, seeing Joe Borwick come into the Wellsprings with his fiancée (*and what a nice-looking couple they made*, Jess thought bitterly) and then her own uncontrolled emotions rising as though she was the wronged woman in the scenario. *How laughable*, she thought now. Anyway, she shoved that to one side and continued to try and recall the incident, closing her eyes tightly, but to be honest the bang on the head must have affected her recall because there wasn't much more to tell after she and Joe had had their exchange in the car park. She couldn't remember getting into the car nor the trip down Pendle Hill and definitely not the crash. Maybe headlights behind. Not sure. All she knew now was what other people had told her.

She gave up. It would either come back or it wouldn't.

'Hey-frickin'-ho.' She sighed, letting her head drop softly back into her pillows.

Dougie had told her that her mother was looking after Lily and Jason and the children had been kept off school. They had been at the hospital most of the night but Marj had taken them home in the early hours once it was confirmed Jess wasn't too seriously injured. They were due to come back to visit soon and when Jess heard the curtain slide open it was that trio she expected and wanted to see.

Her eyes fluttered open.

Joe Borwick stood there, sheepish but concerned.

'Joe.' Her throat was dry again.

'Sarge.'

'Jess will do.'

'Jess.'

Her eyelids closed as a wave of weariness cascaded over her, but then she forced them open. 'I seem to have you to thank for my quick rescue.'

'Only a bit,' he said modestly. 'It was always possible the brake fluid hadn't come from your car.'

'But it had . . . so thanks.'

He shrugged. 'Just doing my job, ma'am,' he smiled.

'As if. But yeah, thanks.' She frowned, perplexed. 'Why did you follow me out of the restaurant?'

'Wanted to talk – to explain, I guess.'

Jess inhaled unsteadily. The pain in her right boob made her shift uncomfortably and tears moistened her eyes. 'Life's a shit,' she said.

'It can be.'

Then she uttered a harsh laugh which also hurt her boob, making her wince.

'Sore tit,' she explained. 'Seat belt.'

'Ahh.'

'Truth is, Joe, I want something I can't have and it's probably best I can't get my hands on it, if you'll pardon the expression. I—' She stopped abruptly.

'You . . . what? Really like me?' he ventured.

'Duh! But nothing's going to come of it, Joe. Nothing.'

'Life's too complicated and all that?'

'Bob on, matey.'

'Things could be simplified.'

Jess held up her right hand sharply. 'Hold it right there.' She looked sadly at him. 'Let's leave things be. I have a marriage to save, two kids, a daft mum with a daft dog, no real home as yet, a new job I want to succeed in and you have your own plans, problems and relationships, I guess.'

God, this was exhausting her, trying to string all these words together into something resembling coherence.

'Jess.' Joe leaned forwards and gently took hold of her left hand, the one in the back of which a cannula had been inserted to connect to the drips by her bedside.

She snatched the hand away, almost dislodging the needle and pulling over the drip which swayed slightly but didn't overbalance.

'Sorry,' he said. 'A bit forward.'

'Joe – nothing's happened between us so far other than our eyes meeting across a pile of burning tyres, so let's keep it that way, then no one gets hurt or offended or uprooted or shocked shitless.'

'You sure have a nice turn of phrase.'

'You should hear me on a Sunday.'

'Right, but OK, there is one thing . . .'

'And what's that, Joe?'

He looked into her eyes with those fantastic grey eyes of his. 'Us . . . don't forget us.' He kissed the tip of his forefinger and held it in her direction – a tiny gesture that seemed to hit her like a truck. It astounded her to her core. Her mouth opened to say something, probably something totally inappropriate that would have landed both of them in the mire. She was glad no words escaped because at that exact moment, the cubicle curtain opened.

'Josh!' she exclaimed.

'I felt like I interrupted something.'

Josh sat on a chair by the bed. He held Jess's right hand, clasped gently between the palms of his hands.

'Just work,' Jess explained. 'Plus thanking him for pressing the panic button.' She clamped up then, realising that if she began to explain the how and why, it might be a tad awkward, given that Josh was her husband.

She spotted a slight frown cross Josh's face, but he didn't pursue anything.

'So how are you doing?' he asked.

'Hurt, tired, but in one piece more or less so I can't complain too much.'

'That detective – Doolan – said your brake pipes had been cut.'

'Looks that way.'

'So, out of the frying pan into the fire?' Josh said coldly.

She knew what he meant. People seemed to want to kill her wherever she went. London, Lancashire, you name it.

He gave a deep sigh, then changed tack. 'I tried to get back last night but the trains were on strike – I phoned every hour to see how you were going on, though.'

'A nurse told me. Thank you.'

'I'm just sorry I couldn't get here before now.'

'I know. It's OK.'

Strangely she was beginning to feel very uncomfortable with her hand being held between his. She kind of didn't like it any more, even though she wanted to. She withdrew it slowly and scratched an imaginary itch on her forehead. Her big problem was that the issues she had with Josh – his unfaithfulness, the fact she'd found him buying jewellery for his lady friend (aka secretary) and then his reluctance to move north for her safety – always seemed to hang around like a bad smell that would not evaporate. Although he'd got himself the new job in Manchester, he despised the daily commute and made any excuse to stay there overnight, which made Jess feel uncomfortable. Was he really meeting clients?

To make life easier they had discussed the possibility of buying a house in or near Preston from which the train connection to Manchester was more reliable, but Jess was reluctant to do that because it would mean uprooting Lily and Jason again and would make her mother's move to help out pointless.

For better or for worse (and Jess sniggered at that thought) Josh would have to get his act together.

They looked at each other.

Once upon a time, looking into his eyes could make her quake inside. Now there seemed to be nothing, not a vestige of feeling, and Jess hated it. She wanted to be in love with her husband and wanted that love reciprocated.

In that moment – probably because of the blow to her head (at least that is what she blamed it on) – she decided to pose that tough question.

'Josh?'

'Yeah?'

She was about to ask if he still loved her, really loved her, but the words never came because, once more, the curtains opened and this time Lily and Jason surged through ahead of their grandmother, and the sight of their dad as well as their mum put an extra charge of electricity in them, with whoops, hugs, kisses and tears of joy. Everything eventually calmed down and the first question Jason asked was, 'Does this mean we can have a new car?'

On a social media site dedicated to all things Ribble Valley, there was a report from the police about an incident the night before where a car had run off the road whilst travelling down Pendle Hill. The police did not post any actual photographs of the crash, but a passer-by had managed to get footage of a very badly mangled, almost squashed, Citroën Picasso being dragged on to a recovery truck.

'Look! I told you,' Lance said. He had been scrolling through Dimbo's phone and found the posts. He and Dimbo were again lounging indolently on the old sofa in the office at Primrose Breakers, both feeling smug.

Mags was behind them like a hovering spectre.

He handed the phone to her and she flipped through the post.

'Doesn't say she's dead, does it?'

In fact, the report was very vague and related mostly to the necessity to close the road whilst the car was recovered from a field and accident investigation work took place. All traffic had been diverted, and the photos had been uploaded by a hill walker. If someone had died, Mags was pretty sure it would have been reported. As it was, all it said was that the driver of the car, a woman in her thirties, had been rushed to hospital. No other car was involved, nor was there any mention of any other person.

'Well, no . . . but if she survived that . . .' Lance said, not finishing the sentence.

'Mm,' Mags said sourly. She looked at the footage again of the vehicle being dragged on to the recovery truck and felt a tremor of excitement at the video. Even if Raker had survived, hopefully she was seriously injured. She glanced at Tommy who was peering over her shoulder at the phone. 'So near yet so far,' she said wistfully.

'We need to be careful now,' Tommy advised soberly. 'The cops'll be gunning for you – us.'

'They won't be able to prove a thing, will they Lance?' she fired at him. 'No one saw you, did they?'

He exchanged a worried look with Dimbo. 'I don't think so.'

'CCTV from the Wellsprings?'

Lance shrugged. 'We were careful and we wore balas,' he said, meaning balaclava masks. 'Dunt matter if a camera picked us up or not, we won't get recognized and we did work on the dark side of the car in shadow. We'll be reet.' He gave Dimbo another uncertain look.

'And it's not as if they're going to find our car, is it? Even if that got caught on camera,' Lance added.

Outside the cabin there was an explosively loud, metallic, tearing and crushing sound, drawing all four sets of eyes to the office window where they saw Steve at the helm of the crane, the grabbing jaws of which had just sunk its teeth into the car Lance and Dimbo had been provided with. The car was lifted and deposited into the other, open set of jaws, this time belonging to the crusher which closed slowly, inexorably around it like a huge Venus flytrap. Then, with more crushing and rending, the vehicle was consumed and a few short minutes later would reemerge on the conveyor belt having been reduced to the size of an old-style school desk, never to be recognized again.

They watched the process from the office.

'Owning a scrapyard is so handy,' Mags murmured with a low chuckle.

'We still need to be careful,' Tommy warned her again.

Mags turned sharply to him, baring her teeth and hissing, 'I know. Don't lecture me,' giving Tommy another quick insight into her personality which had the ability to change almost instantaneously. He said nothing, just noted it. Mags turned back to Lance. 'I take it you managed to deliver those goods to Angela?' she asked, referring to the specially packed sachets of cocaine.

He nodded. 'I did. We need another car, though.'

'Steve'll fix you up with something kosher.'

'And dosh?' Lance pushed it. 'I'm skint and on bail. We pulled a bloody dangerous job for you last night, boss.'

It was then Lance's turn to get yet another glimpse into the fiery soul of Maggie Horsefield, not that he needed reminding of it particularly. She turned to him and it seemed as though her eyes were hooded like a viper's. Then he recalled with a sudden triggering of memory that not very long ago she'd had him tied to a chair with a zombie knife at his throat, threatening to behead him. He swallowed, still able to feel the blade across his windpipe and wondering what it would have been like to have had it sliced open.

'You work for me now, Lance. Don't forget, this is your chance to survive by doing things for me.' For a moment the tip of her tongue poked out between her lips and Lance half-expected it to be forked.

He shook in the sofa. 'Sorry, boss.' His voice was a whisper.

She nodded. 'What you guys need to do now is lie low. We've got something big coming up and we might need you for it, haven't we, Tommy?' Mags then leaned down between the two lads. 'If the cops do catch up with you and you do get questioned, you say nothing, OK?'

They nodded eagerly. Lance said, 'What have you got coming up?'

Mags tapped her nose and said, 'Need to know, but it's a biggie.' She opened her shoulder bag and pulled out a thick wedge of ten-pound notes secured by an elastic band and dropped it on to the sofa between them. 'Split this and don't get too pissed.'

Lance grabbed the money first.

Mags turned to Tommy, purring again. 'Lunch out, dear?'

ELEVEN

Three days off sick was more than enough for Jess. Being cared for incessantly by her mother almost drove her daft, although the way Luna laid her head on her lap and looked up at her with those huge, beautiful eyes was lovely and did aid recovery. The dog just knew she was unwell. Fortunately no mice put in an appearance.

Josh was noticeable by his absence.

He had stayed with her on the day and night she was discharged but was gone the next, not to be seen again. All the usual excuses, which just made Jess chuckle mirthlessly. She knew he could have taken the time off had he wanted. Like a loving husband would have done.

However, her time off gave her some time to look around for a replacement car which was a speedy necessity, something to fill the gap for the time being, just a run around. She also spent some of this enforced 'leisure' time doing house 'viewings' on estate agents' websites, wondering what she might be able to afford if the worst came to the worst and she and Josh split up. If she and Josh stayed together the money from the sale of their home in London – which was going through after a couple of false starts – would have bought a very decent house in the Ribble Valley outright; splitting the equity two ways would mean a very hasty realignment of her sights. It wouldn't be too bad, would require a mortgage but would not be what she had planned.

The other problem was that she was reluctant to leave Bolton-by-Bowland. She had settled in well. The neighbours were nice, the Coach & Horses was close by and beyond excellent, and the rented cottage, whilst probably too small, was cosy. She wasn't sure how Lily and Jason were feeling about it. They had certainly settled at school. Lily had amassed a wide range of friends, even if they included Caitlin; and Jason, being a sports nerd, fitted in brilliantly. The doubt was Josh, of course. She had prepared to ask him that 'lurv' question at the hospital but the kids had interrupted the moment and it remained unasked. She still wanted him as a husband, but thoughts of Joe Borwick had begun to cloud her judgement, try as she might to keep them at bay.

These were all the things that went through her head like a spinning hamster wheel, never ending, never concluding.

By the end of the second day 'off sick' she thought she was going slightly bonkers. Even a walk up on to the fells against her mum's advice – *you might have a stroke or something* – did not clear her head.

On the third day she got her mother to take her to a used car dealer where she bought a very abused Kia which she drove off the forecourt there and then. It would suffice until the insurance on the Citroën was sorted. She also had a proper look around two houses for sale in the village, both nice, both expensive, both beyond her means if she became a single mother . . . which made her wonder if she was just hanging on to the thought of Josh for financial reasons rather than those of the heart.

Damn. This was hard.

When she got home she phoned the owner of the cottage she was renting and asked if she would consider selling. A bit cheeky, but so what?

The answer was a firm no.

Jess thanked her, ended the call, then called the woman something completely unacceptable.

Later she did the afternoon school run in the Kia, hoping she would run into Mags.

She did.

Pure luck. There was a space right behind Mags' Range Rover. She pulled into it and waited a few moments. She could just about make out two figures – Mags behind the wheel and Tommy Moss in the front passenger seat, and because of the direction the cars were facing Tommy was next to the pavement.

Jess decided to go and lean on that side of the car and get a good close-up of Tommy, the big London 'I am' guy. She did and tapped on the illegal smoked-glass window which lowered an inch, just enough for Tommy's eyes to show in the gap.

'What?'

Jess leaned down slightly so her eyeline was level with the gap and could also see past Tommy to Mags who was tilting forwards to look at her, scowling.

'Jess, darling!' Mags said. 'Tommy – open the window a touch more.'

He hesitated then pressed the button, opening the window an inch further.

'Jessica! I heard you drove your car off the road when you were a teensy-weensy bit tipsy. I do hope you're all right, honestly I do. Gosh, your face looks such a mess. I presume you didn't get breathalyzed because, y'know, cops together and all that?'

'It's hard to blow into a bag when you're unconscious,' Jess said. She didn't try to defend the level of alcohol in her body, or the complete lack of it but Mags' remark did jar with her.

Mags chortled.

Tommy just kept on looking at Jess, no expression on his face other than maybe hatred.

'You still here, Tommy?' Jess asked him.

'For the duration,' he said stonily. 'And just so you know, I don't like cops in my face.'

Jess blinked and tried to disguise the fact that she swallowed nervously but retained her composure and said sweetly, 'Just so you know, I don't like villains in mine.'

That made him smirk. 'Tough girl, eh?'

Jess almost said, 'Tough enough to put two bullets into your baby bro,' but stopped herself just in time.

Across the road the school bell rang out.

To Mags, Jess said, 'I just thought you'd be glad to see me up and around again and, I know you'll be curious but just to put your mind at rest, my so-called accident is being investigated as an attempted murder and I fully expect a result soon. See ya!'

She pivoted away from the Range Rover, suddenly feeling unbalanced, and got back into her new car then remembered Lily and Jason wouldn't recognize the Kia so she gobbled a few painkillers, got out and leaned on the roof and waved at her offspring as they came out of the school gates.

Both were shocked by the Kia. Jason warned her, 'This better not be our new forever car. It's a . . .'

Jess stopped a chance of bad language with a finger on his lips. 'It's a filler,' she assured him.

'How many?' Jess asked, completely gobsmacked by the figure just quoted by Dougie Doolan. 'Lay that on me again.'
'Zero.'
'Zero?'
'Correct.'
'Not even a pair?'
'Not even one measly detective,' Dougie said.

Jess sighed miserably. She thought she'd shaken off the headache since the crash but now it came back like a migraine at this news. She tweaked the bridge of her nose between finger and thumb.

'So, let me get this straight, Doug. Neither the CID nor FMIT are going to put a team together to investigate the fact that my brake pipes were cut, handbrake cable was severed, and I could have died as a result?'

Shamefaced, Dougie shook his head.

'Somebody tried to kill me, Doug.'

'I know, Jess.'

Jess was back at work, taking it steady. She was at her desk having dropped the kids off at school and it was now almost 9 a.m. She had a mug of tea on the mouse mat and two slices of toast next to that, slavered with butter. The food and drink had been brought in by an overly attentive Samira and now Jess knew why: to cushion her from the impact of what Dougie had just revealed.

And now, despite her thinly veiled warning to Mags that detectives would be sniffing around in the form of a murder squad, the truth was that there wasn't going to be a murder squad.

'A couple of detectives from FMIT turned up, reviewed the CCTV footage from the Wellsprings and declared it useless – grainy, unfocused images, not possible to enhance in any way; they looked at the remains of your car and though the brakes had been tampered with, because there was no witnesses to the crash itself they decreed that any actual investigation would get nowhere fast and then they quietly effed off back to Blackburn where they're currently investigating a rape/murder and some fallout between low-level gangsters that resulted in a fatal shooting.'

Jess listened to this tale of woe and said, 'No contest, then – me having a crash versus two sexy murders.'

Dougie was sitting opposite her. Samira stood behind him, with Vinnie McKinty at the door. They looked like they were expecting a huge tantrum from Jess and were preparing to flee for their own safety.

It almost happened. It was touch and go. Jess took a sip of the tea – well-brewed, strong, a bit stewed; police station tea, the best in the world. Then she bit a chunk off a slice of thick white toast which was immeasurably delicious.

She munched, swallowed.

'You OK, sarge?' Samira asked cautiously.

Jess raised her eyes at the PCSO, then moved them across to Vinnie – who visibly cowered – then rested them on Dougie.

Jess understood police priorities and resource allocation all too well, especially when there were few enough cops about anyway and everything cost money and time. Murders and incidents which captured the public's imagination and attention were far more likely to get staff chucked at them than a lowly sergeant crashing her car, even if the brakes had been tampered with. After all, she hadn't actually died.

'I need to get my head together,' Jess declared, something she never once imagined she would ever say. She was tough, decisive. She'd been a firearms team leader in the Met for goodness sake and had even made that fateful decision to pull a trigger. Someone who needed to 'get their head together' would never have cut the mustard in that role.

Nor in this role to be honest.

She thought it made her sound weak and indecisive and she didn't like it. Maybe the bump on the head had dislodged everything.

'Give me half an hour, folks,' she told them.

They got the message and left.

When the office door closed, she slammed the palms of her hands down on the desk and said, 'Right,' got up, grabbed a marker pen, pulled out the flipchart from the corner, flipped open the pad and began to do a bit of planning, add a bit of structure for the days ahead.

She liked structure but also knew that life as a response sergeant was often more reactive than proactive because of the nature of the job, but it was good to be proactive where possible – such as leading the raids she'd planned and executed on Maggie Horsefield's drug business – and stuff like that was the icing on the cake. She had imagined that life in the Ribble Valley would have been more laid-back, that it would have been possible to do more pre-planned operations, but so far she was wrong.

She put marker to paper.

Jess rounded up Samira, Vinnie and Dougie, and proudly displayed the scribbled-on flipchart to them.

'First of all, it looks like we are "it" as regards the investigation team concerning me and my car.' She looked at Dougie. 'So being on CID, I know you'll dedicate all your time to this.' She gave him an exaggerated wink.

'But of course . . . er, does this job come with a broom, sarge?' he asked, sounding serious.

Vinnie looked perplexed. 'What do you mean, Doug?'

All three regarded him with amusement. Laying on the patronizing tone, Samira said, 'So you can shove the handle up your . . .'

'Ahh – got it!' Vinnie said. 'My bum.'

'Yep, we're all busy and we'll just have to do the best we can,' Jess said. To Dougie, she added, 'I know you don't come under my supervision and it's not up to me to deploy you.'

'No worries. I'll do my best, even though I've got two house burglaries to attend this morning over Waddington way.'

'Two?'

'Both good class dwellings on a nice estate and two cars stolen from their drives, too.'

'OK. Let's just do this and then we can get going,' Jess said. 'I won't keep you long.'

She turned to the flipchart on which was a to-do list of subjects, each in their own fluffy cloud, like floating sheep.

The cloud in the centre of the board had the words 'My Accident' in the middle of it, in inverted commas, and several lines – like spindly legs – coming out of it, though instead of feet, at the end of each line was an 'action'. Such as, 'Inspect Car', 'Scrap Car', 'CCTV'. Another cloud had the word 'Misper' in it. Another, 'Dawson aka Dimbo' and there was a sidebar, essentially a column, which read, 'Burning Cars', 'TWOC (Jaguar)', 'Royal Family', and 'Lance D', and 'Castle Catering'.

Jess knew it was just a brainstorming list, with not too much structure as yet, but at least it was a start. She looked at Samira. 'You're the doorcam queen,' she said, referencing Samira's persistence once in finding a doorcam recording that led to the uncovering of the murderer of an old man, even though it proved to be an unsettling discovery.

'I thought the CCTV footage at the Wellsprings wasn't that good?'

'It isn't. However, because we know the time of my accident and we know that a car was behind me down the hill and therefore we know the direction of travel of said car, let's make an assumption or two.'

'Ha! Assumptions!' Dougie chuckled.

'I know, but stick with me here. The car drove off down Pendle Hill on Clitheroe Road, which is basically devoid of houses. My assumption is this – and I know I could just be clutching at straws – but what if the driver reached the A59, crossed over on to Pendle Road and went towards Clitheroe?'

'And Pendle Road has plenty of houses on it,' Samira said, getting the gist.

'Spot on! So what I'd like you to do is go door-to-door along there and see what footage there might be from someone's house. You never know.'

'Will do, sarge.'

'Vinnie?' Jess tapped her fingernail on the flipchart. 'Let's you and me do a bit of digging at Castle Catering, eh?'

'Sounds good.'

'Doug?' She looked at the seasoned detective. 'What have you got on?'

'Just the break-ins mainly.'

'Well, you get on with them, then maybe we all meet up back here in a couple of hours and then' – here Jess looked at Samira – 'we turn our attention to Dimbo, the guy who assaulted you; you said you had an address for him?'

'Great,' Samira said.

'Then let's get rocking.'

TWELVE

Castle Catering operated from a unit on a small industrial estate off Chatburn Road. Its two-storey unit sat behind a high fence and looked nothing special. A large refrigerated lorry was reversed up to a roller shutter door and was being unloaded with what looked like pallets of yogurts and other chilled desserts and foodstuffs.

Jess asked Vinnie to park the Defender outside the gates so she could log into the internet via her phone and do a bit of research before knocking on the door, even though she knew Vinnie had already done some background.

The company had a fairly simple website detailing the sorts of catering it did – basically everything from special birthday parties and food to country fairs to rugby club dos and fancy events, and their wide range included English favourites to Halal and everything in between, including the provision of all staff required.

We cater, was their very simplistic motto.

There were some photographs of staff standing behind buffets full of sandwiches, pies, hotpots and cakes, all smiling and wearing aprons with the Castle Catering logo on – a silhouette of Clitheroe Castle with a witch flying over on a broomstick – and all the girls and ladies wore black microskirts and tights.

Vinnie leaned across to see what Jess was looking at, then his finger shot out and he pointed at one of the photos.

'That's her!' he said, indicating a thin woman with bobbed, streaked hair standing behind a seafood buffet of lobsters and other crustaceans. 'My missing woman.'

Expanding the photograph with her finger and thumb, Jess looked closely at her, recognizing her from the misper file. 'Ah, yes.'

She flipped on through more photographs not seeing any of interest, but then stopped suddenly, swiped back, and found a photograph of two women. The caption underneath read, 'Our CEO's, Angela and Margaret.'

And – lo and behold, Jess thought – there was Mags Horsefield standing next to Angela Dart holding up a framed certificate relating to some sort of industry prize for catering innovation, dated five years ago.

She tilted the phone for Vinnie to see. 'Mags.'

'According to the Companies House website, she resigned about four years back,' he reminded Jess.

'Bet she's still involved.'

'I wonder what the catering innovation was?' Jess asked cynically. 'How to make greater profits by selling drugs with your food?'

Vinnie snorted a laugh. 'Probably.'

'Not a terrible idea, though,' Jess said. 'And I know the other woman too – used to go to school with her. Dart the Fart we called her . . . well, I did. Not a great mate.' She sighed. 'Let's go chat.'

Jess had deliberately not phoned ahead to make an appointment because she liked showing up unannounced to gigs like this. She enjoyed seeing people on the backfoot wherever possible. Even if they were innocent of everything, their reactions to cops suddenly appearing on the doorstep was always telling.

It was like entering a huge greetings cards shop with displays and shelves packed with cards of all descriptions, balloons, numerous tacky, sparkly gifts. There was a sales counter at the far end behind which sat a young woman filing her nails and looking at her phone which was propped up at an angle; occasionally she stopped filing and scrolled down the screen. Totally engrossed, she chewed gum loudly, blew bubbles and did not look up as Jess and Vinnie made their way from the front door.

'Reminds me, must get a birthday card for my mum,' Jess said to no one in particular.

They reached the counter and still the girl did not acknowledge them. She was deep into surfing, chewing and filing.

There was a chrome, reception desk bell on the counter which Jess rang twice with the palm of her hand and the girl jumped. She really had been in her own world.

'Ah – what?' the girl said, taking in the two uniforms in front of her. Her name tag said Emma.

Behind her was a door and a large one-way window, behind which Jess assumed was the office.

'Ms Dart, please, Emma,' Jess said. 'She's expecting us.' She added a little fib.

'I don't think so,' the girl said.

Jess took that to indicate Angela was in, which was a plus. 'Tell her Sergeant Raker is here from Clitheroe police station, and PC McKinty.' She jerked her thumb at Vinnie.

'She's very busy.'

'Me too,' Jess said, and slyly kicked Vinnie.

'Me too,' Vinnie added.

'We're all very busy, rushed off our feet, which is why we don't like wasting time.' She tilted her head and gave the girl a sweet smile.

Emma's eyes jumped from one cop to the other, coming back to Jess who said, 'Just get her.'

She nodded, slid off the stool and went through the office door behind her.

A few moments later her head popped back. 'Come on round.'

Even though it was Dougie Doolan's job to catch and put crims into the justice system, on the whole he didn't despise them as such. He fully understood the driving motivations behind a wide variety of crime, particularly the low-level stuff where offenders were often responding to poverty and necessity, such as penniless single mums shoplifting for nappies and food for their kids. He didn't like anyone taking property that belonged to others but he understood some genuine reasons for it.

He didn't have any time for drug dealers who preyed on the vulnerable because far too many times over his long career Dougie had seen too many corpses which could be traced back to that first spliff, ecstasy tab or pill, the 'Go on, try it,' moment, which led ultimately to death. He had no sympathy for anyone who made money from causing misery.

But he rarely hated criminals – with one exception.

It was bad enough taking property that belonged to another but a criminal who entered other people's homes, often wrecking them for no good reason and stealing valuable or sentimental items, sent his anger spiralling.

He utterly despised burglars, whatever their motivation.

And hated the effect the crime of burglary had on victims.

He also hated the modern-day lack of police response to such crimes, the way in which police resources had been diverted away from the core purpose of protecting life and property into the flim-flam crap of today. Sometimes he thought that policing had totally lost its way and a lack of manpower and weak leadership often meant burglaries, one of the most serious of crimes, were never visited, had to be reported by phone and victims rarely even saw the police any more.

That infuriated him.

He was realistic enough to appreciate that solving such crimes was rare and hard to accomplish – which had always been the case – but what had been important was the police always visited the scenes and spent time chatting to and reassuring victims, which was often just as valuable as solving the actual crime.

People liked to see cops. They liked to talk to them. They mostly understood how hard it was to catch villains and often all they wanted was the reassurance that they were important to the police, not just crime numbers for insurance claims, and, Dougie believed, the only way to achieve that was through personal contact, sympathy, empathy. In other words, interpersonal skills.

Which was one of the reasons, and much to his detective sergeant's chagrin, Dougie tried to visit every burglary reported on his patch. It helped victims, it made the police look half-decent and maybe there was just the possibility of securing some evidence along the way.

And that was why he visited the burglaries in Waddington that morning from which vehicles had been stolen, because both properties had been broken into whilst the householders were in bed – extra scary – and their cars stolen from their driveways.

Dougie was sitting opposite a young lady who was still shaking badly with tears flooding down her face.

A victim.

'My husband's away,' she said. Dougie could even hear her teeth chattering. 'He works in the Middle East, teaching . . . stuff.' She sniffed up snottily. 'I teach too. In Clitheroe.'

Dougie nodded.

'It's not so much the car . . . well, it is, I suppose. My husband's pride and joy. A Porsche. We saved forever for it and now it's gone.'

'I'm sorry.'

'I don't apologize for the car.' She blew her nose. She was a pretty lady, mid-twenties, but her runny nose was now red raw. 'We worked hard for it. Gavin being away is a real wrench, especially now.'

She patted her tum.

'Ah,' Dougie said.

'He'll be away for most of my pregnancy. God, I wish he was here!'

'Have you contacted him?'

'Yeah. He was all for jumping on a plane but I told him no. It's just,' she said weakly, 'like I said, not just the car, it's the fact they came into the house for the keys. Came in. Broke in. I don't know, entering my house while I was in bed.'

'It's awful,' Dougie commiserated genuinely, beginning to seethe. He was already suspecting this was a well-planned job, probably professionals, stealing to order. He guessed the car would be well gone by now, sitting in a container on its way to a port. 'And they didn't disturb you?'

'No. Fortunately I was out like a light.'

Dougie had already inspected the entry point, the back door, and it looked as though the offenders must have had a duplicate key for the place – not hard to get if you knew the right people – which would not give CSI much to work with. The car key had been left on the island in the middle of the kitchen. It appeared the thieves had remained downstairs and also helped themselves to a few items from the living room too. They didn't seem to have gone upstairs.

'The thought of burglars in my house,' she shivered.

'Horrible,' Dougie agreed, 'but it is quite rare and, I'm assuming this, I think your car might have been the actual target. The valuables taken from the house itself were probably just opportunistic.' He paused. 'You heard nothing?'

'Not a peep.'

'Do you have CCTV?' He knew she had because he'd spotted a security camera affixed to the inside of the front bedroom window in which she slept.

'Yes, it's connected to my phone. Here.' She handed him her mobile, linked to the camera which overlooked the front of the house. At the moment it showed an empty front drive with Dougie's own car parked on the avenue at the bottom of the driveway. 'Just swipe it backwards and you'll see a red marker on the timeline under the footage at two a.m.'

He did and the timeline graph showed a whole heap of activity around that time. He let the footage run.

The camera was positioned to catch movement on the front driveway, where the Porsche had been parked, but it managed to capture the side of a vehicle cruising slowly past on the avenue, a van of some sort. Dougie could only see the bottom third of it, but it looked like a Transit van or something similar. It went out of shot, presumably to park up further down the avenue. A few moments later two black-clad figures with balaclavas over their heads came into shot.

Crouching, the pair ran up the drive and disappeared from view as they came to the front door. Dougie swiped the footage back and slowed it down frame by frame. It was all quite clear, showing two individuals. The bigger one was definitely a man, quite tall and broad shouldered, that being obvious even though he was running at a crouch.

At first Dougie assumed the other crim, who was slimmer and smaller, was also a man but there was a point at which this person came fleetingly upright and in profile, and without a doubt, Dougie could see breasts.

'A man and a woman,' he said to the Porsche owner.

'Yes, I thought so.'

'Interesting.'

He watched the remainder of the relevant footage. There was a break in the activity whilst the thieves were inside the house, then they appeared shortly after and went to the car, opened it using the remote they'd stolen from the kitchen, and the woman got in. There was an incline to the drive and without starting the car they rolled the vehicle slowly out on to the avenue. The man took up position behind it and pushed, at which point he was joined by two others, men, both in black. They pushed the car along the avenue and out of sight.

Dougie sighed. A sliver of pain arced across his lower chest and back and he fought hard not to react to it.

'They knew what they were after,' he said. 'Can I have a copy of the footage, please?'

She nodded and downloaded a file and sent him a copy via email.

'Obviously you need to get your locks changed,' Dougie advised her. 'I can arrange a locksmith if you want?'

'That would be great, thanks.'

'And look, I know this is a big shock, but it seems to be a one-off, so try not to worry, which I know is easy for me to say. I do have another address to visit nearby, though.'

'Same thing?'

'I think so.'

She swallowed then shrugged philosophically. 'Hopefully they won't be back here.'

Angela Dart's office was full of inflated balloons relating to someone's upcoming sixtieth birthday, all secured by weights to the floor to stop them floating up to the ceiling. It was like entering some sort of wonderland. As Jess and Vinnie came in, Angela Dart was inflating another with helium gas from a cylinder.

The woman's back was to the officers but she must have been aware they had stepped in and she said, 'One sec,' as the pink balloon grew in size to take on the shape of a large penis and testicles with a line of silver dots from the tip of the balloon.

Jess blew out her cheeks. 'Tasteful.'

Vinnie said, 'Crikey blimey,' as the erection continued to grow.

There was no mistaking what the balloon represented and as Jess scanned other already inflated balloons she saw more examples of male – and female – genitalia and quite a few boob ones, too.

Finally the balloon Dart was blowing up reached full size and she slid it off the gas cylinder, and whilst tying it expertly she turned to face the officers.

'Hen party, plus bride-to-be's sixtieth. Quite a combination,' Dart said. 'I think it's going to be a hoot!' She led the erection across the office, attached it to a weight and allowed it to settle and sway amongst other like-minded balloons. She then edged behind her desk and sat.

'Wow,' Jess said.

'We cater for everyone,' Dart said, then smiled thinly. 'Even the police.'

It was at that point Jess said, 'Angela Dart?'

Dart squinted at Jess and the penny dropped with her too. 'Jessica . . . er . . . ?'

'Easterby, as was. Now Raker.'

'We were at school together way back,' Dart said. She didn't mention them being friends; they hadn't been because Angela had been best buddies with Maggie Goss, as was, now Horsefield, and both girls heartily despised Jess mainly because of the very immature love/lust triangle with Mags, vying for the attention of a young, rather dim lad who was great in bed. It had got nasty on occasion and Angela had encouraged Mags to punch Jess's lights out.

'Yeah, we were,' Jess confirmed.

'Anyway, water under the bridge, eh?'

'Absolutely,' Jess said positively.

'So, what can I do for you?'

Jess looked at Vinnie and nodded.

'Oh, yeah,' he said, having been a bit transfixed by a large pair of inflated boobs wobbling behind Dart. He got back on track but they remained a slight distraction to him. 'I'm investigating a missing person. A lady called Janet Moyser.'

On the name, Jess waited for a reaction from Dart, but there wasn't one. No blink. No tick. She was either a skilled actor or the name didn't mean anything to her. Dart screwed up her nose slightly. 'Doesn't ring a bell. Am I supposed to know her?'

'According to my enquiries, she worked for you,' Vinnie said.

Dart reckoned to think. 'Still a no.'

'You don't know who works for you?' Jess asked, slightly accusingly.

'People come and go. We only have half a dozen full-time staff and the others, waitresses and such like, are on zero-hours contracts and they come and go; some are regulars, some work when it suits.'

'I'd like you to check your records for this lady, Janet Moyser,' Jess insisted firmly.

'What's this got to do with her being missing?'

'Maybe nothing,' Jess admitted, 'but we'd really like you to help us out here. Her disappearance is a cause for concern and we do know she definitely worked for you because there is a photo of her on your website.'

'Ah, OK.' She didn't seem to quite like that.

Jess saw her reaction and quickly added, 'We've downloaded the photo,' just in case Dart felt inclined to delete the post.

'What we want to know is the names, dates and venues she worked at for you over the past year,' Vinnie said.

'Easier said than done.'

'How about you give us a list of all the people and organizations you've catered for over that period. I'm assuming that's possible?' Jess said. 'With dates.'

'We need to follow up all leads,' Vinnie added.

'You might need a warrant . . . GDPR and all that,' Dart said stubbornly and the atmosphere changed slightly, became chilly.

'Seriously?' Jess said. 'Now I'm very intrigued. Why wouldn't you just help us?'

'Client confidentiality?'

'Bollocks,' Jess said with a snort of laughter. To Vinnie, she said, 'Go and get a warrant, PC McKinty. I'll stay here.'

'No, no, no, that won't be necessary,' Dart relented. 'Look, I'm just watching my back, OK?'

'In that case, we will get a warrant,' Jess said.

'No, look, it's fine,' Dart relented. 'You can look at the order book plus all the casual staff records which are all on cards.'

'Angela,' Jess said, 'I should bloomin well think so.'

Dart shrugged unhappily.

'Oh, by the way, I also saw a photo of you on your website with Maggie holding some sort of certificate between you. Small world, isn't it? You both being owners of this place.'

'She isn't involved any more, she resigned.'

Jess chuckled. 'Course she did.'

They were ushered into another office which was packed with boxes containing serviettes, plastic cutlery and other party essentials. There was a table and two chairs where Jess and Vinnie sat.

'She'll still have something to do with this business, I bet,' Jess murmured, thinking out loud about Mags. 'It's one heck of a way to distribute drugs, don't you think?'

'Definitely, sarge. Delivered to your table, silver service.'

The door opened and Dart entered bearing a sheaf of order forms held together by a massive crocodile clip, plus a ledger and an iPad. She placed the items on the table. 'Orders for the last twelve months and last year's actual jobs. On here,' she said holding up the iPad, 'are our employee records for all casual zero-hours staff. I've had a quick look and Janet Moyser is listed but I'll be honest, I don't know her.' She laid the iPad on the table.

'Thank you,' said Jess. 'Do you recall if you've provided your services to the Duchess of Dunsop and Newton at Wolf Fell Hall near Chipping?'

Dart pretended to think. 'Yeah, I think we have.'

'What would that include?'

Dart pouted and shrugged. 'The usual – nibbles, buffets, drinks, that sort of thing – and some sit-down meals.'

Jess was going to add, 'And drugs hors d'oeuvres?' but held herself back. 'OK, we'll take a look, thanks.'

Samira had watched the very grainy footage from the Wellsprings' CCTV cameras overlooking the car park. Two dark figures creeping up and disappearing behind Jess's Citroën where they then presumably cut the brake lines and pipes. The two figures then scuttled away – like cockroaches, Samira thought – across the car park where they went out of shot. Not long after Jess left the restaurant, had her conversation with Joe Borwick, got into her car and drove away, followed moments later by another car of indeterminate make which had to be the one that tupped her on the way down the Pendle Hill. The registration number wasn't legible, and though the model was not easy to make out Samira thought it could have been something like a Vauxhall Corsa.

She knew and remembered all these details as she parked on Pendle Road and began her house-to-house enquiries regarding doorcam and CCTV footage. She didn't mind doing this, a job often avoided by many cops because it was a bit dull, but as a wannabe cop in the making it was just another excuse for her to do what she totally believed all police officers should do as much as possible and that was talk to people. Any excuse. She liked doing it, being naturally nosy.

However, because of the time of day, most of the houses she called at were unoccupied, but she managed to spot a few cameras and put notes through doors asking people to give her a call when possible.

Two people who did have doorcams were at home. Samira had a quick look at the footage but neither camera had detected anything of note.

She got to the end of a row of houses feeling slightly frustrated but then had a light-bulb moment by putting herself into the mindset of two individuals who had cut Jess's brake pipes and tried to kill her.

'She was employed a dozen times by Castle Catering in the six months before she disappeared,' Vinnie said, referring to the notes he'd made on his pad. 'Twice a month – ish.'

'And we can link those occasions to twelve events the company catered for,' Jess said, checking her notes. She ran a finger down them. 'They all seem to be society dos, for want of a better phrase, not twenty-firsts or kiddies' birthday bashes.'

'Yeah – balls, dances, charity dos, that sort of thing. Black-tie jobs, including three at Wolf Fell Hall.'

Jess was on her mobile, searching the internet. 'The kind of things you see in the society pages of glossy mags, as you discovered. Good work, by the way.'

'Thanks, sarge.'

Jess found entries for the events at Wolf Fell Hall on its own website. She flicked through the photographs. All the functions were over six months old.

'Well, well, well, very interesting,' she said.

She slid the phone over to Vinnie who looked through the photos. 'Now you think there's enough to go back to the hall?'

'Enough to go and chat to the duchess for a start, even though I doubt we'll get much from her.'

'I wonder if the Armstrong-Bentleys are still at the hall,' Vinnie said.

'Well, going off the photos, it seems to be their second home, pretty much.'

'But we have no proof of anything,' Vinnie said despondently.

'That's where all good investigations begin,' Jess said. 'From ground zero.'

THIRTEEN

'That was probably the best fun I've had in a long time,' Mags said breathlessly as she slid off Tommy after once more experiencing one of the most amazing orgasms that only he seemed capable of engineering. Jeeps, he was good and again, despite herself, found she wanted him more and more.

'Kind of you to say,' Tommy breathed modestly, feeling his heartbeat subside.

Mags snuggled up to him, nuzzling and licking his neck, 'That's not what I meant. Going back to basics is what I'm talking about. Entering people's property in the dead of night, stealing stuff. God, that is such a buzz.'

So much of a buzz that after she and Tommy (assisted by Tommy's two enforcers) had stolen a Porsche and a Maserati and then stashed the cars to await onward transportation, they'd been so hyped up they had rushed back to Mags' house and essentially banged the living daylights out of each other.

That euphoric feeling had been somewhat interrupted by Mags having to drive Caitlin to school, but on her return, still feeling the buzz, Mags had remounted Tommy and fired him up, and, after a few hours' kip, had done it all again.

'Oh, right,' Tommy said, now completely deflated.

'Sex was pretty good too,' she teased him. 'I wouldn't want to make a habit of it, though.'

'The sex or stealing cars?'

'The sex is a habit, but nicking cars is too fraught with danger. It's a young kid's game and, as a one-off, fab.'

'I know what you mean.'

'Hell, tiptoeing through someone's house, knowing they're upstairs asleep, that is so special.'

'You're not wrong, Mags.'

Tommy had suggested this idea prior to his trip north. He knew someone who exported stolen sports cars and thought it might be fun to get Mags, with her connections, to source a couple of motors that were on this guy's list, one being a classic Porsche, the other being a Maserati.

The Porsche was easy as one of the part-time teachers at Caitlin's school drove one and she also knew a guy in textiles who owned a Maserati.

With a bit of planning they had stolen the cars which were currently on their way in a container to Hull docks for onwards transportation to Europe to the collector in the Netherlands. It was a twenty-grand payday, split between the coffers of the Moss gang and Mags. Not a life-changing amount, but nice, tidy pin money.

It was the next heist – something much bigger, spicier and more challenging than a couple of house burglaries and car thefts – that was going to net them both serious money, and plans for that were well advanced now.

There was just one element to it that stuck in Mags' craw like a chicken bone: a certain woman, a certain wife, a certain bitch . . . a certain Leanora Moss, Tommy's wife.

Her involvement in it made Mags extremely uncomfortable, not least because any mention of Leanora triggered something inside Mags because she knew, deep down, that Leanora had sent that drunken man to rape her in a toilet cubicle, a claim that could not be proven, but which Mags knew to be true.

It couldn't be proved because the attacker, the would-be rapist, was now dead, knifed by Mags and now mincemeat amongst the hardcore foundations of the now defunct HS2 railway line. Tommy had done that disposal and so far, several months down the line, no enquiries to trace the missing man had ended up on Mags' doorstep.

But Leanora – she of the big boob job, trout-pout lips and mega arse-tuck – was unfortunately key to the disposal of the objects from the planned heist, which Mags had initially pitched to Tommy months back and who had loved the idea although he needed Leanora along for the ride. Her background, according to Tommy, gave her the contacts needed to fence the items and the deal had already been set up much to Mags' annoyance, although she had to breathe in and accept the way things were. But once this was all over, Mags had her own plans as to how Leanora was going to be dealt with and it wouldn't be pretty.

'I suppose I need to get up,' she told Tommy. 'Can't spend all my time being impaled.'

Tommy laughed.

Mags' mobile phone started to ring.

She sighed, answered it, listened, frowned and looked at Tommy as she asked the caller, 'Do we need to be worried, Angela?'

Jess directed Vinnie to the kitchen when they arrived back at the station, saying, 'You know the score: milk, no sugar,' then walked to the sergeant's office, the door of which was slightly ajar. She stopped herself from entering as she could see Dougie Doolan's back to her. He was standing, facing out of the window with his hands on his lower back, fingers splayed. He was stretching and rotating his hips, making a painful wheezing noise as he did.

Jess watched him, puzzled by what she was seeing.

Maybe an older man doing some stretching exercises? But then he stopped mid-rotation and seemed to slump forwards, putting a hand out on the windowsill in order to stop himself tipping over.

Jess quickly stepped in, but Dougie must have heard her, recovered and twisted around innocently as if to convey nothing had happened, although he could not keep the agony off his face.

'What's going on, Doug?'

'What do you mean?'

'All the twisting, the groaning, the painful looks.'

'Nowt, OK? Just a knackered old bloke's aches and pains.'

He and Jess maintained tense eye contact, both seeming to dare the other to speak. Finally Jess capitulated. 'Whatever.'

Dougie relaxed but there was one last flinch on his face before it returned to normal.

Vinnie appeared at the door, a mug in each hand. 'Doug, didn't know you were back. Can I get you one?' He placed the mugs down on the desk.

'No, no, I'm fine.' Doug eased himself into a chair, as did Vinnie. Jess sat behind the desk.

'Let's hang on for Samira, see if she's found anything of interest,' Jess said.

The trio had a general chat about nothing, and as they did Jess began to feel an overwhelming, unstoppable weariness crawling over her. She put it down to the 'accident' which perhaps had taken more out of her than she admitted. Even though she'd emerged relatively unscathed, it could not have been good for her. She realized that once she'd seen this tour of duty through to its conclusion without too much drama she needed to pick up the kids, get home and put up her feet and chill with the nice bottle of white wine currently in the fridge and dive into the box of chocolates she'd been saving for a rainy day. Also maybe have another long hot bath. She was beginning to stiffen up like an ironing board and wasn't looking forward to inspecting the bruises which were blossoming all around her body.

She heard Samira coming down the corridor, humming to herself.

Jess looked at Dougie and Vinnie then at Samira as she came through the office door with a triumphant expression beaming on her face.

'Hey, guys, and sarge,' she said breezily.

Suddenly Jess slumped forwards, not unconscious but overcome by fatigue. Even as she did it, she felt silly but couldn't stop herself.

Samira was first to react. 'Sarge?' She ran around the desk.

'I'm OK, honest,' Jess said, though her brain was light and everything was unfocused.

Maybe banging her bonce on the car as it did its flips had caused some as-yet undiagnosed damage.

Samira bounced on to her haunches beside Jess, deeply concerned, taking hold of Jess's hand tenderly.

Both Dougie and Vinnie were now up on their feet, neither sure what to do but Dougie said, 'Maybe the crash is catching up with you?'

'Yeah, yeah, maybe.' Jess pursed her lips and exhaled as her mind began to clear. She smiled at Samira and gently withdrew her hand from hers. 'I think I'm OK now, just a blip.'

Samira stood up. 'Sarge,' she started to say.

Jess held up a hand. 'It's OK, love.'

Jess was no fool, though, now realizing that taking just three days off sick wasn't quite enough. She rarely took sick leave, had had maybe ten days in total over her whole career. She hated doing it, something in her psyche that made her a workaholic but she also knew that she'd get no thanks for being at work when not feeling a hundred per cent, particularly following a nasty accident. She knew she had to get home and do those relaxing things she'd been thinking about.

'I need to head home and chill,' she admitted a bit weakly.

'Yes, you do,' Samira confirmed.

Jess grinned lopsidedly at her, a young woman she had come to admire so much and who she now counted as a friend.

'Everything here can wait,' Doug said.

'You're what's important,' Vinnie added.

'You look after us,' Samira said, 'so let us return the favour. There's nothing spoiling here, as Dougie said.'

Decision made. 'I'll go and pick up Lily and Jason, then go home. I'll book off on sick leave, maybe take tomorrow off, too.'

'Take as long as you need,' Dougie told her.

That said, being off sick made her feel guilty. She couldn't help it but she was determined to take the rest of the day off and the next day and do nothing. At least that was the plan.

She was early picking up Lily and Jason, so had about half an hour sitting in the car outside the school, slumped down in the driver's seat of the tiny Kia, listening to the radio.

She let her mind go as blank as possible. She didn't want to think about anything, just lose herself in the music coming from Jazz FM.

Even when a car pulled up directly in front of her, nose-to-nose, bumper-to-bumper, she couldn't even fake interest even though it was a big black Range Rover driven by Mags with tough guy Tommy alongside her.

She assumed Mags had parked there by accident perhaps not recognizing the Kia but then remembered that Jess had been in the Kia when they last butted heads a few days before.

Jess couldn't be bothered to raise her eyes, feeling too weak for any verbal jousting with Mags. She settled even more deeply into the seat, folded her arms, closed her eyes.

If she expected Mags not to have a dig, she was wrong.

The tap on the window proved that.

Jess turned her head slowly, not least because she now had a raging headache and any sudden movement would have sent sparks flying around her skull, and opened her eyes just as slowly, her face showing how annoyed she was at the interruption.

Jess mouthed, 'What?' silently.

'Window,' Mags said.

Jess allowed her eyes to do a roll, then opened the window. 'Hi, Mags.'

'Jess, darling . . . I, we,' she pointed to Tommy who jerked up a middle finger at her, 'were wondering how you were after that little accident?'

'Hundred per cent.'

'I can see you're back at work.' Jess was wearing a hoodie over her police uniform. 'So you must be OK.'

'I am. Thanks for your concern. That it?' Jess asked bluntly.

'What?' Mags seemed taken aback, amused and disappointed. 'Not in the mood to threaten me? I'm still waiting for that army of detectives to swoop in and interview me.'

'They'll be round, don't fret,' Jess promised.

'Right.' Mags paused and looked slyly at Jess. 'You do know we could work together, you and me?'

Jess almost burst out laughing. 'Mags! You do know I'm always wired up, don't you?'

'Ha! Such a tease. Still, think about it.' Mags tapped the car roof, then walked back to the Range Rover.

'God, I wish I had been miked up,' Jess murmured to herself and resumed her comfortable position, turned up the jazz a touch and waited for the school bell to ring.

Lily and Jason were magnificent. They instantly picked up the vibe from Jess that she wasn't in a great mental and physical state, and when they arrived home Lily ran a hot, bubbly bath with subtly scented candles arranged around the edge and some mood music whilst Jason sorted out the wine and chocolates and ordered pizza, of course.

Jess thanked them both as she made her way from her bedroom wrapped in a fluffy dressing gown, then once in the bathroom allowed it to slither off her shoulders on to the floor, then stepped into the bath, sliding into the water which swilled up and over her body like silk. Then she just lay back, closed her eyes and listened to the music.

She had a couple of refills of the bath as the water cooled but finally decided she needed to haul herself out. Her joints, limbs and muscles felt weary and weak as she took her own weight and eased herself over the rim and reached for the towel that had been warming on the radiator.

Whilst drying herself, she stood up and, using the bathroom mirror, inspected her bruises and swellings.

The whole right-hand side of her torso must have smashed repeatedly on the inside of the car as it bounced down the hill. Her skin was an ugly mass of purple and off-yellow blotches all the way from her shoulder, down her rib cage and to her buttock and outer thigh.

'Dear God, what a battering,' she said.

She said that knowing it could have been much worse. She was lucky to be alive and able to hunt down whoever it was who had tried to murder her. And hunt them down she would.

The warning on the packet read, 'Can cause addiction. Contains opioid.'

Jess shrugged and tipped three co-codamol tablets into her mouth and swallowed them with a couple of mouthfuls of the chilled wine. She refilled the wine glass and carrying the now half-empty bottle from the kitchen into the living room she slumped down in her outrageously comfortable bunny onesie in one corner of the settee and lifted her feet, clad in matching bunny slippers, on to the pouf.

The pizzas had arrived – two between three of them – and Lily brought them in from the kitchen, placed them carefully on the coffee table whilst Jason brought in the extras he had cheekily ordered, the chicken wings, chips and a cola. He'd left the huge tub of ice cream in the freezer for later.

It was all totally inappropriate food but exactly what was needed when feeling down in the dumps and just plain hurting all over.

She and the kids tucked in like ravenous vultures.

Later on, draining the last of the wine into her glass, Jess sat back, rubbed her full belly and blew out her cheeks.

Lily and Jason had decamped to their respective bedrooms after the feast but would be back down later to break open the ice cream.

But for now, with the TV turned down low, Jess was alone, exhausted and she closed her eyes.

Until the front door bell rang.

With an exaggerated eye-roll Jess answered it to be presented with a huge bouquet of flowers. At first she couldn't tell who was holding them until they slanted sideways and a beaming face appeared.

'Samira!'

'Sarge – I hope you don't mind, but these are from everyone on the shift and . . .'

'You drew the short straw by having to deliver them?'

Samira giggled. 'I volunteered. I got the long straw.'

'Thank you so much,' Jess said as the flowers were thrust forwards by the PCSO who, now off duty, was in jeans and a blouse. 'Come in.'

'It's OK. I don't want to intrude. We just wanted you to know we're thinking about you.'

'That really is so kind, but you're not intruding. I'm touched, so come in.'

'Thanks, sarge.'

Jess shook her head. 'As you know, off duty it's Jess.'

'Gotcha, Jess.'

Jess beckoned her in and went into the kitchen. 'I'll put these in a vase.'

She balanced them in the sink for a moment, still in their wrapping, and looked at the blooms which were quite magnificent and found herself 'tearing' up a little. She turned to Samira. 'They are beautiful, I'll send everyone a text with a photo of them to say thanks.' She opened her arms and gave Samira a hug and then, before she burst into a fully fledged flood of tears, pushed her away gently and said, 'I do have a vase somewhere.'

She couldn't find it but promised Samira she would do later. She offered her a drink – Samira was teetotal – and they went back into the lounge where Jess quickly cleared up the empty pizza boxes and shoved them to one side.

'The kids have been looking after me,' she explained, 'in their own inimitable way, bless them.'

'Where are they now?'

'Upstairs, headphones on, in their own worlds.'

Samira nodded then said, 'Sarge?'

Jess noticed the hesitation and the return to the more formal use of her rank.

'I know I shouldn't and I know you're off sick . . .'

'But?'

'I could do with showing you something, if that's OK?'

Jess was intrigued. She knew Samira well enough by now to realize that what she needed to tell her would be important. 'Go on.'

'It's just because I thought you'd want to know.'

'Samira – just tell me.'

'OK, OK. You know you asked me to do house-to-house on Pendle Road?'

'The doorcam queen,' Jess smiled.

'Yep, anyway . . . let me skip back slightly: the CCTV footage from the Wellsprings wasn't that great, as we know, but good enough to give us an idea what sort of car followed you off the car park – a small hatchback, possibly a Corsa, maybe grey in colour.'

'Yeah.'

'And it's likely that the occupants of this car were the ones who did your brakes.'

'Yeah.'

'Well, thing is, I went to every house on Pendle Road, which may or may not have been the route taken by this car after coming off Pendle Hill.'

'Just a guess,' Jess said.

'Anyway, I didn't get anything of value from any of the houses on Pendle Road, so far. There are still a few to revisit, by the way.'

Jess sipped her wine, said nothing.

'So, I put myself in the shoes of someone who had just planned, then executed a terrible crime and believed they'd got away with it and I wondered what I would do if I was successful.'

'What would you do, Samira?'

'Celebrate, that's what I would do.'

'Understandable.'

'Obviously, being a good-ish Muslim, I don't drink, but if I wasn't I'd probably like to raise a glass of beer or something and settle my nerves after committing such an audacious crime, particularly against a cop.'

Jess sipped her wine, intrigued.

'So I just thought there might be the possibility that whoever did this thought, 'We need some booze.' They might go to a pub or they might not. Or they might call in at an off-licence on their way home, or as I prefer to call it because of the rats they are, their lair.'

'Not a bad line of thought.'

'And guess what?'

Jess licked her lips. 'Don't keep me in suspenders, Samira.'

'A light grey Corsa pulled up on the car park of Elletson's offie on Shaw Bridge Street, right in front of the shop, approximately seven minutes after you were driven off the road, from the direction of Pendle Hill. I went back to where you came off and drove it myself just to check the timings – it took me eight minutes. And I know it's all approximate and maybe circumstantial . . .' She paused.

'Get on with it!'

'Anyhow, this car, this Corsa, pulls on to Elletson's car park seven minutes after your accident and parks right under one of the CCTV cameras at the front of the off-licence. Two people get out, enter the shop and are immediately picked up by the four cameras inside. These two people get a few six-packs of lager, a bottle of whisky and go to pay for it, so one of the cameras is actually pointing directly at them as they buy stuff over the counter. They also buy crisps, nuts, sweets, chocolate and ciggies. They then leave in the car.'

With a slightly shaky hand, Jess placed her wine glass down.

Samira took out her phone. 'I didn't get a chance to show you at work because you weren't feeling well. Anyway, I downloaded some of the footage from the shop and pasted it into this bit of video.' She handed her phone to Jess and said, 'Press play.'

She held the phone landscape-style, tapped play and watched the action unfold.

Her mouth popped open and a shiver flitted through her as she watched and recognized two young men buy stuff. There was no sound but it was obvious the pair were laughing and joking.

Jess watched it twice, feeling everything inside her tighten up like a fist around her guts, squeezing until she was almost breathless.

Then she looked at Samira who was watching her reaction with trepidation.

Jess handed the phone back. 'Is this all logged as evidence?'

'Yes.'

'Bloody good work, Samira,' Jess commended her and saw her flush with modest pleasure. This lass, Jess thought, was going to make one hell of a cop one day if she had anything to do with it. 'Dave "Dimbo" Dawson and Lance Drake, well I never,' Jess said vehemently.

'I know. What do you want me to do about them?' Samira asked.

'Have you shown the footage to anyone else yet?'

'Just Dougie.'

'What does he say?'

'Sit on it until you're back at work.'

'Mm, it'd be a shame not to strike while the iron's hot.'

'Don't you come back any earlier than you need to,' Samira cautioned Jess, picking up on the look of determination in her eyes. 'You need to be better.'

'I want to arrest them, I want to feel their collars,' Jess admitted. 'I'll probably be better tomorrow,' she added with a conspiratorial wink.

'Sarge! Really! Get yourself better!'

Jess smiled. 'Have you checked the car's number on PNC?'

'Registered to some guy in Accrington.'

'Get someone over there to pay a visit.'

'Will do.'

'And in the meantime we need to go and speak to these jokers, don't we? You said you have an address for Dimbo?'

'I have.'

'And perhaps we make a house call to the bail hostel where Lance is supposed to be residing.'

'That's in Accrington too, isn't it?'

'Yeah. I want serious words with him anyway.'

'Look.' Samira leaned in seriously. 'Please don't come back until you're one hundred per cent.'

'Somehow, Samira, I'm rejuvenated.'

The PCSO sighed.

'Anyhow,' Jess said, 'how are you? How's life?'

'Fair.'

'Boyfriend?'

'On the run from my father pretty much, but I'm not going to let him win on that one.'

Jess knew that whilst Samira was serious about her religion, she had a very modern outlook and would not kowtow to her father who wanted to be the one who chose her husband. Jess knew her dad did not approve of her choice of boyfriend but Samira was having none of that and there was a bit of a power struggle going on within the family. Her dad, also, wasn't keen on her being in the police, certainly in a front-line role.

Jess knew Samira was strong enough to power her way through all that family pressure.

'Go, that girl,' Jess said and, slightly inappropriately, raised her glass of wine to her.

As she took a sip, there was another knock on the door.

Jess answered to be faced by another massive bouquet of flowers in the hand of a lady from a florist in Clitheroe – Jess could see the logo of her van.

'Mrs Raker?'

'That's me.'

'For you.' Smiling, the lady handed the flowers over. 'Please enjoy.'

'Thank you.' Slightly nonplussed Jess backed into the lounge and looked at Samira. 'Fancy!'

'Someone's popular tonight.'

Jess cradled the bouquet carefully in the crook of her elbow and eased the little greetings card out of its clasp. She held the envelope in her teeth and extracted the card. The message had obviously been written by the florist and read, 'To J, Hope you're feeling much better, Love J.'

She gave a little smile as she took the flowers through to the kitchen and placed them with the ones Samira had brought. 'Josh, bless him. I'm going to need another vase.'

'That's nice,' Samira said, knowing about Jess's fraught situation with her husband. 'That's got to be a good thing.'

'Yes, it has,' Jess agreed.

Samira left a short time later and Jess set about doing some major flower arranging before settling on the settee again with more wine and sent a text to Josh to thank him for the flowers, feeling a nice, warm glow for once.

FOURTEEN

The next knock on the front door came about a quarter of an hour after Samira left.

Having raided the freezer for the ice cream, Lily and Jason were back up in their rooms and Jess didn't really expect to see them again before bedtime, so she stretched out on the settee and settled down to watch the soaps. Total indulgence. Brain dead, loving it.

She was also feeling quite a bit better in herself. The co-codamol had kicked in assisted by the wine. Samira's visit had also helped.

Jess half-thought it might be her mother at the door even though she had spoken to her briefly just after Samira left to ask if she would run Lily and Jason to school next morning and be ready to pick them up afterwards. She said she would. Jess was determined to go back to work and arrest Drake and Dawson and expected to have a long, busy day.

Other than it being her mum at the door, Jess could not think who it might be.

It was a surprise to see Dougie Doolan in his off-duty clobber of neatly pressed jeans and a well-worn leather jacket.

'Doug!'

He looked pale and skinny, his complexion a kind of yellow-grey, his sagging double chin even more pronounced than normal. His eyes had a yellow, unhealthy tinge to them.

'Jess, look, sorry to bother you.'

'That's fine, come in. I'm only watching TV.'

'Thanks.'

She led him in and gestured to the armchair.

'I'm so sorry to bother you.'

'It's OK.'

'It's not work, by the way.'

'OK.' She had already worked that out.

'I haven't told anyone,' he said. Jess could see his hands were shaking. 'Not even Helen,' he said referring to his partner. He interlocked his fingers to stop his hands shaking.

Jess waited, fearing the direction this was going to go.

'And especially not my bosses,' he said. 'I know you've noticed.'

'I've seen you in agony, yeah,' Jess confirmed. She was feeling really apprehensive now.

'I . . . er . . . fibbed to Helen on a couple of occasions recently, said I was working overtime.'

Jess almost wanted to butt in and say, 'You've been going to medical appointments, haven't you?'

But she didn't have to.

'I'd seen my GP and got one of those two-week referral things the NHS do for suspected cancer diagnosis.'

Jess swallowed.

'Well, big dos, little dos, I got stuck in a bit of a queue so I forked out privately for blood tests and scans and all that.' He smirked. 'Cost me a fortune.'

'And?'

His head drooped and he shook it sadly. 'I have got cancer.'

Jess blinked and clamped her teeth together as she went dithery. 'OK.'

'Pancreatic.' He raised his eyes which beseeched hers. 'Literally no chance of a cure. Advanced. Maybe got four months if I'm lucky.'

'Oh, Dougie.'

She swept across to him, knelt on both knees and enveloped him in a long, tender hug. At first he was stiff to her touch, then he succumbed and she could tell he was trying to stifle sobs. She clung on and eventually he submitted to them. Finally, she drew away from him.

'Thank you. I needed that. I've been bottling this shit up and I haven't told a soul.'

Jess reversed on to the settee. 'You must tell Helen. She needs to know, has a right to know,' she said firmly.

'I know.'

'Dougie, I'm so sorry.'

'And we had such a good thing going,' he laughed, wiping his face dry with a pristine white handkerchief from his pocket.

'We certainly did,' Jess agreed. 'So – on the spot – what are your plans?'

'Not sure. Tell Helen.'

'And make the most of what time you have left?'

'Goes without saying.'

'Can you retire?' Jess asked. She knew he had a lot of service under his belt but wasn't certain exactly how much. She assumed he had enough service to take his full pension and a lump sum or maybe a sick pension which Jess thought, but wasn't certain, was enhanced.

'I can.'

'Are you going to?'

He sighed. 'I suppose. Kinda like the job, though. Keeps me going.'

'Do it. Spend time with Helen,' Jess urged him, and with a twinge inside her couldn't help but think fleetingly about Josh and their teetering relationship. Yes, it was fucking odd, but even in that quick thought and as perverse as it seemed, she felt slightly envious of Dougie and Helen. Not at the cancer part, which was an unspeakable tragedy, but of their opportunity to spend valuable time together, to be open, honest, tell each other their innermost thoughts and feelings, hopes and what terrorized them, what made them ecstatic. Once, she and Josh had that, but life and circumstance seemed to break it up like ash being rubbed away between a finger and thumb.

She shook that away and concentrated on Doug.

This had to be all about him and Helen.

'You could be out of the door in a fortnight, sooner even,' Jess said. 'I can ensure that.'

'You trying to get rid?'

'Far from it. Is it financially viable?'

'I guess. Still got a small mortgage but my life insurance would pay that off . . . to be honest, Jess, I haven't really given it any thought. My head, as they say, is a shed.'

'I understand.' She closed her eyes. 'I'm so sorry, Dougie.'

'Life's a funny old thing, isn't it? One minute you're maybe in sight of retirement, next you're in death's rifle sights.'

Jess had only known Dougie Doolan a matter of months but his news was like a gut punch, and when he left half an hour later she really did feel like she had been winded by a fist and was glad to sit down and glug more wine.

She always knew that serious life events happening to other people often made her think she should reassess her own existence; usually it stuck for a week or two then dematerialized as day-to-day living got in the way of good intentions.

Perhaps this time she should not allow that to happen.

Perhaps she should face the Josh/Joe Borwick conundrum head-on and take it as it fell. Whatever, it would be silly to allow things to drag on with no-one happy, and if there was one thing Jess prided herself on it was being a realist.

If it wasn't working and couldn't be fixed then it should be taken to the knacker's yard.

Something then happened to make Jess really realize the truth of that line of thought.

She sat back, mulling about Dougie. They had come up with some sort of action plan for him as regards work and personal life, something for him to take away and ponder. Something with a bit more substance than he'd turned up with at her door.

As these thoughts filtered through her mind, her phone vibrated as a message landed. She looked. It was WhatsApp. Without opening it she saw it was from Josh, no doubt responding to the thank-you she had sent him earlier about the flowers. She tapped on the message which opened and showed Josh's actual response which was three question marks: ???

Jess was getting a bit tired of feeling the pit of her stomach churning, but it did.

???

She dropped the phone and dashed into the kitchen to reread the card attached to the bouquet.

It was signed, 'J' with three kisses, 'XXX'.

Jess would much rather have had a stress-free evening but obviously it didn't work out that way.

The visit from Samira got her adrenaline pumping with the distinct possibility of feeling the collars of the 'two little shits', as she had moved on to calling Dawson and Drake who had almost killed her. Dougie's visit with his tragic news had hit her hard, and then finally receiving the message from Josh who hadn't actually sent her the flowers and she was cross with herself for even imagining that he had done.

She didn't reply to his questioning WhatsApp but instead tried to kid herself that she had absolutely no idea who the mysterious 'J' could possibly be, even though she was now certain who it was.

So there was a lot of conflict going on inside her mushed-out brain cells: annoyed Josh hadn't been the sender of the flowers; annoyed also by the person who had sent them.

At least Lily and Jason eventually descended from their rooms to spend an hour cuddling up to her on the settee which felt great because both were also wearing furry onesies, so it was like three little bears all nice and cosy and the love they shared was truly warming.

Finally Jess went to bed after downing a couple more co-codamols, a slug of bourbon and a couple more chocolates.

She slept better than she thought she deserved and was up early, back at work behind her desk at 6 a.m., working on her plans for the coming day which included the 'two shits' arrest and a revisit to Wolf Fell Hall.

However, the problem with being a response cop was that events rarely unfolded in the way you would have liked, and other things came along that required your attention more urgently than your own urgent list.

She had taken in her own toastie loaf and was sitting at the desk munching thick toast and washing it down with coffee, whilst quickly skimming the overnight logs.

One message was flagged for her attention – that the road policing department had concluded the examination of her Citroën, removed sections of the braking system for further forensic analysis, plus the owner of the garage to where the car had been taken now wished to have it removed as soon as possible. Jess knew it was no good for anything other than scrap now and quite liked the thought of taking it to Primrose Breakers and get Mags' lackey, Steve, to drop it into the crusher and pay Jess whatever the metal was worth. Other scrapyards were available but Jess was tempted to play a petty psychological game with Mags who she believed even more strongly was behind the sabotage of the Citroën.

This was something she and Samira had discussed the evening before because neither of them thought that Lance or Dimbo would have had the temerity to do the brakes off their own initiative.

The pair, Jess said, were being controlled by a sinister force that went by the name of Maggie Horsefield, who – Jess also suspected – was being driven by the even more evil force that was Tommy Moss.

And the first step into opening that can of worms would be to arrest Lance and Dimbo and get some skilled CID interviewers on them. Jess thought both lads would crack easily under the right pressure.

However, the message from the traffic department about moving her car wasn't the thing that knocked Jess off her proposed course of action that morning.

As she munched her toast and looked forward to arresting the two lads, which in turn would get Mags squirming very uncomfortably, her desk phone rang.

She checked the caller ID display. It was an internal number, the inspector's office at Blackburn.

Which probably meant the lovely Inspector Brian Price was on the other end.

And that immediately knocked some of the new-found vigour out of her.

'Thought you'd gone off sick,' Price huffed without any foreplay.

'Just needed a break, so an evening did it, thanks for asking,' she told him tersely.

'You need to update the duty states,' he said, 'so everybody knows.'

'On with it, sir.'

'Good. I was wanting to speak to PC McKinty. Is he on duty?'

'Yes, out on patrol.' Jess had spotted Vinnie's own car in the backyard so knew he was on but hadn't yet seen him. 'Can I help instead?'

Price snorted. 'Doubtful. You never seem to have a grip on things, do you?'

Everything inside Jess tightened up, but she stayed cool. 'Go on, sir, give me a go,' she said, almost mimicking Oliver Twist asking for more.

Price paused. 'I want an update on that misper he's been dealing with – forever, it seems. The divisional commander is starting to get jumpy. Progress, sergeant?'

'Well, strangely enough I can help you out on that.'

'Really?' He sounded surprised.

'Really,' she confirmed.

'Go on.'

'You probably won't like it,' she warned him. 'However, with a tail wind and a bit of luck we will be following up on some information we gleaned yesterday which points to the missing woman's involvement waiting-on at some events at Wolf Fell Hall, which may include crossing paths with our two minor royal friends who seem to frequent the place.'

'No, no, no,' Price cut in patronizingly.

'Sir?'

'Steer away from that place. You already have a complaint hanging over your head from your previous intervention there. Is it truly worth stirring up that hornets' nest?'

'Sir, we both know that making a complaint is often like flak to fool a missile that's on its way up your arse. If we really want to know what happened to our misper – and I do – then we need to go and ask sometimes awkward questions of people, whoever they are, and unless the divisional commander directly orders me not to, then I'll be knocking on some big doors later.'

'Be it on your own head,' Price said.

'I'll take full responsibility for the police doing the job it's supposed to be doing.'

'Mm . . . What else are you doing this morning?'

Although Jess was reluctant now to share anything with Price, she thought there wouldn't be any harm letting him know she intended to try and arrest the pair of miscreants responsible for doing her car, based on CCTV footage found by Samira.

'Samira?' Price said. Jess imagined him screwing up his face unpleasantly as he tried to recall exactly who that was. Then he said, 'Oh, that brown one?'

And that was the end of the phone call as far as Jess was concerned.

After slamming the phone down without a further word, she sat back fuming. 'And you're the tosser one,' she muttered, daring him to ring back. She knew he wouldn't.

'Who would that be?' a voice from the office door asked.

Jess looked up quickly at Samira's face grinning around the doorframe. Jess waved her own problem away with a little gesture. 'You don't want to know.'

'So you came in, then?' Samira said, entering the office.

'Strike whilst the iron's hot and all that.'

'Excellent.' Samira rubbed her hands together excitedly but Jess could not help but feel sorry for her and others like her who joined up wanting to do a decent job of being a cop, or PCSO, or support staff, and then coming across idiots like Price. Most colleagues were good and decent; some though, like him, were not.

Jess also knew that Price had been good mates with PC Dave Simpson, the officer who had turned out to be the baddest apple in the barrel. Not that there was anything specifically to suggest that

Price was equally bad – like all other officers on the Clitheroe section, he had been scrutinized, investigated and interviewed by detectives following the revelations about Simpson, and nothing untoward had been unearthed about him or any of the others – but Jess, who was experienced enough to know that bad cops usually hid their corruption well, couldn't help but be wary of him. She was hesitant about sharing too much with him even though she knew she really didn't have a choice. Price was her boss, end of.

It was a work in progress.

However, first things first. 'You ready for a round-up?' she asked Samira.

'Definitely – but how are you feeling?'

'Good enough to send someone ahead of me to do the dirty work, me being a sergeant and all.'

'Fair enough.'

The conversation was then brutally interrupted by the thing that truly did put Jess off her planned course of action, the thing that being on response that could never be ignored: life.

HQ comms cut in over the radio: 'Patrols Clitheroe, treble-nine, house fire Henthorn Road, persons trapped,' the operator reported coolly but urgently, adding, 'Fire service en route.'

Jess shot up from her chair, grabbed her gear. Samira had already dashed to the locker room to get her stuff and met Jess in the corridor as she sprinted to the back door of the nick, responding to the message and also asking Vinnie for his whereabouts and his ETA to the incident. A traffic car also called up and reported he was on his way from the A59.

Jess and Samira jumped into the sergeant's car, Jess at the wheel. With blue lights on she swerved out of the yard, round on to Station Road, sped on to Parson Lane just below the castle and turned right at the roundabout to head west out of Clitheroe, over the railway bridge which had a kink in it, on to Bawdlands and then left on to Henthorn Road, which was narrow with terraced houses either side.

As soon as they turned the corner they spotted flames leaping out of a terraced house from a downstairs window and licking up the front.

Vinnie was already there in the Defender.

As were a quickly gathering number of neighbours, watching on helplessly because the house was truly, spectacularly ablaze, the flames belching out as if coming from a dragon's mouth.

Jess stopped behind the Defender and she and Samira got out to face a desperately worried Vinnie who rushed up to them.

'Mother and kiddie trapped in the upstairs front bedroom.' He gasped. 'The fire looks like it's taken hold of the whole of the ground floor which consists of an open plan room with an exposed staircase going up the middle. She's well trapped and it's an inferno.'

Jess hustled her way through the onlookers, listening to Vinnie at her ear and also radioing to ask for an ETA for the fire service.

'Get this lot right back,' she shouted at Vinnie and Samira over the roaring sound of the flames, concerned about how close the people were to the front of the house. She yelled, 'Get back, get back. It's dangerous and you're in the way!'

She didn't mince her words.

Vinnie and Samira got straight in, herding the onlookers backwards whilst Jess spun on her heels to face the burning house and immediately saw the shape of a woman cowering at the front bedroom window with a babe in her arms.

Suddenly the window panes cracked and burst as the flames from the ground floor window fried them.

The woman in the room screamed and disappeared from view.

'Fire brigade, where are you?' Jess said to herself, then into her radio said, 'Confirmed at least one adult and one child trapped in the house fire, Clitheroe, upstairs rooms and the fire is spreading rapidly.'

'Have you evacuated adjacent and nearby properties?' the operator asked.

'Not my priority at the moment,' Jess responded. 'Fire service ETA, please?' she asked again, then turned to the crowd and shouted, 'Anyone got any ladders?' above the sound of the flames, plus screaming from several of the onlookers.

'Me.' A guy put up his hand.

'Go get,' Jess gestured urgently, then turned back to the house. The woman and child were back at the window. She was dodging the flames and screaming, 'Save my baby, save my baby.'

Jess got as close to the house as she could, but the heat was beating her back with its intensity.

'Is there anywhere you can find cover?' she shouted up through cupped hands. 'Get low down, the fire brigade is almost here,' she lied but could hear the sirens somewhere in the distance.

She wasn't surprised she was unable to have a meaningful conversation with the woman, who must have been terrified beyond belief.

What Jess didn't expect was for the woman to come to the window and suddenly hurl out the bundle that was her baby.

One of those slow-motion moments.

The baby, wrapped tightly in a blanket, sailing through the flame-licked air, twisting and rotating like a misshapen rugby ball.

The woman's face, still terrified, but horrified by what she had just done on instinct.

The realization that throwing a baby out of a first-floor window didn't mean that the tiny thing would travel the distance to where Jess was actually standing.

It basically flew out about four feet then began to plummet towards the pavement.

Jess reacted instinctively, hearing the collective shriek of horror from the crowd behind her.

She knew she was going to miss it, even if she got to it before it smashed to the ground, she knew she would let it slip through her fingers.

A prospect which, in that nanosecond, made her determined to catch the kid.

She surged forwards, moving more quickly than she had ever done in her life. Arms outstretched, her brain computing the speed she needed to achieve, the angle at which the baby was flying, like she was going to catch that rugby ball that had been booted from the opposite side of the pitch.

She got it, took it, twisted into a sideways roll, came up on to her knees with the baby cradled in the crook of her arms. Safe. She stood up unsteadily, looked up at the window and made momentary eye contact with the woman who acknowledged her with a nod of the head then backed away from the flames into the bedroom.

'Oh no, no, no,' Jess uttered desperately. There was no way she was now going to allow this woman, this mother, to succumb to whatever horrific death awaited her up there, smoke inhalation, or burning to death, or both.

Behind her the first fire tender arrived, disgorging the firefighters like a swarm of army ants. Jess raced to them, one of which was Joe Borwick. 'First floor, now!'

Joe nodded.

Two firefighters ran past with a long ladder, followed by two more unfurling a hose pipe.

'Save her, Joe,' she implored.

'We will,' he promised.

FIFTEEN

With the road cordoned off and some sanity restored from out of the chaos, Jess leaned against the sergeant's car and watched an ambulance pull away as a paramedic closed the rear doors, giving Jess one last glimpse of the dishevelled mother and baby in the back rescued and alive from the terraced house, which was now little more than a burned-out shell.

She turned back to the scene. The house was being tamped down by firefighters and lots of smoking, saturated rubbish that had once been carpets and furniture was being heaved into the street to help the process.

Joe Borwick strolled towards her. 'Good catch.' He grinned. 'Well done.'

'Thank you.' Jess wasn't in any mood for compliments or flirting. At the time of catching the baby, something she hadn't realized was that she'd gone down hard on her right knee which now was sore and tender to the prod. More bruising, she guessed, to add to the rest from the car wreck.

'But what in God's name are you even doing at work?' Joe demanded.

'Working?'

'Back too soon, if you ask me.'

'Matter of opinion.'

He was now standing right in front of her.

'Any early indications on the fire?' she asked, trying not to notice him.

'Deliberate. Accelerant, I'd say. Arson and attempted murder.'

'That's all I need.'

'We'll probably know for certain in a couple of hours, once the forensic guys have done a bit of sifting.'

'That's good.'

'Even though you shouldn't be at work, I'm glad you are. It's good to see you,' Joe admitted.

Jess levelled her eyes at him. 'You should not send me flowers.'

Joe's lips popped open slightly. 'There was nothing contentious in the note, I made sure of that,' he defended himself.

'Other than the fact your initial is J, as is my husband's.'

'Oh yeah,' he said a bit dimly.

'I thanked *him* for the flowers and guess what?'

'They were from me?'

'Something like that.' Her head twitched slightly. 'Joe, this is not happening. The record's stuck.'

'But I think I love you,' he whispered after checking the coast was clear.

She sighed. 'You don't even know me and you're seeing someone else. I can't say I wasn't gutted when I bumped into you at the Wellsprings, but I'm over it, OK? I've got kids and a hubby and I need to make that work because I've caused them enough heartache already. Let's get off this hamster wheel.'

He nodded. 'Fair dos.'

'Sarge?'

Jess turned. It was Dougie Doolan.

'Anything for me here?'

'I'll let Joe tell you.' She pushed herself away from the car.

It was well after 9 a.m. by the time Jess got away from the scene of the fire, which, as Joe Borwick suggested, looked like an arson/attempted murder scenario as the background story emerged of a broken relationship, domestic abuse and assaults leading up to this morning. Jess was under no illusions that the police would probably self-refer to the IOPC because it seemed there was ongoing stalking involved which hadn't been effectively dealt with.

She returned to the police station.

Samira and Vinnie were still at the fire, co-opted into traffic control, and Dougie was also there, so it seemed that the plans for the day were probably scuppered.

This was frustrating but gave her chance to do more admin catch-up.

It was almost impossible to get Joe off her mind, though, because as well as being on her mind, he was also under her skin. But the 'flowers' incident, as she now thought of it, was a step too far at this stage. She creased up inside wondering what would have happened if Josh had been at home when they'd been delivered. As it was, with him being in Manchester, Jess had managed to fudge the issue – also known as lying. She told Josh the bouquet had come from work colleagues and she'd thought it had come from him. She'd destroyed the accompanying card and combined the flowers with the ones that *had* come from work. Lying felt bad, but was necessary. A little shiver ran through her at that, something she wasn't proud of.

The mountain of paperwork in her in-tray made her a bit queasy too. She needed some uninterrupted time to deal with it. But first she logged back on to her computer, ensured the incident log regarding the fire was up to date, then went on to the internet to see if she could find out where the Armstrong-Bentley brothers were that day. They had their own website which told a lot about their mansion in Surrey and also listed their engagements. She smiled grimly when it showed they were still at Wolf Fell Hall where they were due to attend a fancy ball and charity auction that evening and they would be there next day, too.

'Excellent,' she said and reached for her in-tray.

'This one, then?'

Mags stood in front of Tommy Moss, holding up a full-length, pencil-thin black dress in front of her, checking out whether he approved of it or not. *He bloody should*, Mags thought, *at two grand*. This was the fourth one she'd displayed and so far they had all got a shake of the head from him which was beginning to brass her off. Plus he wasn't entirely focused on the fashion parade, which she understood.

Today was going to be a big day. A long day.

They were going to a ball.

Then a charity auction.

And then they were going to pull a heist. A big one. Worth millions.

'That one's OK,' he said, feigning some interest.

At fucking last, she thought.

'Should I try it on?'

Tommy nodded. His phone buzzed. He'd been holding it on his lap, waiting for calls. He checked the screen. 'Got to get this. You try the frock, darlin',' he said, as he stood up and crossed to the window.

Slightly infuriated – *Frock? Darlin'?* – Mags' mouth went very tight. She spun in a huff and went into the generous, curtained-off changing room, walking past the lady assistant who had been taking a back seat in all this because, frankly, these two customers terrified her.

They were in the first-floor changing room of a very expensive dress shop in Whalley, the pretty, ancient town south of Clitheroe. Mags had shopped here on many an occasion, pumping plenty of money into the business over the years, and rarely came away from the place without something new and dynamic to wear. Usually she did her shopping solo, or occasionally with her best friend Angela Dart, with no pressure and all for pleasure. Today, trying to please Tommy, who was also finalising details for the night ahead, was simply stressing her out.

Trying to please a man, she realized, simply wasn't her thing.

She stepped into the spacious fitting cubicle and dragged the curtain closed with an angry swipe.

But then she felt a little frisson of fear, which she knew was ridiculous.

Since being attacked in that toilet cubicle, going into enclosed spaces, even ones as large as this one, freaked her out. She had been – literally – caught with her knickers down on that occasion. She pulled the curtain open a touch so she could glimpse Tommy by the window and hear his murmuring voice as he made the arrangements. Mags' only problem was that she was sure Tommy was on the line to Leanora.

And her hatred of Leanora was becoming a bit tsunami-like.

The woman was definitely going to have to go, one way or the other.

Mags was dressed in slim, cut-off jeans and a low-cut blouse, both items showing off her attributes, she hoped. Her boobs (enhanced, but not over the top) and her nicely tapered legs which came down from her tucked-up bum. Whereas Leanora's bodywork was completely OTT, Mags thought her own was just *mwha*!

Before she could slither into the black dress, her phone rang.

She sat on the two-seater sofa in the changing cubicle and took the call from an unknown number.

She didn't speak, assuming it was a scammer and she always waited for them to speak first, but usually they just hung up with an automated, 'Goodbye.'

She was about to hang up when a voice at the other end said, 'Mags?'

She recognized the man immediately and shot to her feet, turning to the wall and keeping her voice to a harsh hiss. 'You do not call me on this number, ever!'

'I apologize but I don't have the burner phone to hand. It's just a quick call, anyway.'

'Don't you know how this works? You should! A call less than a second long can be traced. You're a c—' Just in time she stopped herself from uttering the word 'cop'. She was aware of the shop assistant hovering, possibly within hearing distance. 'Be quick.'

She listened. It was only a short message but one which made her stiffen upright. She hung up without any acknowledgement, then moved to the gap in the curtain, hoping to catch Tommy's eye.

Finally she said, 'Oi!'

Tommy looked up from his conversation. Mags beckoned him over urgently.

He ended his call, walked over and poked his head through the gap. He'd been expecting Mags to have the new dress on and be asked for his opinion but was surprised to see her standing in her underwear, hands on hips.

'Now I like that look,' he said, smirking.

'Get in here now.'

'OK.' He sidled into the changing room unsure what to expect, but what she whispered in his ear made him shake his head.

'We need to do something,' she told him. 'If either of those two nut-jobs blab, I'm stuffed and so are you, babe.'

'You know your problem, Mags?' Tommy asked. She didn't and waited for the revelation. 'For a big-shot crime queen, you are too close to the front line for comfort if the say-so of a couple of low-life dickheads can incriminate you. Generals usually stay well back from the action.'

'Finished the lecture?' she asked. 'We could both be up shit creek here, so what are *we* going to do?'

Tommy looked her up and down, clearly aroused by the vision of Mags in her frilly, skimpy underwear. She stood there unashamed, suddenly liking his eyes doing what they were doing. She slid her own hand down the front of her knickers.

'So what are we going to do?' Her voice had become throaty.

Tommy's nostrils flared like a bull's.

'I've got two top enforcers out there,' he said, referring to the guys he'd brought up from London with him. 'I suggest we put them to good use.'

'I agree.' Mags slid a bra strap off one shoulder.

Tommy blinked and turned to the shop assistant who, wide-eyed with disbelief, was watching the quick build-up of sexual tension.

'Fuck off,' Tommy ordered her.

She scuttled out.

Tommy closed the curtain, unfastened his belt and bore down on Mags who had a very dirty grin on her face. 'Sex in a changing room,' she said. 'That's a first.'

'This is what is known as being proactive,' Tommy said.

It was an hour later, mid-morning, and he and Mags and Tommy's two guys from London, Chambers and Deerman, were sitting hunched over a table in the McDonald's on the Ribble Valley Business Park just off the A59. They were all munching on breakfasts and thoroughly enjoying the food. Mags usually avoided fast food but conceded that as a one-off it tasted delicious. Tommy wolfed the food down, ravenous after the sex in the changing room. She had drained him and he simply could not get enough.

'OK,' Chambers said. He and Deerman had been the pair who'd abducted Lance Drake on his release from prison and Chambers was the one who'd been bitten by PD Flynn and still limped from that injury. Both were now pretty bored up north, although they would be used later as part of the team for the heist, which they were looking forward to. Their usual stomping ground was south London where, on a daily basis, they acted as last resort tax collectors for the Moss gang.

And they were good at it, intimidating people who owed money, usually gambling debts or protection money, and often going in 'the old way' as they called it, by snapping fingers and smashing knees with baseball bats.

Yes, they missed it, but they were also very trusted employees of the Moss gang, affiliated to Tommy in particular who liked them hovering in the background when he was doing business. Not that Tommy wasn't intimidating enough – he was frankly terrifying when he had to be – but when it came to doing the actual business he liked to step away to be in a deniable position.

The pair grinned over their hash browns. They knew what Tommy meant by proactive.

Tommy went on. 'You've met both these guys.' He pushed a scrap of paper across with two names on it: Lance Drake and Dave Dawson. Deerman drew the paper towards him and spun it around.

They read it and nodded.

Chambers said, 'How proactive?'

'They are a threat, a clear and present danger,' Tommy replied, naming an oldish but favourite film of his, and using a phrase he was fond of. He thought it made what he was ordering his enforcers to do sound like a noble thing. 'Remove them from the equation.'

Jess was kept updated on the house fire and the condition of the victims. The mother was in hospital, suffering minor burns and smoke inhalation; she was stable and would survive. The baby, caught by Jess, was unharmed and alongside her mum in hospital. Jess relived that moment quite a few times that morning, and it would haunt her for a while to imagine the consequences of not catching the child.

That sent a shiver down her.

Dougie Doolan and another detective were already on the trail of the boyfriend of the woman – he was the prime suspect for the fire and Jess guessed his freedom would be short-lived.

Other than that it was a fairly normal day for response cops.

Two more PCs had come on duty, one at 8 a.m. and one at 9 a.m., and they were immediately deployed to a burglary and some overnight damage at a shop.

Finally, around midday, the house that had been set on fire had been made safe and sealed and the police could then back off, which meant an exhausted Samira and Vinnie could withdraw from the scene as the road was reopened.

They arrived back at the station together, bedraggled and reeking of smoke, not having had chance of a brew or refreshment break since coming on duty. Neither moaned about it, it was just part of being a street cop, but Jess sent them to grab something to eat and drink. They returned about half an hour later.

Jess had made the decision to put the visit to Wolf Fell Hall on hold until the next day. The remainder of the shift was going to be dedicated to arresting Dave "Dimbo" Dawson and, hopefully, Lance Drake.

Vinnie looked disappointed, but was happy enough to be going after Dimbo. Jess shooed them out of her office. 'Away you go, lock up a pair of baddies for me.'

SIXTEEN

Samira had been a PCSO for just over three years and become increasingly effective in that role around Clitheroe town centre, getting to know its denizens by simply walking around, chatting and trying to solve problems. She was a great people person, always ready to listen. But she was also canny and knew that being an effective cop – because that's how she saw herself – was about getting people to open up and divulge information without too much prodding.

This was how she had managed to find out Dawson's current address. She knew he was a frequenter of the pub scene in town so she had meandered around a few of the pubs and collared a couple of people who she knew hung around with him. She spun a bit of a white lie – just need to chat with him about his car insurance – and without trying too hard she nailed an address, a council flat on Low Moor to where she directed Vinnie in the Defender.

'I'd really have liked to have gone to Wolf Fell Hall this afternoon,' Vinnie whined a bit.

'Do you really think either of those Hooray Henrys could have had something do with that lady's disappearance?'

He shrugged. 'You know, when paths cross and all that, questions need to be asked.'

'Do you think she's dead?' Samira asked bleakly.

'I do,' Vinnie answered just as bleakly. 'However, I think arresting those two scumbags for trying to kill the sarge should be our priority today.'

'Agreed.'

He skirted around the town centre and a couple of minutes later was travelling along Whalley Road.

They needed more supplies of beer, crisps and a few microwaveable pizzas which, whilst truly awful concoctions, could be washed down with the lagers. Lance traipsed around from Dimbo's council flat on Low Moor to a small supermarket on Whalley Road. He filled a hand basket with mostly rubbish, the kind of things he'd survived on most of his short adult life and was now paying for in terms of bad skin and horrendous shits. While Lance did the shop, Dawson stayed on the settee engrossed in playing a video war game on the TV.

Lance went through the self-service checkout, proud to pocket a couple of bars of chocolate without paying for them, but did fork out for the rest of the items. Small wins were always important to him.

He was feeling excited, though. He knew there was going to be a big job tonight, having eavesdropped on a conversation between Mags and Steve at the scrapyard, picking up a few snippets from it. He expected to be given some sort of menial role on the periphery of the job, which was OK with him. He was in favour with Mags, more or less, but although he could see she despised him he wasn't going to let her down. He valued his life too much.

Outside the supermarket he flipped up his hoodie, put his carrier bag on the ground between his feet and began to construct a roll-up with the new set of ciggie papers and tobacco he'd just bought. He enjoyed a roll-up more than a properly produced cigarette, liked the whole process of making them and that first drag of pure smoke straight from the tobacco into his lungs. He knew he was poisoning himself and that with his lifestyle, diet and bad habits he'd be unlikely to live to a ripe old age, but he was fine with that.

As he lit the ciggie, he looked up, inhaling that first, sweet, smoky lungful.

The shop was set back slightly from the road with a narrow car park in front of it. Lance was standing under the awning where the trolleys were parked and the cash machine was located.

He saw a car cruise slowly by.

Two people on board – driver, passenger.

Neither looked in his direction but they didn't have to for him to recognize the car and the occupants, Chambers and Deerman – the two guys Tommy Moss had brought up from London. The ones who'd kidnapped him in Accrington Asda, the ones who'd stood around whilst Mags threatened to slit his throat. Two guys who properly terrified him. Real hard villains from the Smoke. Guys who would happily break limbs or attach testicles to mains electricity and flip the switch. Hard guys in a different class to himself and Dimbo who were essentially cowards from the sticks who were happy to put the boot in when someone was already down.

Lance had one of those strange, uneasy sensations jitter through him as he watched the car roll by. Like a sweep of pins and needles all the way down to the tips of his toes, otherwise known as dread, a feeling exacerbated when the passenger pulled a black mask on over his head.

The car turned into Littlemoor Road.

Lance urgently patted his pockets for his mobile phone. Twice. It wasn't there.

'Oh, shit me!' he said, visualizing the phone on the chair arm in the flat.

Abandoning the shopping and discarding his cigarette, he ran, skidding around the corner to see the car turn into Beechwood Avenue on which Dimbo's flat was located.

Lance came to a stop, then sprinted up to the opening of Beechwood and peeked around the corner, trying to stay out of sight.

He didn't like what he saw.

After pulling on the balaclava mask, Chambers reached forwards and, keeping the pistol out of sight between his knees, checked the magazine – full – reinserted it into the handle and cocked it so that a round slid smoothly into the breech. He thumbed on the safety catch and sat up as Deerman parked outside Dimbo's flat. They knew they were at the right address, having done a swift drive-by half an hour earlier to pinpoint the place.

Deerman now pulled on his balaclava and they looked at each other through the eye-slits. They nodded, then Chambers got out, walked quickly around the car and up the short pathway to the ground-floor door of the flat, still with a pronounced limp from his altercation with PD Flynn.

He held the pistol tightly to his outer right thigh, and as he approached the door he thumbed the safety catch to 'off'.

He didn't expect the door to be locked, didn't bother knocking, didn't feel the need to be polite.

Lance watched this, then sank to his knees behind a parked car, peering through the windows. Suddenly he could not even find a breath, but then he looked over his shoulder towards the sound of another car approaching from behind. A cop car.

Lance dropped even lower out of sight.

The police car went past and neither occupant spotted him. It turned into Beechwood Avenue.

Chambers stepped silently into a short hallway off which was a small bathroom, one bedroom.

Ahead was the living room from which emanated the loud sounds of a gun battle, army versus army, from the video game Dimbo was playing on the TV, totally unaware of the intruder creeping towards him. Even if he had been aware he would not have turned around because he would have assumed Lance was returning with the shopping. The TV set was under the window, the big screen facing back into the room. Dimbo was sitting upright in the middle of the settee with his back to the door. He jumped and jerked as his whole body swayed with the flow of the exciting game, even ducking as a character shot at him.

Chambers paused for a second, at which point Dimbo became aware there was someone behind him. He didn't turn, just said, 'You got me fags, Lance, matey?'

Chambers immediately understood the meaning of what that meant: Lance was also at the flat, something he hadn't known before that moment.

Then he paused no longer.

He took two strides up to the settee and placed the muzzle of the pistol against the back of Dimbo's skull.

Vinnie pulled the Defender in across the road from Dimbo's flat. Both he and Samira had clocked the stationary car outside the flat, but because Vinnie had parked slightly behind it and at a diagonal all they could see was the outline of one person on board behind the wheel and could not say for sure if the person was wearing a hood or not. All they could see was a dark shape.

But yet . . . there was something odd about the car.

Odd meaning suspicious.

'One of Dawson's mates, you reckon?' Vinnie asked Samira.

'Possibly.'

Both were on the same wavelength.

Samira said, 'Let's say hi.'

As they opened the Defender's doors in unison, the front door of Dawson's flat also opened and Chambers came hurtling out, limping fast.

Vinnie swore.

Chambers, with the balaclava still over his head, screamed something at Deerman as he sprinted towards the car; he raised his pistol and fired off a couple of loosely aimed shots in the direction of Vinnie and Samira.

'Get down!' Vinnie yelled, ducking after the two bullets whizzed above his head.

Samira didn't really need to be told. She'd already dropped to her haunches behind the engine block and was instantly on her radio, calling the job in: shots fired at police, plus a quick description, plus the make and model of the car the gunman had got into and was now being driven away in.

She was good, very, very good at quickly processing information and keeping her cool in mega-stressful situations.

Vinnie scrambled back into the Defender, starting the engine.

'What are you doing?' Samira asked, astounded, making to grab the door handle.

'Think I'm doing?' He slammed the car into first. 'Goin' after them.'

'Don't be a fool,' Samira shouted but before she finished speaking the Defender was moving. Adrenaline, red mist and tunnel vision had all combined in a perfect storm within Vinnie into an elixir that made him reckless in his desire to nail bad people.

The door handle came out of Samira's grasp and the door slammed shut by the forwards momentum of the Defender as Vinnie set off.

Vinnie was on his radio now.

'In pursuit,' he said into the mic, already breathless. 'Vehicle on to Langshaw Drive towards Peel Park Avenue.'

In disbelief, mouth agog, Samira watched him go, the word 'Pillock' on her lips.

She looked across the road at the open door of Dawson's flat.

Jess was on her feet and running on the words, 'Shots fired.'

Grabbing her gear, she found herself once more hurtling along the corridor towards the back door of the nick where she met Dougie Doolan coming back in, empty-handed from his bid to arrest the arsonist ex-boyfriend in relation to the house fire.

'Another fire?' he asked, bemused by the rush of Jess's figure.

'Shots fired,' she said, sidestepping him, knowing that he probably hadn't heard because detectives, in her experience, were notorious for using personal radios only when it suited them.

'Jeez, where?'

'Outside Dave Dawson's flat on Low Moor,' Jess said as she bundled past him, still threading herself into her gear.

'Coming!' Dougie said.

By the time he'd said that, Jess was already behind the wheel of the sergeant's car, doing several things at once: starting the car, putting on her seat belt, crunching it into gear and transmitting over the radio. She needed to be an octopus.

Dougie swung in alongside her as the car started to roll as HQ comms intervened into the situation, warning Vinnie to back off from the pursuit.

Jess cut in then and also warned him to hold back. She didn't want anyone hurt.

Vinnie, on the other hand, didn't seem to be hearing anything other than blood pulsing through his brain. He was only driver-trained to a standard level with the additional qualification of being a Land

Rover and personnel carrier driver. He did not have the necessary authority to pursue other vehicles, even if the occupants had shot at him.

Deep down he knew all this. He knew the dangers of car chases and why the police were reluctant to get involved because if it all went awry, it was rarely the offender's fault, even if it was. The police were always to blame.

However, Vinnie was driving and chasing on a visceral level, even though he knew he shouldn't be.

Not only that, a Land Rover Defender was hardly built for car chases.

But Vinnie, as the saying goes, screwed the arse-end off it.

He was behind the car along Peel Park Avenue, feeling the rattle of the steering wheel in his hands. His jaw was clamped tight between his terse transmissions, such as, 'On Goosebutts Lane,' 'Now Pendle Road towards the A59 . . .'

At the other end of the radio, the comms operator at HQ was instructing him to pull back and desist.

He ignored her, just gripped the wheel more tightly. 'Bastard shot at me,' he grumbled.

Then, 'Got 'em!' he uttered triumphantly as the car ahead swerved off Pendle Road on to High Moor Road, which Vinnie knew led up to the home ground of a local football club.

He transmitted this development as he turned and followed in the cumbersome Defender. By the time he had straightened the wheel he then had to slam-on because the car had stopped slap-bang in the middle of the road, the passenger door was opening and the gunman was getting out and twisting around to face Vinnie, bringing up the pistol which he held gangster-style parallel to the ground and jogged towards Vinnie, firing at the windscreen.

For a moment, Vinnie's world came to a stop of complete disbelief as his recklessness crumbled into dread.

The first bullet crashed through the left side of the windscreen and imbedded itself into the passenger seat headrest. The second came through the glass six inches to the left of the first, this time smashing into the dividing bulkhead panel between the front seats and the prisoner transport cage.

Vinnie ducked as he realized too late he had stupidly bitten off more than he could chew and, transfixed, watched the gunman over the top of the dashboard as he approached. He fired again, this time the bullet ricocheted off the bonnet, into the windscreen and angled up steeply into the roof of the cab.

Vinnie sank lower, now a trembling mess.

The gunman yanked open the passenger door, aimed the weapon at Vinnie's head and pulled the trigger.

Blue lights, two-tone horn plus the car's own horn all combined as Jess careened through the streets of Clitheroe, weaving through traffic, driving mostly one-handed, bursting out of junctions without stopping or even seeming to check, just driving on pure instinct, skittering around corners until she made it across town and turned up Pendle Road.

Jess didn't like that Vinnie had gone horribly quiet.

She shared worried looks with Dougie who was holding on tight to his seat belt.

Samira warily entered Dawson's flat. Her mouth dry. She stood just inside the threshold initially, looking along the hallway towards the living room from which she could hear the sounds of the video game: shooting, loud explosions.

Far too real for comfort.

'Dave? Dave Dawson? Dimbo? Are you in there? This is PCSO Patel from Clitheroe nick. Dave? I'm coming in.'

The Defender was ahead, stationary in the middle of the road. Both the driver and passenger doors were open, but there was no sign of Vinnie.

Jess pulled in behind. She and Dougie climbed out of the sergeant's car.

Jess mee-mawed at the detective to stay put. He had no body protection on and though Jess was only wearing a stab vest, it was at least something, though wouldn't stop a bullet.

She drew her baton and flicked it hard with a wrist action to extend it to its full length, then she arced wide and made her way at an angle towards the Defender, very much aware there was no sign of Vinnie or the car he'd been chasing.

She was still not liking this scenario one bit.

Finally, she got to the open driver's door and looked into the cab,

Death on Wolf Fell   177

seeing the bullet-shattered windscreen and where the slugs themselves had imbedded into the headrest and bulkhead.
No Vinnie, but no sign of blood either.
Then a figure appeared at the front grille of the car – Vinnie heaving himself upright.
Jess rushed around to him.
He looked at her, visibly shaking, pale beyond white, then he retched, turned away and staggered a few steps before sagging on to all fours and vomiting.

Six hours later Jess walked into the sergeant's office and could not be bothered to peel off any of her uniform, even though over the course of the day it had become heavier and heavier and more cumbersome. She thumped down on the chair with images of the day just gone flipping through her mind like a black-and-white film on an old-fashioned projector.
From getting the puce-faced Vinnie back up to his feet and brushing him down – with no real time to truly engage with him or listen to his woes – then attending Dawson's flat which was a major crime scene now, quickly sealed by Samira in spite of her shock on discovering his murdered body.
After that it all went into multi-task mode as the influx of cars and cops went through the roof.
The police helicopter appeared from its base at Warton on the Fylde coast; roadblocks were set up at strategic positions on the road network in and around Clitheroe, but also as far afield as the North Yorkshire border, the M6 and Blackburn.
Uniformed cops, including armed officers, swarmed into town and were initially deployed by Jess who, actually loving this, held the fort and directed ops for the best part of four hours non-stop, a role which included crime scene management both at Dawson's flat and the location at which Vinnie had been ambushed.
Jess revelled in it all because things like this had been her bread and butter in the Met and tested her knowledge and skills and abilities to their limits and her capacity to hold things together until the big hitters arrived on their high horses and inevitably took over.
She was ably assisted by Dougie – 'Bless him,' Jess had thought at one point, seeing him wincing with pain but remaining resolute in his desire to keep going – and Samira who grafted hard and

responded efficiently to every order and instruction given; and also Vinnie who, once he'd cleared his head and compartmentalized his terrifying incident, got on with the job.

Jess had other PCs on her patch who all responded superbly to her directions.

Inspector Price put in an appearance and seemed to be on the verge of butting in, but also seemed to be overwhelmed and uncomfortable by everything that was happening, like a bunny in the headlights. His reaction puzzled Jess but she didn't have time to dwell on it. For the moment, task was all, getting stuff done.

Thoughts and feelings were on the back burner to be dealt with when appropriate.

She loosened off her gear as she sat there, feeling grubby and in need of a long hot shower, probably followed by a long cold beer and a JD chaser.

She was just mulling over this prospect when Vinnie appeared at the door.

'Sarge, you got a minute?'

'Course I have.'

He closed the door behind him and sat in the chair opposite Jess who said, 'You did good today, Vin.'

He shook his head despondently, looking at the floor then raised his face. 'I don't think I did.'

'Take it from me, you got on with the job and sometimes that is more important than anything.'

'I mean, what was I thinking? Chasing them, no plan what I'd do if I cornered them, which I sort of did . . .' His voice tailed off weakly. 'I was terrified.'

'Anyone would have been.'

'You wouldn't.'

'Don't you believe it.'

'All that stuff you went through in London. Facing armed, violent men, having a colleague murdered right next to you,' he said, referencing some of the incidents he knew Jess had dealt with down south.

'Vinnie.' Jess leaned forwards. 'I was shit scared.'

He sighed, not really believing her. 'When he opened the door and pointed his gun at me, oh God, Jess . . . I thought that was it! I thought I'd never see my kid get born.'

'But it wasn't it, was it? He'd run out of bullets or his gun jammed or whatever . . . fate . . . and you are still here to tell the tale and then you got on with it. You had your moment, then you pulled it together and now we have time to reflect on it and learn.'

'I felt like a coward.'

'Chasing armed men is not cowardly, Vin, it's damn brave. Bit reckless, maybe, but certainly brave and you need a right royal rollocking for the red-mist syndrome, but I'll leave that for another day.'

'But what if everyone finds out I brought back my breakfast? I'll be a laughing stock, never live it down.'

Jess grinned. 'I won't tell and nor will Dougie.'

'Thank you.' He sounded relieved.

'My suggestion? It's been a long day, get yourself home, hug your wife, get a beer, a takeaway, feet up, chill. See how you feel tomorrow, because that's going to be a long one, too, and also if you want to speak to a counsellor . . .'

'*No!* Nothing like that . . . I don't think, but thanks. I'll take your advice and get home and see you in the morning.'

'You're very welcome.'

'I presume the royals are on hold,' he said as he stood up.

'For the time being.'

He left, but before Jess could pick up her phone, Samira pivoted into the office and plonked down. She drew in a very deep breath, then exhaled, fanning herself with two hands telling herself, 'Cool down, relax, babe.'

Jess waited.

Eventually Samira came back to earth and said, 'Wow!'

'Wow indeed.'

'A . . . like . . . proper murder, gangland style.'

'Yup.'

'Never thought I'd see anything like that in this neck o' the woods.'

'Can happen anywhere.'

'So it seems.'

'Are you OK?' Jess asked after a pause.

'Suppose.'

'Suppose? What does that mean?'

'I'm still in shock. Dimbo's brains blown out all over the settee and the TV screen.' She shivered. 'It was dripping with . . . matter, I suppose you'd call it.'

'You dealt with it well. Most cops never see anything like that in their whole career.'

'I know. Hell, eh?'

'Hell, yeah.'

Samira paused. 'Is Vinnie all right?'

'He will be,' Jess promised.

'Big day all round,' Samira said.

'Yep.' Jess raised her eyebrows. 'That it?'

'You want rid of me?'

'I want to go home, to be honest, but I have a couple of jobs to do first.'

'Message understood.' Samira started to stand up.

'I'm always here for you, you know,' Jess said.

'Yeah, I know. If I crack, you'll be my first port of call.'

Both ladies chuckled. 'You off to meet up with your boyfriend?'

'I think so.'

'Is he a listener?'

'Well he's not a talker, that's for sure.'

'Then download,' Jess suggested.

Samira nodded and left the office. Jess's hand hovered over her phone but didn't quite reach it as Dougie Doolan hobbled in and took a seat.

Jess looked over his shoulder. 'Anyone else in the queue?'

'Eh?'

'Nothing,' she said, managing a grin and just for a moment realizing how much affection she had for these people. She'd come into their lives unexpectedly and been unreservedly welcomed, although she had ruffled the feathers of a few. She'd loved her life in London until it all went sour and now she had no desire to return. 'Where are we up to?' Jess asked Dougie, who she knew had been mingling with FMIT and CID detectives all day.

'Not sure.' He shrugged. 'Dawson's one of the pair who cut your brakes, so we need to speak to Lance Drake urgently. It looks like a mobile phone of his was in Dawson's flat and is being examined now. He hasn't even been to the bail hostel in Accy yet and his ankle tag still hasn't been activated. Probably in the Ribble.'

'No one's seriously thinking Lance killed Dimbo, are they?'

'It's a line of thought, obviously.'

Jess screwed up her face. 'From the description Vinnie and Samira gave, it sounds more to me like the two lads who did the runner from the Transit van, one of whom we know because PD Flynn almost bit his bum off and he got locked up. The gunman they saw legging it from Dawson's flat was limping so we know who he is and he's got to be one of our first priorities – and maybe that's worth exploring with Tommy Moss, too?'

'I agree. It seems all gang related, and somewhere in the mix I'm sure one of the ingredients is Mags. All very sordid.'

Jess mulled it over. She had given the detective superintendent in charge of the murder enquiry as much as she knew, including her own speculation. It seemed odd that Dawson had been murdered as part of a drugs feud of some sort. She knew he was at the bottom of the heap like Lance was, a mule, a gofer, with no influence at all, although he would be liable to be involved in squabbles at that level which could be mean and nasty, but to be cold-bloodedly assassinated, for want of a better phrase, seemed highly extreme.

She sighed.

'Sometimes people get killed just because they know too much,' Dougie said, obviously thinking along the same lines.

'Yep, they do,' she agreed. 'I suppose there are quite a few reasons why he could have been shot,' she admitted. 'It'll all come out in the wash. Anything more on the car the shooters were using?'

'No. False plates and it's not been found yet, if it ever will be.'

'Right. So, tomorrow? What's the plan?'

'FMIT move in upstairs en masse. Support unit will be here for the door-to-door and searching stuff, et cetera.'

'The circus hits town?'

'Absolutely.'

Jess smirked. 'The irony.'

'Of what?'

'A drug dealer gets wasted and a full murder squad moves in. I get my brake pipes cut, and zilch!'

'I know. It's wrong.'

'And not only that, if FMIT had moved quicker and done something after my incident, Dawson might still be alive, which I also find hard to deal with. I know he did my car but he shouldn't be dead because of it.'

'You're too generous, Jess.'

'Don't get me wrong, I wanted my pound of flesh from the little sod, but, y'know, through the channels of justice, not murder . . .' She stopped talking abruptly, her mind whizzing all over. 'Doug, did you ever arrest Dawson for anything?'

'Yeah, a couple of times. Burglary and a bit of low-level dealing. Why?'

'What was he like?'

Dougie pondered that for a moment. 'A pussy, a pushover, why?'

'He admitted stuff easily?'

'After a bit of manoeuvring, yeah, he was a piece of cake.'

'So, if we had managed to arrest him for cutting my brake pipes, do you think he would have confessed?'

'Undoubtedly.'

'OK, and as we suspect, he probably didn't try to kill me off his own bat?'

'Unlikely.' Dougie leaned forwards, interested.

'And it's very unlikely that Lance did it off his own bat, either, would you say?'

'Correct.'

'So they acted on orders? That's a good hypothesis, yeah?'

Dougie nodded.

'So whoever gave them their orders, when that person knew, or thought they knew, or got wind somehow, that Lance and Dawson were going to be arrested they might have got the jitters, do you think? I've had experience of dealing with Lance in custody, as you know, and he's a blabbermouth too, especially if he thinks it's going to save his own skin.'

Dougie was getting on board with this. 'A bit of judiciously applied pressure, coupled with the prospect of going down for life, could have meant Lance and Dimbo would have named names. That said, there's a flaw in your argument.'

'I know,' Jess admitted. 'That flaw being that whoever ordered the hit on me didn't know that we were going to arrest Lance and Dimbo. And, and, and,' she went on, 'something that's troubling me a bit, too: backtracking a bit – how would Lance and Dimbo know I was even at the Wellsprings that night? They wouldn't, unless someone told them.'

Those horrible words dangled in the air for a few moments.

'OK, OK, OK,' Jess said. 'Let's not get too hung up on this. First off, it wasn't a secret that I would be at the Wellsprings. It was a bit of a social do.'

Dougie's face was creased with misgiving.

'However,' Jess reluctantly said, 'no one knew except me, you, Samira and Vinnie that we were going to arrest Lance and Dawson for the attempt on my life. Did they?'

And even as she said those words, she hated the twisted path her thoughts were leading her along.

'But I know someone else who did . . . anyway, it's probably bollocks, Dougie. However, I do think we should concentrate on finding Lance because, and I know this all sounds bonkers, he could be next in line for the chop and we have a duty of care to him to lock him up for his own safety, silly as it seems.'

'I agree.' Dougie glanced at his watch. 'First thing tomorrow, eh?'

'Even before the cuckoos upstairs start to stir,' Jess said, pointing at the ceiling, meaning FMIT and CID. 'Are you up for an early start?'

'I'll be in at six.'

'Me too. The FMIT briefing is scheduled for eight, so a couple of hours rooting around for Lance won't do any harm. I'll message Vinnie and Samira.'

They nodded in unison, decision made.

Then Jess's business face softened. 'How are you, Dougie?'

'Today's a good day, but who knows what tomorrow will bring? But I intend for it to be a good one.'

SEVENTEEN

On the journey to the charity meal, followed by an auction (and then a heist) they behaved rather like a bickering old couple rather than a pair of slick robbers. The atmosphere in the back seat of the very roomy old Rolls-Royce taking them was as chilly as ice and there was as much space between the couple as Mags could physically make it as she hunched up by the door.

The frigidity had begun hours earlier, after they had screwed in the dress shop then briefed the two enforcers at McDonald's. In setting up the fine details of the heist for later, Tommy had spent far too much time talking on the phone in hushed tones to Leanora, as well as other parties it had to be said, which didn't bother Mags, but the wife part did and she detested it, like a disease creeping over her, ripping her innards apart.

She hated that she had fallen for Tommy, that they'd gone beyond simple animal lust; she hated herself for allowing this to happen, to actually have feelings for him instead of the usual screw 'em and leave 'em philosophy which had served her well for years.

But above all, she hated Leanora, Tommy's nasty, dangerous spouse.

And she had come between her and Tommy.

The coldness had been going on all afternoon.

The initial catalyst had been Tommy's phone call at the dress shop – pre-changing room fuck – and then the series of phone calls and eventually Mags losing it and saying, 'I don't see why we need her, I just don't! Surely you must have the contacts, for God's sake?'

'I've told you several times,' Tommy said, annoyed and instantly reverting to a patriarchal caveman tone of voice. 'She has the contacts in Europe that I don't. She's set up the deals and as soon as the job's done tonight, she can move the items within hours.'

The explanation did not placate Mags who could feel a double-cross coming in her pee.

'Look,' Tommy said, realising he might have overstepped it with the mansplaining, 'I don't like it either, babe. I'd cancel if everything wasn't in place, but it is, y'know – the people, the lines, the cash . . . a lot of very dangerous individuals are expecting to get what they paid deposits for, and I mean Mafia dangerous, and I don't want to piss them off just because you don't like my wife; opportunities like this don't come along often, so we've got to take it.' His eyes pleaded with her.

'Afterwards, the bitch is ditched, OK?'

Tommy swallowed with a clunk, knowing that would be easier said than done, but he nodded.

'Say it,' Mags insisted of him. 'I. Will. Ditch. The. Bitch.'

'I will ditch the bitch,' he repeated but not in a way that filled Mags with confidence, but at least he'd said it.

They were travelling to the event in the back of a very spacious old Rolls-Royce that Mags owned and kept mothballed at the back of a garage on one of her used car sales sites. It had belonged to her father before her and had been his pride and joy for a while until its lack of practicality and instant recognizability became apparent. But he'd been reluctant to sell it and had kept it under cover for many years now. Mags brought it out for occasional posh social outings such as tonight's, and Steve, who was a mechanic by trade, had given it the once-over, valeted it and was doing the chauffeuring.

'OK, good.' Mags relented and slid coyly across the expanse of leather seating to Tommy who wrapped his arm tenderly around her shoulders. She kissed him on the cheek.

'Let's enjoy the first part of the night,' Tommy suggested.

'And then rob the bastards blind, eh?'

'That's my girl,' Tommy said, then, 'ooh, is everything all go for Whalley?'

'Hundred per cent,' Mags assured him. 'That town's gonna be on fire.'

Even after Dougie had gone, Jess stayed at her desk doing even more catching up and all the while processing what the day had thrown at her.

She also whizzed through a stack of paperwork – where the heck did that all come from? – after which she was ready to leave. She stood up, still in her full uniform and gear and thought about it for a moment, then decided to go home with it all on, so in the morning she could simply roll out of bed and the cottage at 5.30 a.m., ready to hit the streets.

Just as she was about to start the Kia, Josh rang.

'Hi, babe, how's it going?' he asked.

Jess closed her eyes. 'Busy. Only just about to set off home. You?'

'Busy. Gonna be stuck in Manchester again.'

Jess bit her tongue, metaphorically speaking. She had been about to blurt, 'Whatev,' but tried to remain sweet. 'That's a shame.'

'I'll be back for the weekend, though,' Josh said hurriedly. 'Maybe we can do something? Bowland Knotts? The coast? Take the kids to Blackpool? What do you think, babe?'

At least he seemed to be trying and the prospect of a donkey ride and amusement arcades sounded quite fun. She tried to sound enthusiastic. 'The kids would love that.'

'Anyhow, got to go. Love ya!'

He ended the call before she could respond but she was happy about that because she wasn't totally sure she could have mirrored the 'love' sentiment.

She took her time driving home and she knew why, as daft as it sounded. She wanted Fireman Joe to call her. She knew he had her number but she didn't have the courage to call him, especially after she had pretty much ditched him at the scene of the house fire; not that she wanted him to come crawling to her, or she to him. What she did know was that they needed to talk seriously, which would probably scare the living daylights out of him, and would also terrify her too.

She parked on the charred road outside the cottage and clambered wearily out of the car and went in the front door, failing to notice the lone figure loitering by the war memorial opposite the Coach & Horses.

It cost good money to attend the dinner and charity auction, but Mags was convinced it was worth it as she looked around the other guests from her table of ten.

The main attraction for the attendees wasn't the meal or the auction itself but the opportunity to do a bit of paid hobnobbing with members of the royal family, the Armstrong-Bentleys, who seemed to use Wolf Fell Hall as a second home. Mags had interacted with the brothers a few times and found them completely dull and uninspiring, other than for their insatiable desire for cocaine. They paid handsomely for their fun.

However, as the evening progressed she glanced at them once or twice through narrowed eyes at their position on the top table alongside the duchess and other distinguished guests, and wondered if either of them did have any connection with the disappearance of Janet Moyser. Mags hadn't even known anything about Janet going missing and learning of it from Angela Dart following the visit to Castle Catering by Jess Raker and her gangly sidekick bothered her not one jot, but she was curious to know if either of the daft brothers knew anything about it. Maybe she'd ask them at some stage. Or not. She wasn't all that fussed.

The meal at Wolf Fell Hall was good. She and Tommy stuck to fizzy water and avoided alcohol because they needed very clear heads for later when their fun would begin.

Until then, they watched, listened, smiled and bid for a few things just to show willing.

Tommy, who was a football fanatic (a big Arsenal supporter, Mags learned for the first time that evening), couldn't help himself bidding for the two soccer-related lots in the auction – signed and framed football shirts, one by the Preston North End first team, the other by the Blackburn Rovers first. Mags had watched his enthusiastic bidding with a quizzical, screwed-up expression accompanied by a sad shake of the head when he jumped with delight and pumped the air on winning the bid and then returning to the table with the two shirts and a deliriously happy look on his face, like a fucking boy, Mags thought.

'Why the hell?' Mags began to question him, then held up her hands in defeat, but couldn't help but add, 'Neither of these teams are at their zenith, even I know that and I don't like football. And five hundred quid each?'

'Go well with my collection,' he said proudly.

'Your collection?' Mags' voice contained a high degree of disbelief.

'Got about two dozen of these and loads of football memorabilia, but most of it is from top clubs and players from London.'

'On your walls?'

'Yep, and display cabinets.'

'I never knew that.'

'You wouldn't, would you?' he said. A remark that stung because no, she wouldn't. She'd never even seen Tommy's house. She knew it was a big one, close to Wimbledon Common, but no, she'd never been there. Their affair had been conducted mainly in the back seats of cars and rooms in budget hotels. Having Tommy visit her at her house in Hurst Green was a big thing for her. She had never even been close to his.

'Anyway, it's money for a good cause, isn't it?' he said defensively.

Mags shook her head. 'Whatever.' She knew that a lot of what was raised would be skimmed off into the duchess's coffers, though the duchess would at some stage in the future make a big deal of doling out some measly cheques to some worthy local causes. Mags reached for her glass, needing a drink, only to be disappointed to be reminded she was drinking water. Suddenly she wanted to get this night over and done with.

Tommy's mobile phone vibrated as a message arrived.

He glanced at it, then said, 'Need to call back.'

'Leanora?'

'Yeah, just details, nothing to worry your pretty arse about.'

The evening dwindled away to nothingness, really. Fizzled out with a whimper rather than a bang, which suited Mags and Tommy. Steve was on standby in the Rolls but they hung back to watch a few of the other attendees leave before calling him in from his location in the car park of Chipping Village Hall, about five minutes' drive from Wolf Fell Hall.

As the pair waited for the Rolls to arrive they made their way to the front steps to ensure they were seen shaking hands with the duchess and the two royals who were saying goodbye and thanks to everyone departing who had made the evening such a profitable success.

Mags and Tommy needed to be seen leaving with everyone else.

'Thank you so much for inviting us,' Mags said graciously to the duchess who with a combination of alcohol and cocaine whizbanging around her brain was unsteady in the extreme. Her eyes could hardly focus, which meant that in the next hour or so she would be flat-out in her apartment in the west wing of the hall.

The duchess replied incoherently but managed to stay upright.

Mags and Tommy moved on to do the same with the Armstrong-Bentleys who were in much the same state as the duchess – drunk and drugged up.

Obviously Mags didn't mind too much, as the brothers were experiencing her product, but as she shook their hands, she wondered again whether either or both of them had anything to do with Janet Moyser. Mags didn't care one way or the other, really, because her main train of thought related to their two bodyguards who were skulking about behind their charges, both looking mean and nasty and seemed as though alcohol and drugs had bypassed them so far that evening.

They could possibly be a problem.

As she and Tommy edged away from the formalities and went to the front steps, she mouthed her misgivings about Harker and Leighton.

Tommy said, 'My thoughts, too.'

Then the old Rolls-Royce made a sweeping turn in the gravel and came to a halt in front of them with a squeak of the brakes. Steve – who had gamely dressed up for the occasion in a grey chauffeur's suit and matching flat cap – got out and opened the rear doors for Mags and Tommy.

Tommy handed his prized auction lots to Steve, who put them into the boot, then slid in alongside Mags who said, 'Let's get this shit over with, shall we?'

Jess's mum and dog left about 11 p.m. Jess was glad to see her go. She'd wanted a bit of selfish time with just her and the kids, but prising her mother out of the house was like trying to scrape a barnacle off the hull of a boat.

But she couldn't complain really, so she tolerated her and listened to her latest exploits in the village where she had quickly become part of the community fabric, on this committee and that charity group. She was the kind of woman who fitted in anywhere and Jess envied her that as she herself was more introverted and didn't mix particularly well.

Although her mother always told her not to bother – *it's safe here; this isn't London, you know, this is Bolton-by-Bowland* – Jess always insisted on accompanying her on the relatively short walk home after dark. It was just one of those things Jess felt obliged to do and after locking the front door she walked with Marj and Luna to her house, waiting for them to actually enter it before returning home

Her mind – again – was on many things during that short stroll, and when she reached the garden gate she was preoccupied with mush not tuned in to anything specific.

Then she was.

Jess had left the standing lamp on in the living room.

She was certain she had.

But now she could see through the net curtains covering the front window that the room was in complete darkness. No light on.

Jess stopped and frowned. Had one of the kids come down and turned it off? Unlikely. Last time she'd peeked into their rooms, both had been spark out.

Then there was movement. Just a shadow and the net curtains wafted ever so slightly.

She took the two strides up to the front door and saw that the wooden frame had been jemmied open around the lock.

Someone had broken in.

Jess careened straight into the lounge. No hesitation as that overwhelming maternal conditioning, plus the one about defending your property, kicked in simultaneously. The combination made her a very dangerous woman.

Even as she burst through, her sense of smell picked up something different: a combined tang of cigarette smoke, weed, alcohol, sweat and urine.

'Fuck's here?' she screamed and crashed into another person in the dark and it wasn't one of her children. The shock of that initial impact had a massive, immediate effect on her and she began swinging haymaker fists in from side to side, smashing into whoever that person was, pummelling them, feeling them crumble under her ferocious blows until he or she was on their knees, cowering, covering up their head with their hands and forearms, mewing, 'Stop, stop, please stop.'

Finally, shaking, Jess took a step back and fumbled for the light switch.

Petrified by the commotion, noise and the screaming, wailing man, Lily and Jason tumbled down to the foot of the narrow staircase into the living room, fear and horror etched on their young faces. They found their mother kneeling on the spine of a man, pinned face down on the wooden floor.

'It's OK, guys, it's OK,' Jess panted, trying to reassure them. Her police uniform was hanging on hooks by the front door. She looked at Lily, whose face had crumbled, then at Jason behind his sister on the stairs.

'Mum!' Jason cried.

'I said it's OK, I got him.' Just to make this point, she put her weight down on her knee, on his spine, between his shoulder blades. This was obviously a very risky manoeuvre for the person being held and could crush lungs and heart and break bones and possibly cause death, but just at that moment Jess didn't care if the individual on the floor died or not. She was on the scale way beyond enraged and was struggling not to beat the person into a pulp and screw the consequences. *No one, no fucker*, she was thinking, *breaks into my house.*

She took a breath, an extra moment to regain her self-control, and suddenly the red mist lifted a touch and she eased back on the pressure from her knee but yanked the guy's arms roughly behind his back and said to Lily, 'Get my cuffs will you?' She pointed to her utility belt on the hook and nodded encouragingly at her daughter. 'It's fine, love, I've got him. He's not going anywhere.'

As if to confirm that, the prostrate figure exhaled a loud breath which sounded like a death watch beetle had crawled into his lungs.

Lily tiptoed over his outstretched legs and found the rigid handcuffs in their leather pouch on Jess's belt and handed them across. Jess expertly stacked the intruder's wrists behind his back and applied the cuffs – tight – before heaving him over on to his back, not caring about the pain she was causing him.

She glared down at him and demanded, 'Have you come to finish the job you started?'

'What d'you mean?' he whimpered.

'To kill me, to murder me?'

EIGHTEEN

'I don't want anyone killed, understand?' Tommy Moss made it clear to the assembled team as he slammed the fully loaded magazine into the butt of his beloved, and occasionally used, Ruger SR semi-automatic pistol. There were ten nine-millimetre rounds to play with. He had bought it clean from an arms dealer in Brussels and had brandished it a couple of times and fired it twice in anger, injuring other villains without police involvement. He knew the complete irony of his words as he slid the gun into the waistband of his black jeans and took the ski mask from the trestle table next to him.

His words were even more ironic because this team of six, including his two enforcers from London, Chambers and Deerman, were similarly dressed and bearing arms of some description or other. Tommy knew this escapade had every chance of becoming a shooting match if things went tits up, but he didn't want it to happen. 'Shooting is the last resort,' he said, selecting an extendable baton from the table and sliding it into a leather loop on his belt. 'I don't mind anyone getting a clonk on the head or zapped in the face by one of these,' he then selected a can of pepper spray, 'or brought down by one of these,' he picked up the last item on the tabletop, which was a Vipertek stun gun, hand-held, about the size of a chunky mobile phone. He put that into his back pocket.

'What about those two security guys?' one of his team asked. His name was Gus and he was Tommy's second-in-command.

'Leave them to me and Mags,' Tommy said, jerking a thumb at Mags who was pulling on a black hoodie to match the black jeans she was now in. She had been armed with a two-inch barrelled revolver. 'We all know plans go to rat shit once things start happening, but once me and Mags have dealt with the occupants of the hall as we've discussed before, there's no reason why we shouldn't pull this off nice and neat.'

And there wasn't. The guys in front of him were his best 'Action Heroes', as he called them. Tough, no-nonsense operators, all with military backgrounds other than his two London thugs, all of whom would be well reimbursed for their efforts and who would then melt into the background after the job to somewhere warm and sunny where they owned nice villas and had legitimate businesses to run. They didn't want people to die either because that always made the cops try just that bit harder.

They had assembled in a disused industrial unit on Fiddlers Lane outside Chipping. It was a property Mags had been renting through various firewall companies for a few months and was lying fallow with the intention of it becoming a cannabis growing and production plant. It was behind a high wall, hidden away from prying eyes, and had been in a handy location for this latest endeavour which needed to be as low-key as possible.

'OK, you've each got your map of the hall?' Tommy checked.

There was a series of nods. Tommy knew this job was pretty last minute but he was certain there was every chance of pulling off one of the biggest art heists in history, certainly in the UK, and without too much collateral damage. 'So, boss,' Gus asked, 'are we sure there'll be no other staff or security bods knocking about, going to surprise us when we get there?'

'The irony, Gus, is that the owner of the place is so strapped for cash she's almost broke, but yet she owns one of the most extensive art collections in the country and isn't allowed to sell it because of the terms of her dead husband's will. So, no, she doesn't have any staff, other than the ones hired for functions like tonight.' Here he looked at Mags. 'And they are all owned by us and they'll be gone when we get there anyway.'

Mags nodded.

'OK, Tommy,' Gus said. He was checking his pistol, a big old Browning 9mm from his army days.

'So, once again – we go in, me and Mags neutralize the occupants, and as we're doing this you guys should have already started loading the vans with the artwork as planned, OK? Do not fucking kill anyone, OK? I don't mind violence per se, but not too much. You all know the score.'

'Blah, blah, blah,' one of the men mimicked Tommy, making them all laugh.

Tommy grinned. 'This will be a piece of cake, boys.'

He and Mags watched the men prepare themselves, then turn towards the three black vans that had been brought in for the job. There was a lot of artwork to steal and hopefully the vans would be large enough for it all.

'Pretty impressive,' Mags said quietly to Tommy. 'Pulling this all together so quickly. Consider me awestruck.'

He smiled at her.

'Where's your wife, though? The lovely, frigid Leanora?'

Tommy pulled a face. 'This bit ain't her scene. She doesn't like to get her long, manicured nails chipped.'

'But you're happy for me to do so?'

'You, babe, are a different kettle of fish.' He winked at her and fitted his ski mask properly.

He was a crushed young man. Jess could have accurately written his life story the moment she met him some months before when she had arrested him in possession of three hundred grand's worth of cocaine which, although Jess did not ever prove it, belonged to Mags. Then he was eighteen, from a broken home, had bad experiences with 'uncles' all through his life, had no role models, and crime was just something he did without a second thought.

And now he was crushed by even more bad decisions and the misplaced belief that being a gofer for a major drug dealer was preferable to working a steady, albeit lowly, job in a cut-price supermarket with regular pay and hours. He'd been lured by the prospect of an easy lifestyle, being a tough guy, perhaps, but then discovering he was at the very bottom of a dung heap. And not all that tough.

Lance Drake's face looked as though it had imploded as tears cascaded down his face, his mouth distorted by terror and loss.

Jess looked at him scornfully, a pathetic individual who had even pissed his own pants at some stage in the day, hence the reek of urine.

'No, no, no,' he begged as Jess heaved him up into a sitting position and propped him against the understairs cupboard door. 'I didunt, I didunt,' he said through his squished-up face. 'I didunt come to kill you, honest . . . I dint know what to do, who to go to and I had nowt to run wi', no real brass, nowt,' he sobbed.

'But you broke into my house, MY house,' Jess snarled. 'Where my kids live, where I live.'

'Only because . . .' He snuffled.

'Because what?' Jess demanded.

'Because you're the only person I knew I could turn to who'd keep me safe.'

Taken aback by this, Jess leant against the settee, looked down at Lance. She was still shaking but now regaining control and there was slightly less likelihood of Lance receiving a fatal kicking from her now.

Lily and Jason were kneeling on the settee, peering over fearfully at the scenario.

Jess glanced at them. 'You two OK?'

Neither seemed OK, but both nodded bravely.

'Tell you what, go grab any snacks and pop you want, then head back up to your rooms and watch a bit of TV or something – but do not mention this on social media, please promise me that.'

Jason flew into the kitchen like a shot, reappearing clutching crisps and cola, stepping across Lance's outstretched legs, then running upstairs. Lily was a little slower, clearly more affected by the danger. Still, she appeared armed with goodies, pausing at the foot of the stairs.

'Bloody hell, mum, you're a good fighter,' she said admiringly.

'Thanks – but only when I'm protecting someone I love.'

Their eyes met. Jess gave her a little nod, acknowledging the look of love. Lily was much tighter with her affections than Jason and this tiny, but significant, gesture meant a lot to Jess.

'What are you going to do with him?' Lily asked.

'Bang him up . . . now off you pop.'

After one more scared look at Lance, Lily went up the narrow stairs.

Jess waited a moment or two, listening to check if Lily had gone into her room, then turned her attention back to Lance who was almost hyperventilating in his effort to control his sobbing.

Jess had no sympathy. 'Calm down,' she told him, 'and tell me what's going on.'

'They're going to kill me, I know it, I just know it.'

'Who's they – and why?' Jess said. 'And consider yourself under caution.'

'Help me. Will you help me?' he pleaded pathetically, although to be fair Jess knew that maybe he wasn't being all that pathetic, not if folk were out to slot him.

She played him. 'I'm not sure I can. Depends on why I need to help you.'

'You know they came for Dimbo.'

Jess waited, allowing the lure of silence be a trap for Lance.

'Well, yeah, they did, and if I'd've bin wi' 'im, I'd've been killed too, but I saw 'em first an' I legged it.'

'Saw who?'

'Those two London tossbags, Cheech and Chong or whatever they call 'emselves; friggin' finger-breakers, that's what they are.'

'Names.'

He divulged the names and, of course, one – Chambers – instantly registered with Jess as the lad who'd been arrested by PD Flynn and his fangs, the one who had subsequently been released through lack of evidence.

'OK, they're finger-breakers and bad lads, but why are they

coming after you and Dimbo – may he rest in peace, obviously, or more likely, perpetual hell? How do they even know you? What the hell are they doing up here, Lance?'

Lance sniffed back a particularly stalactite-like length of snot and swallowed it down disgustingly into the back of his throat. 'They work for that Tommy guy, the one who's screwin' Maggie Horsefield.'

Jess felt her own throat go dry and she tensed up. 'And you're working for them, too, aren't you, Lance?'

He nodded.

'Confirm to me in actual words: you work for Maggie Horsefield.'

He did.

'Is she the one who got you bail from remand?'

'Yeah, through her brief, obviously.'

Jess inhaled a long breath, suddenly feeling rumblings of excitement in the pit of her stomach as all those loose ends which had been waving so tantalisingly in front of her eyes like fronds of vines in a Tarzan film were suddenly in reach and now, maybe, there was a way to plait them, then climb up them to get to Mags – although Jess knew that pinning all her hopes on the jabbering wreck in front of her was pushing matters a little too far maybe.

But it was a start.

'But I didn't know, honest,' Lance said.

'Know what?'

'That I was working for her.'

'How do you mean?'

'Like, y'know, when you arrested me. I were just a delivery boy, didn't know who the real boss was until I got on remand, then I found out it was Maggie Horsefield and believe it or not I felt safer in a cell cos I knew she wouldn't a forgiven me for losing all that stash to you lot.'

'You actually thought you were safer inside?' Jess asked incredulously. 'On remand?'

'I know, sounds stupid when you say it out loud, but I think I were and then I got bail without even asking for it!'

'Where's your ankle tag, incidentally?'

'Mags cut it off with bolt cutters that were in the back of the Land Rover. It were never gonna work anyway cos she has someone inside who can switch it on and off or whatever.'

'Mm, OK. Then what happened?'

'Those two London gits caught me and next thing I know I'm tied to a frickin' chair on a plastic sheet and Mags was gonna slit me throat with a zombie knife, she were, but you guys showed up and we all legged it.'

Jess shook her head in amused disbelief. 'So I saved your pathetic life?'

Lance's head dropped forwards and he said a muted, 'Yeah.'

'Then what happened?'

'I pleaded for me life, dint I? Told her I'd do anything.' His eyes angled up towards Jess. 'She said she wanted you frightened, to back off hassling her . . .'

'Hence the cars on fire, outside here and outside the nick? And the silent phone call?'

'Yeah, all me, doing it for her. Then she got some info that you'd be up at the Wellsprings and got me and Dimbo to do your brakes.'

That ice-like feeling, the glacier slithering down her body, shimmered through Jess again. 'To kill me?'

'We even tupped you off the road,' Lance admitted.

'And then went to buy yourselves a celebration drink,' Jess added bitterly. 'Job well done, eh?' She got a grip of herself. 'How did you know I'd be up Pendle?'

'Dunno. Mags knew, that's all I know, someone told her. A cop, I think.'

Jess did not like that. 'You're under arrest for attempted murder, Lance. You don't have to say anything, but . . .' She began to reel off the caution in full this time.

Moments later Jess was on the phone to the HQ comms room, a direct line, explaining who she was, where she was and what she wanted – a section van to be dispatched to her house to transport Lance to Blackburn police station custody office.

'I need transport,' she said.

'Stand by,' the comms operator replied, putting her on hold. Jess rolled her eyes, standing in front of Lance who was still hanging his head in shame.

'C'mon, c'mon,' Jess intoned impatiently, holding back a sudden urge to kick Lance.

'Sergeant Raker?' another voice cut in, in place of the initial comms operator. 'Inspector Allen, comms inspector here.'

'Hi, boss.'

'Your request for prisoner transport?' Allen said and even in those few words, Jess knew something was amiss. 'Bit of a problem, I'm afraid.'

'That being?'

'Every section patrol in the Ribble Valley and many from Blackburn are tied up at a serious public order incident and a possible firearms one, too, in Whalley.'

'Whalley?'

'Yes, sarge, so you might have to release your prisoner.'

'Don't let me go, please,' Lance implored Jess. 'That'd be like feeding me to the wolves and I don't want to be torn to shreds. That's why I came to you for help, Sergeant Raker.'

'To save your own skin?'

'Yup, I'm a coward when it comes to it,' Lance admitted freely.

'At least you're honest about it, Lance – and there's no way I'm letting you go.'

Relief flooded across his face.

'On the understanding that you tell me everything you know about Maggie Horsefield.'

'I don't know that much,' he baulked.

'Oh no, deal is I want to know everything you did prior to me arresting you, even if you didn't know you were working for Maggie. Every drug pick up, drug drop, every location, the name of everyone you came across, d'you understand?'

He nodded less than eagerly.

'Otherwise I'm going to take you right now and drop you off at her front door.'

Lance gave a nose-snort of derision.

'What's so funny?' Jess demanded, not amused.

'You, dropping me off at her house.'

'How's that amusing?'

'Because she isn't there.'

'Why would that be?'

'It's tonight, sarge.'

'And where exactly is she?'

'Pulling a job with her gangster boyfriend.'
'What are you saying?' Jess demanded.
'Already said it,' Lance shrugged.
'OK, then, what job?'
'That stately home, or whatever they call them big country houses.'
'Which stately home?' Jess asked, although she was already getting a bad feeling about this.
'Wolf summat.'
'Wolf Fell Hall?'
'Yeah, that's it.'
'What's the job?'
'Nicking pictures.'
'Pictures?' Jess queried. 'You mean paintings, artwork on the walls?'
'I guess.' He shrugged again.
'Mags and Tommy are going to steal valuable art from Wolf Fell Hall?'
'Yeah, he's got a team up from London to do it.'
'Are you sure? How do you know?'
'I overhear stuff, I'm a sneak,' he said proudly. 'They're going to pull the job after some charity ball thing at the hall, after everyone else's fucked off.'

Jess checked her Fitbit and did the calculations in her head, quick style. Nearly every cop in the known universe was tied up in Whalley dealing with public disorder and searching for a gunman, so there was literally not a soul to help out. Her cop instinct fired up her insides and all she wanted to do was somehow get over to Wolf Fell Hall and catch them, or at least disrupt a crime about to be, or being, committed and obviously nab Mags and Tommy Moss in the bargain. The latter would be extra sweet.

'You're not bullshitting me?' Jess demanded of Lance. He shook his head. She called up the stairs. 'Lily? Can you come down, love?'

Jess got on to the control-room inspector again.

Lily came tentatively down the stairs, pausing about halfway down, watching as Jess contorted herself into her police gear over her civvy clothes, trying to make the phone call at the same time as threading her arms into her stab vest, hi-vis jacket and also trying to fasten her utility belt, until she finally looked imploringly at Lily. 'Can you give me a hand?'

After a moment of hesitation, Lily jumped down the last few steps, grabbed the belt and started to fasten it.

The phone connected. 'PC Sue Ellis, Lancashire Constabulary Control Room, may I help?' Clearly the call had been diverted.

'Inspector Allen, please . . . this is Sergeant Raker over in Bolton-by-Bowland. I spoke to him a few moments ago.'

'Oh, apologies, sarge,' PC Ellis said. 'He's very busy dealing with a serious ongoing incident in Whalley. Can I help you?'

'Sorry, what's your name again?'

'Ellis – PC Sue Ellis.'

'Hi, look, Sue,' Jess said brusquely, 'I'm off duty at home. I've locked up someone breaking into my house and I've now got information there's a robbery taking place at Wolf Fell Hall near Chipping involving a serious London gang. I'm turning out to it from home in half a uniform but I need backup.'

Ellis hesitated. 'All patrols in your area are tied up with the incident in Whalley.'

'I know! What about the helicopter or a spare ARV?'

'Let me check. How good is your intel?'

Jess looked at Lance. 'Excellent, and like I said, a London-based gang are pulling the job,' then to gild the lily a touch she added, 'known for extreme violence.'

'OK, hold the line.'

Lily stood back, admiring her uniform-fitting work.

'Thanks, my love, now can you phone Gran? Hopefully she hasn't gone to bed yet.' She knew her mum liked a smidgen of whisky before turning in.

'Why?'

Before she could answer Lily's question, PC Ellis came back on the line. 'I'm sorry, the helicopter isn't available and the nearest ARV is in Blackpool.'

Jess didn't swear but came close. 'Look, I'm turning out to this job, whatever, so log that, will you – Wolf Fell Hall – and if anyone comes free, please deploy them as urgent backup.'

'Will do, sarge.'

Jess hung up.

Lily kept looking at Lance, then back to Jess. 'What are you going to do with this creep?'

'Take him with me, of course.'

'You are not!' Lance protested.
'Just watch me, fella.'

'Samira, sorry to call you this late,' Jess said, her face grimacing to reflect the apologetic tone of voice she was using. She had dragged Lance out of her house by his collar with one hand, pinning him face-against her car and restraining him there with her hip whilst she unlocked it, and had her mobile phone to her ear using her other hand to call Samira's number.

'That's OK, sarge.' The PCSO did not sound weary or pissed off to hear Jess calling at such a ridiculous time.

And from the background sound of it, it seemed Samira was travelling in a car.

'Hope I haven't interrupted anything.'

'No, just heading home from a secret tryst with my boyfriend since my dad banned him from our house, although it'll be plainly obvious what I've been up to.'

'You can always tell dad you were at work, if you want,' Jess suggested.

'How's that?'

'Where are you, first?'

'Almost home. Clitheroe.'

'Look, I know this isn't good, but do you have any uniform with you?'

'In the boot as always – jacket, cuffs, baton, torch and such.'

'And what are you wearing now?'

'Jeans, T-shirt – look, why, sarge?'

'Right, you can say no to this if you want and I won't think any the less of you, but, long story short, I've arrested Lance Drake – no, don't interrupt – he broke into my house and I'm looking at him now.' Jess had managed to manoeuvre her prisoner into the back seat of the Kia and was now standing by the open door.

'He broke into your house!' Samira almost exploded.

'I'll explain later . . . thing is, he's told me that Maggie Horsefield and Tommy Moss are pulling a job at Wolf Fell Hall as we speak, supposedly a big art heist, and there is literally no one to turn out to it, so I'm going to go, even if all I do is prevent or disrupt it.' She paused. 'All I'm saying is . . .'

'I'll be there!' Samira interjected.

'Right, good lass. Meet me in the car park at Chipping Village Hall. I'm setting off from home now.'

'On my way, sarge.'

With a grim smile and thinking, *damn, she's a good 'un*, Jess activated the child locks on both rear doors then went round to the driver's seat and fired up the little car. 'You do nothing, you don't move, nothing,' she warned Lance over her shoulder then she switched on her PR, which she'd brought home with all her other bits of uniform, and immediately heard the crossfire of numerous transmissions from the ongoing firearms and public order incident in Whalley where it seemed the police were being run ragged.

A car drew up beside her – her mother. Wrapped in a fluffy dressing gown over her jim-jams but with trainers on her feet, Marj got out accompanied by Luna. Jess watched her approach in the side mirror, and wound down her window.

'You have got to be kidding me!' Marj declared.

The front door of the cottage opened. Lily and Jason stood there in their night things like abandoned waifs in a Victorian novel.

'Sort 'em, Mum, please. I need to go. Explain later.'

Marj angled her head and looked into the back of the Kia. 'Is this the little twat who broke in?' She glowered at Lance, who cowered.

'Mother!'

'Bring him back so I can punch his lights out.' She jabbed her finger angrily at him, causing Luna to react to her furious voice and body language by jumping up and placing her paws on the car window and snarling with teeth bared. Lance cowered even further.

Jess gave a half-grin and said, 'I will.'

With that, Jess put her foot down and set off. She mulled over whether or not to call Dougie Doolan and Vinnie McKinty but decided not, whilst also feeling a surge of guilt at calling Samira, but that was done now, so it was too late.

With tape covering the registration plates, the three black vans moved out in a line from the industrial unit. Tommy and Mags in the lead van, Tommy driving.

Tommy retested the encrypted radio system between the team,

each individual member having their own set. The signal would work effectively up to a radius of two miles, then would drop off bit by bit, so was good enough for tonight's escapade. It worked fine.

Mags was charged up high. She slid a hand on to Tommy's thigh and looked at him through the eye-slits in her ski mask. He looked back and pursed his lips into a kiss through the mouth slit, which even Mags had to admit made him look extremely creepy. Like some sort of serial killer in a film, an image that had a reverse effect on her adrenaline.

As expected, the gates of Wolf Fell Hall were still wide open – probably hadn't been closed for a dozen years – and the vans cruised through them, down the wide driveway and circled to a stop outside the once magnificent house.

'Here we go,' Tommy said into his radio.

They debussed and jogged up the front steps into the hall. Each man had studied the floorplan of the hall and had the layout imprinted precisely into his brain along with where the artwork could be found. They split like a well-rehearsed air display team into various hallways whilst Mags and Tommy went straight ahead and took the central flight of stairs on to the landing, then veered left along a wide corridor to the large suite at the very far end of that wing which Mags knew belonged to the duchess.

They moved silently along and entered the suite, the door to which, like all the other doors in the place, was unlocked.

Mags stepped in first.

A very inebriated and drug-addled Carolynne, Duchess of Dunsop and Newton was sitting at a huge dressing table in an old-fashioned, flimsy gown which looked like an ancient wedding dress. She was continuously running a brush through her thinning hair, having removed her wig, and her make-up was smeared over her features like a clown having a particularly bad day.

She spun on hearing them enter, almost tipping out of her chair as she swung around. She emitted an ear-piercing scream.

Tommy shoved Mags sideways and lurched towards the duchess with his stun gun which he applied to her upper chest and zapped her, sending a high voltage through her.

Her body jerked like she was being defibrillated, then toppled over and crashed stiffly to the floor, dragging several bottles of perfume and cans of hairspray with her, clattering all around her stunned body.

Tommy continued to move quickly, flipped the duchess on to her face, pulled her arms behind her and jerked his head to beckon Mags. She handed him strips of preprepared gaffer tape which Tommy wound expertly around the duchess's wrists and ankles.

'You've done this before,' Mags commented.

'Don't ask,' was all he mumbled, flipping the skinny, almost weightless woman on to her back. Mags then handed him a shorter strip of tape which Tommy applied over the duchess's mouth as she came round from the shock.

She started to wriggle desperately so Tommy gave her another zap of electricity which instantly stopped her moving.

Mags and Tommy stood face to face. Mags peeled up her mask to reveal her lips, then did the same to Tommy's and kissed him passionately, truly on fire from what was going on, slurping her tongue into and around his mouth.

Then she stopped suddenly.

'You know what happens as soon as this is over, don't you?'

He nodded, pulled his mask back down and they both stepped out into the hallway.

NINETEEN

'We need to find the bodyguards,' Tommy said. 'They won't be as easy as the drunken and drugged-up duchess,' he warned Mags.

They hurried along the hallway.

'The royals have always stayed in the same two suites down on the East Wing and Harker and Leighton were always in rooms adjacent,' Mags said, refreshing Tommy's memory of details she had gone out of her way to find out. 'Down this way.' She had spent a lot of time researching titbits like this over the last few months, getting to know the ins and outs and whereabouts of the residents of Wolf Fell Hall.

They reached a ninety-degree corner on to the East Wing and slowed down, listened.

'Once we've done these guys it'll be plain sailing,' Tommy said. 'You OK for this, babe?'

'More than OK.' Mags stopped suddenly and pointed at a door. 'Harker's room.'

Tommy stopped and held up a finger: wait, listen.

Then he nodded. She took hold of the huge, globe-like, gold-coloured door handle and turned it slowly. It went all the way – another door unlocked – and she pushed it slightly, opening it a fraction.

Tommy touched her shoulder, indicating the prearranged entry they had discussed, him in front, pistol drawn, her behind.

She slowly pushed the door open to reveal the immense bedroom beyond and the ancient four poster bed which was swaying like a schooner in a hurricane as the naked couple on the bed engaged in riotous intercourse.

The surprise being that the couple was Harker and Leighton, with Leighton on all fours and Harker kneeling behind him wearing a latex mask.

Mags and Tommy, for a moment, were dumbfounded.

But only for a moment. With an incredulous shake of the head Tommy stepped across to the bed and jammed his stun gun against Harker's rib cage, discharging its voltage at exactly the same moment Harker achieved his own peak, and Tommy could only wonder what the guy experienced as 50,000 volts shot through him as he ejaculated.

Tommy quickly placed the stun gun against Leighton's side and zapped him too.

'What the hell goes on in stately homes?' Mags asked. 'Who knew?'

'I'll bet this stuff doesn't appear in the pages of *Country Life*,' Tommy said as he got to work trussing up the two rigid men with Mags' help.

By the time they'd done it, the bodyguards' wrists and ankles were zip-tied and gaffer-taped and, having removed Harker's mask, their mouths were taped over and the tape was wound around their heads like bandages. They did not want these two guys getting free in the next fifteen minutes or so.

They left the pair squirming like beached dolphins and threatening all sorts of inaudible, mumbling threats behind the tape covering their mouths.

'Go!'

Mags' hand was once again on a doorknob, this time on the door she believed led into the suite used by Bruce Armstrong-Bentley, the younger brother.

On Tommy's word she twisted the immense gold knob and the door swung open. She stood aside. Tommy entered, Mags following, and they went down a short hallway into a lounge area furnished with once-magnificent but now decrepit furniture.

The lounge was empty.

Bottles, glasses, trays of half-eaten food were scattered around, with half-snorted lines of coke on an occasional-table top.

Mags pointed to a closed door and said, 'Bedroom.'

'I wonder what we'll find behind that?' Tommy asked.

'Well, so far we've seen Miss Havisham and a scene from *Pulp Fiction*, so who knows?' Mags said. 'Let's just hope it's not something from *Silence of the Lambs*.'

The bullwhip arced through the air and connected with a sickening crack, causing an instant slit in the girl's delicate skin, drawing blood alongside the other dozen or so criss-crossed whip marks on her pale white back.

The whip drew back for another blow, like the line of a fly-fishing rod.

The man brandishing the whip did not hear Mags and Tommy enter the bedroom, nor did the cowering, sobbing, naked girl who was on her knees in a foetal position, her hands wrapped around her head, face pressed into the threadbare carpet.

For a few moments, Mags – who thought she had seen most things in her life – could not believe what she was witnessing: an overweight, naked man with a fat, wobbling arse, drawing back the whip to inflict more horrific punishment. In his free hand he held a glass of Champagne, which he raised as a toast and threw his head back with a roar of filthy laughter. But then a bullet hole appeared between his shoulder blades and, still clutching the whip, Bruce Armstrong-Bentley pitched on to his face, almost in a position which mirrored the girl in front of him. Blood suddenly pooled underneath him, emptying his chest cavity via the exit hole made by the track of the soft-tipped bullet through his sternum.

Mags looked slowly at Tommy who had his pistol in his hand, lowering it inch by inch.

She couldn't see the expression on his face under his mask, but she guessed at it.

Neither she nor Tommy could have been described as law-abiding citizens. They had made people suffer, tortured them on occasion, but what they had seen in front of them had been a step too far, even in their perverted world.

But Mags said hoarsely, 'You just killed a member of the royal family.'

'I killed a guy abusing a girl,' he said bluntly. 'We need to move on.'

Tommy spun away, slotting the pistol back into his waistband, and without a backwards glance he left the room.

Mags hesitated a moment, catching the girl's eyes as she peered back terrified from her position. Mags scooped up a blouse and a pair of jeans from the floor which she assumed belonged to the girl, tossed them towards her and said, 'Do one, lass.' She took one last glance, then followed Tommy.

Tommy rushed along the hallway to the next door along and stopped outside, believing this was the room of the older brother, Edward. Tommy tried the handle. This door was locked.

There was no shortcut from Bolton-by-Bowland to Chipping, so Jess sped out of the village towards Sawley, then did a sharp right and went on the narrow, twisty roads towards Grindleton. She veered a dogleg through Waddington and via Twitter Lane crossed Higher Hodder Bridge, on to Birdy Brow with Longridge Fell looming ominously to her left in the darkness, before finally reaching Chipping.

It was a long time since she had raced along these roads in a car at night. In her teenage years she had owned a souped-up Vauxhall Cavalier – that she had done up herself – and had blasted at ridiculous speeds around these very roads and lanes with her mates; back then she had known them intimately . . . until of course, and this wasn't something she was proud of or ever spoke of, she drove at speed through a hedge into a field whilst well over the drink-drive limit and ran away from the scene, no actual harm done but leaving the car wedged into another hedge. She had lived in perpetual fear of the cops tracking her down and sticking a breathalyzer into her mouth, but they never showed. She recovered the car later, got a mate to repair the hedges and took the vehicle to a scrapyard – ironically Primrose Breakers – big lesson learned.

Tonight there was no alcohol involved, just a prisoner and a heist.

She swerved up into the front car park of Chipping Village Hall and wasn't surprised to find Samira had already arrived.

Tommy put his shoulder to the locked door. It was big, made of heavy oak and didn't budge. He swore and banged loudly on it.

'Maybe leave it?' Mags suggested.

Tommy nodded and turned, and as he looked past her along the hallway he swore again.

Mags spun to see a figure striding along towards them, dressed in a velvet dressing gown over luxury cotton pyjamas and grey suede slippers: Edward, the other low-ranking royal.

Problem was he was carrying a double-barrelled shotgun aimed right at Mags and Tommy.

'I demand to know what in hell is happening here!'

Tommy eased Mags to one side and said, 'Put the gun down, you idiot.'

Mags knew this man was also very drunk. She had watched him imbibing alcohol all evening at the charity auction and knew this confrontation would not end happily.

He brought the shotgun up to his shoulder, aimed it somewhere between Mags and Tommy and pulled the trigger.

Mags flinched and gasped, expecting to feel the horrific splatter of pellets thudding into her body.

Nothing happened.

'What the hell!' Edward said furiously and tilted the shotgun to look along the double barrels and chambers and realized his rookie error. 'Damn safety catch!'

He thumbed the catch off and brought the weapon back up to his shoulder.

Tommy shot him twice in the chest.

* * *

'What's happening, sarge?' Samira asked enthusiastically when Jess got out of her car. She tried to get a look at Lance in the back seat but he was shrouded in shadow, hunched over and with no desire to show his face. He had been completely silent on the journey over as Jess had been constantly on the radio to try and prise some backup from somewhere.

'He broke into your house?' Samira asked incredulously.

'Yeah, but not for the reason you might think. Anyhow, more of that later. Thing is, there's something big going down at Wolf Fell Hall . . .' Jess succinctly explained it and what she planned to do, which, she admitted, seemed slightly reckless even to her, and again she gave Samira the option to opt out.

'I'm in,' the PCSO said without hesitating.

Jess nodded.

First, though, they dragged Lance out of the Kia, unfastened his cuffs, marched him to a lamppost, made him hug it, then re-cuffed him.

'You can wait here,' Jess said.

Lance tipped his head back and propped his chin on the lamppost to look skywards. 'I don't think I'm going to shimmy up that, somehow,' he said disconsolately.

Jess patted his cheek. 'Good boy.'

Moments later in their own cars, they drove out of the car park.

Stunned, but still functioning, Mags jogged out of Wolf Fell Hall right behind Tommy, but it didn't take her brain long to default back to her version of normality. Maybe she would have hesitated to shoot the whip-wielding royal in the back but she was very much on the same page as Tommy when he gunned down the shotgun-wielding one. As a new splurge of adrenaline entered her system she felt reenergized, and a grim expression came to her face because she really was enjoying this.

All that had to be done now was ensure that the vans were filled with stolen art and then go.

As she and Tommy reached the front door, two of his team were manhandling a large gilt-framed painting between them across the foyer. They stopped to let the guys pass and carry the painting out and down the steps to slide it into a waiting van.

Tommy ran up and down the three vans, checking.

The team had done well. Each van had been efficiently packed with paintings from the walls, large and small, plus various items from display cases.

Tommy had a quick word with Gus, patted him on the shoulder, then turned to Mags. 'A few more pieces and then we're gone.'

'We need to get a move on,' Mags urged him.

'Ten minutes, max,' he promised.

'OK.'

He was as good as his word and was at the back of each van as the doors were slammed shut on the stolen goods, then sprinted to the lead van in which he and Mags had arrived.

Just as Tommy was about to move off, the bright headlights on main beam of a fast-moving car hurtled towards them and skidded nose-to-nose in the gravel, ensuring that the van had no place to go. Two figures got out of this car.

TWENTY

Steve had parked the old Rolls-Royce in darkness behind Chipping Village Hall again whilst waiting for his boss to return from the heist, or to respond to whatever instructions she gave him. He wasn't exactly certain what was required of him but he would go with the flow, whatever.

Settled down in the soft leather upholstery behind the vast steering wheel, which reminded him of the helm of an ocean-going yacht, he played with the old radio and tape deck in the dashboard and even found some ancient cassettes in the glove box. He couldn't tune the radio into anything other than static, so he tried the cassette player, inserting an album of country classics which he assumed had belonged to Mags' father rather than her.

It started off well for a couple of songs – Hank Williams warbling away, then the amazing voice of Patsy Cline – but then something went very wrong with Dolly Parton. The singing became distorted, then complete gobbledygook, until finally there was a terrible crunching sound and the tape stopped.

The machine was eating the tape, and with a certain degree of reluctance Steve pressed the eject button and cautiously withdrew the cassette, finding that the tape was trapped like very long linguini in the workings and cogs of the machine.

He tried to extract it and amused himself by trying to deal with old-fashioned tech that had tried to devour itself.

It was as he tried to rewind the tape on to the cassette using a ballpoint pen to turn one of the spools that he saw the flash of headlights at the front of the village hall, followed shortly by another flash, obvious that two cars had pulled in to the car park. Maybe a lovers' tryst.

He wound down his window and tried to eavesdrop. There were voices but they were indistinct, as the village hall separated him from them.

They didn't stay long and soon the headlights from both cars swept away and there was silence again as the sound of their engines disappeared.

All was quiet for a moment.

He was about to continue with the ancient art of repairing a cassette tape when he heard a loud howl of anguish from the front of the hall.

Jess had no plan because she had no real idea what she was going to encounter, but if it was truly a heist she was rushing headlong into, then presumably there would be vehicles of some sort involved.

And also the probability of running into dangerous, desperate individuals.

But first things first.

Her car was ahead of Samira's as they raced towards the gates of Wolf Fell Hall, which gave Jess an idea.

Not a great one, admittedly, but an idea.

She stuck her arm out of the window and flapped it up and down in a Highway Code 'slow down' gesture, hoping Samira would see and understand the message, coupled with brake lights.

She did and the two cars stopped at the gates. Jess dashed back to Samira.

'How do you feel about leaving your car here, at a slight angle and blocking the gates so no vehicle can easily get out?'

'Er, I don't mind, but it also means no vehicle can get in either,' Samira pointed out practically.

'Good point,' Jess accepted. 'However, backup's not exactly rushing our way.'

'Fair enough, let's keep winging it here.'

Samira gave her a thumbs-up. Jess ran back to her car and drove forwards a few yards. Samira edged her car between the gate posts at an angle, then got into Jess's car.

From the light cast by the spotlights at the front of Wolf Fell Hall, Jess saw the three vans parked up nose-to-tail in the turning circle and saw two people get into the lead vehicle.

'It's happening,' she warned Samira. 'Any firearms used or displayed at all – *any* – we back off and let them go, OK?' Jess said.

'Yep,' Samira said nervously.

The two ladies exchanged a tense glance. Samira was blowing out her cheeks as she tried to preserve some degree of calm. Jess had asked Lance about firearms but he claimed to have no idea, so Jess had to acknowledge that she and Samira were possibly plunging into a very dangerous situation.

But that's what cops did.

When others might run away, they had to run towards.

Jess always saw this as part of the contract she had between herself and the community she served and she would never, ever, shirk that duty, but neither was she stupid about it.

'Hang on,' she warned Samira, and put her foot down, driving the Kia down the wide driveway towards the hall and coming to a skidding halt at the front of the lead van. As she stopped she said, 'Me one side, you the other.'

By the time those words were out of her mouth she was heading for the passenger door of the van and Samira, just a second behind, aiming for the driver's door, so when they reached the van they were almost in sync and yanked the doors open in unison.

'Out of the vehicle now!' Jess screamed at the hooded figure.

'You can screw yourself,' the figure screamed back. Jess instantly recognized the voice: Mags.

On the other side Samira reached in and snaffled the keys from the ignition.

'Ya stupid bitch!' the man behind the wheel snarled at her: Tommy.

'If the cap fits,' Samira responded to an insult she had received many times. Not aware who she was dealing with, not that it would have made any difference, Samira grabbed Tommy's right arm and tried to drag him out of the van.

On the opposite side, Jess said, 'You're under arrest, Mags,' and reached for her upper arm, almost mirroring what was happening on the opposite side of the van between Samira and Tommy.

Mags squirmed out of the grip and swore vehemently at Jess whilst trying to twist and turn and reach for her revolver which she'd put in her waistband just before getting into the van.

Jess saw the movement and made a more concerted effort to get hold of Mags so she could not writhe as much, but Mags suddenly exploded like a firecracker, punching, screaming and kicking out sideways at Jess, who had to back off and duck and weave to avoid the barrage of blows.

On the other side, Samira – much to her amazement – managed to drag Tommy out and he crashed down sideways on to his knees, but the fall knocked Samira backwards a few steps and she lost her balance and toppled on to her backside.

On the periphery of their vision, both officers were aware that the occupants of the other vans in the line were getting out of their vehicles and it would probably only be seconds before the two cops were surrounded, outnumbered and overwhelmed, and unless Jess could negotiate arrests, which seemed very doubtful, they would have to hold up their hands and beat a hasty retreat, even if the villains were unarmed.

But then everything changed.

Initially, no one spotted the figure in black emerge from the shadows under the trees at the far edge of the turning circle, armed with a lightweight, compact Skorpion machine gun, often called the world's favourite pistol.

Had Samira not staggered away from Tommy as he tumbled out of the van, she would have taken four bullets in the back. But because she fell, she left Tommy open and vulnerable as the figure from the bushes fired a brief burst from the Skorpion, all of which hit the intended target – Tommy Moss.

The slugs formed a rising diagonal line up from his heart and tore out his throat.

When they struck him, he had been on one knee, trying to stand up, angry at Samira, but he fell back against the van, clutching his wounded chest and neck and slithering down into a heap. And with one twitch of his legs he was dead.

Samira scrambled away on all fours, her toes skidding in the gravel, but she was unable to get up as her hands slid in the sharp stones. Finding herself prostrate by the side of the van she did the only sensible thing and rolled underneath it.

Tommy's team also did the only sensible thing. They scattered in all direction like a Catherine wheel, running into the darkness of the grounds as the solitary figure opened fire again, just a short blast to strafe Tommy's van, putting bullet holes in its side.

On the other side of the van Jess had just about been holding on to Mags, who had been struggling like a trapped leopard, but they had almost comically stopped mid-struggle when this new factor came on to the scene. Both women dropped to their haunches.

Twenty yards short of the lead van, the figure came to a halt on the gravel, stood there, legs shoulder-width apart, breathing heavily with the Skorpion ready for use, then began to walk forwards with purpose.

Ten yards from the van the figure stopped again and pulled off the balaclava hood, tossed it to one side, and revealed the face underneath.

Jess raised herself slightly so she could see along the bench seat of the van, through the open doors, and what she saw shocked her: a woman, and from what she could make out, a very good-looking one, even though her hair was scraped up tightly away from her face into a bun on top of her head.

However, the expression on her face wasn't remotely pretty as she snarled, 'Maggie Horsefield, you are dead, you cheating, husband-stealing bitch.'

'Who the hell's that?' Jess gasped.

'Shit,' Mags said.

'Who is it?' Jess asked again.

'Leanora.'

'Who the hell's Leanora?'

'Tommy's missus, Leanora Moss.'

'I know you're over there, Mags,' Leanora shouted. 'Next to that cop. She isn't going to protect you, and what I advise you to do,

Maggie, is step away from her so she won't get hurt, then come out and walk towards me.'

'Screw that,' Mags said, from her crouching position.

Instead, Jess stood up shakily. 'I'm Sergeant Raker from Clitheroe police station,' she announced to Leanora. 'My colleague is over there. I want to know if you've hurt her.'

'She's in one piece, but my shit of a husband is dead and now I want Maggie Horsefield and then I'll be happy and gone.'

'Not going to happen,' Jess said. 'You must put your weapon down, then we can talk and end this madness.'

Leanora paused as though she was considering this, then said, 'Sergeant Raker? Jess Raker?'

Jess didn't like the sound of that, but said, 'Yes.'

'You killed Terry Moss, didn't you?'

It was Jess's turn to pause before replying. 'Yes.'

'Well, fancy. Now we've both killed a Moss. We're very much alike.'

'Don't think so – now put the gun down,' Jess insisted.

'Nah. I need Maggie to step up to the plate.'

'Like I said, screw that,' Maggie said, ripping off her ski mask. She shoved Jess out of the way and stood up, this time getting her hand around the gun in her waistband. She drew it out, brought it up and aimed through the middle of the van and began to fire, yanking back the trigger, quickly discharging all six bullets in the chamber in the general direction of Leanora. But being so badly aimed and so affected by recoil, most of the bullets went skywards through the van roof, none of them anywhere near Leanora who, cold as ice, simply didn't move, just waited for Mags to finish and then re-aimed the Skorpion.

On her knees and peeking along the footwell of the van, Jess saw Leanora was uninjured and was about to return fire, but probably with more accuracy than Mags' terrible efforts, which were like a cowboy on speed.

With her right hand, Jess whipped Mags' legs from underneath her and brought her crashing down with a scream like some sort of kid's trick on a mate. Jess then crawled alongside her, wrenched the revolver from her hand, grabbed her hoodie top and, finding strength from somewhere, pulled Mags alongside the van as Leanora opened fire for just short of three seconds. But one thing

Jess knew from her extensive firearms background (which included having fired several seized Skorpions down police ranges) was that although three seconds or less was only a short time it was long enough to empty a magazine which had discharged several bullets already.

And so it proved.

Leanora emptied the magazine and had to somehow replace it, which gave Jess the opportunity she needed to pull Mags up on to her feet and, using the cover of the van, push, pull, prod and direct her up the steps towards the hall.

'Move, move, move!'

And as she did this, she felt Mags suddenly become lighter and found that Samira had managed to roll all the way underneath the van and had joined Jess in her effort to drag Mags to safety.

'You OK?' Jess managed to ask, relieved to see Samira moving.

'Just. That guy's dead, though,' she said.

No more words were said as the trio stumbled towards the front door of Wolf Fell Hall, but just as they reached the threshold Samira tripped and went down head-first, losing her grip on Mags' clothes. It was just as well because about thirty yards behind them, having fumbled a bit as she replaced the magazine, Leanora had rushed up to the van, and, standing over the body of her late husband to which she gave one contemptuous kick in the ribs, she'd leant on the bonnet to stabilize her aim at Mags and the two cops helping her to run away and flicked the weapon on to single-shot mode and aimed down the barrel.

The moment after Samira tripped there was a shot, and Mags screamed as the bullet from the Skorpion skimmed her outer right bicep, gouging a deep, bloody channel and then tumbling through the air to imbed itself in the wall.

'I've been shot!' Mags uttered, sinking to her knees, gripping her arm and looking plaintively at Jess, who said, 'We need to keep moving, Mags or you're dead for sure, and maybe us too.'

And just to make that warning a reality, Leanora fired another shot which missed Mags' skull by about an inch.

Jess knew there was no time for discussion. Once more she grabbed Mags' clothing and dragged her unceremoniously across the tiled entrance foyer into a ground-floor hallway, followed by

Samira scrambling on her hands and knees as more single bullets crashed into the walls and woodwork around them.

This was the hallway Jess had been taken along by the duchess when the Armstrong-Bentley brothers had been kicking off, and Jess swung the wounded Mags into the same drawing room which had been the scene of the brothers' conflict that morning. She didn't dwell on it, but wasn't surprised to find that the room was still in the exact same state of disrepair it had been on that day, with shotgun holes in the ceiling and smashed furniture strewn around. No effort had been made at a clear-up.

Mags slumped on to an armchair and looked fearfully down at her arm which was bleeding quite heavily.

'I've been shot,' she said again. 'And Christ it hurts.'

Jess ignored her whining and stood in front of her and waved the revolver in front of her face. Jess knew it was a two-inch barrelled, six-shot revolver and that Mags had fired every one of the bullets at Leanora because, as this was ingrained in her after years on the firearms branch in the Met, she had counted them. 'Do you have any more ammunition for this?'

Mags was very, very pale, possibly on the verge of going into shock.

Jess wasn't greatly sympathetic and asked the question again.

'Yuh, yuh,' Mags said weakly and dug into her pocket and came out with four .38 shells which looked as though they'd been home produced.

'That it?'

'Might be one more . . .'

'Jeez, c'mere,' Jess said abruptly and plunged a hand into Mags' pocket and pulled out another two bullets. She then flipped open the chamber, emptied out the used ones on to a chair and expertly slotted the new ones into the six chambers. She then looked at Samira, who was watching her with horror. 'You look after her,' she pointed at Mags, 'and see what you can do with the wound . . .'

'What are you going to do, sarge?' Samira could not keep her eyes off the revolver which, though small, looked deadly to her. And was.

'Going back out there,' Jess said after taking a breath. She winked at Samira. 'Use some of this furniture to barricade yourselves in here and only let me back in.'

'Sarge . . .'

'I'll be fine.' She looked at Mags who seemed to be wilting visibly. 'This officer will try to help you. I'll call an ambulance and ask for backup, OK?'

Mags nodded, her eyes like a puppy dog that had been kicked.

Jess turned to leave, but Samira grabbed her. 'Be careful, please.'

'Don't worry,' she said.

Steve edged around the corner of Chipping Village Hall, his curiosity getting the better of him eventually, wondering who had emitted that anguished howl and saw a young man with his arms wrapped around a lamppost. With a furrowed brow Steve walked slowly towards him, trying to make sense of what he was seeing in the darkness.

The figure was sobbing, but must have heard Steve's approach and turned to look.

Steve recognized Lance instantly in the yellow light of the fluorescent lamppost.

Lance also recognized Steve.

'Oh God, mate, help me, help me. Cops have left me here.' He rattled the handcuffs against the lamppost.

Steve grinned. 'Well, well, well, what have we here?'

Jess took a steadying breath before spinning out of the door into the hallway. The gun, which she had glanced at, was of indeterminate make, probably had a sordid history of being used in numerous shootings and did not look in great condition, but at least it worked. Revolvers were less prone to malfunctioning than semi-automatic pistols, as Mags had proved when she'd taken six wild potshots at Leanora. And the ammo had worked too, so at least that boded well if Jess had to actually fire the damned thing – which she fervently hoped she would not have to. Even as Samira closed the door behind her, in her mind's ear Jess could hear the jarring tones of Inspector Price's voice as he bellowed at her gleefully, finding something that would finally bring her down – unless, of course, she found the 'something' that could bring *him* down. And in another train of thought Jess was already preparing her defence if it came to it because if she emerged from this in one piece she aimed to come up smelling of roses.

She moved cautiously along the hallway combat-style, with the gun held in her right hand, her left-hand cupped underneath in support, taking her time, arcing the weapon side-to-side in front of her, finger on the trigger so that if it had to be pulled there would be no time lapse, the response instant.

And, not even deep down, she was enjoying this, sliding along like a panther, controlling her heart rate and her breathing and the flood of excitement. She was enjoying it right up front.

She reached the junction where the hallway met the grand foyer of the hall and stopped, going tight to the wall, bringing the gun up in front of her chest before taking the chance to have a very quick look around the corner. She'd been outstanding at this sort of thing, both in training and live scenarios, taking that less-than-a-second glance and having to report back exactly what she had seen with her sharp eyes and switched-on brain. She was glad to see that skill had not completely deserted her as she jerked back and analysed everything she'd seen in that microsecond.

Basically nothing dangerous.

The front door of the hall was open and the foyer was deserted. There was a trail of blood spots from Mags' arm wound from where she and Samira had continued to drag her across the floor, but nothing else.

One more glance: all clear.

Jess stepped into the foyer and took the long way to the front door, sticking to the walls until she reached the front door, where once again she stopped and went tight to the wall, caught her breath, and looked. Nothing appeared to have changed at first, but then she saw only one van remained of the three that had been parked there in a line – the one Mags and Tommy had been in. The other two had gone.

Still she remained extremely cautious, took careful steps out through the door, slowly across the terrace to the front steps of the hall down to the parking circle where this van remained. There was no sign of Leanora, nor anyone else, but still she did not relax as she very, very carefully went into a defensive crouch and edged around the front of the van where she saw that Tommy Moss's body was still lying there.

Keeping her eyes peeled, she knelt beside him, knowing there wasn't any point in checking for a pulse. Even so, she did. There was none.

* * *

She called it in whilst standing on the front steps of Wolf Fell Hall, but even so it seemed that any backup was still very distant, particularly when Jess confirmed that no police officer had been injured – but she did insist on an ambulance for Mags.

Then she turned slowly and walked back into the hall, wondering if there was any fresh hell to find in there because it worried her there was no sign of any of the occupants in the hall. Her first port of call, though, was back to Samira and Mags in the drawing room.

She rapped on the door. 'Samira, it's me – let me in.'

There was no response. Jess knocked again. 'Samira, PCSO Patel, open the door please.'

Again, nothing. Jess turned the door handle and pushed, fully expecting to find that Samira had barricaded herself in as Jess had told her to, but the door, whilst unlocked, did not move, so Jess put her shoulder and weight to it and heaved through, finding her way barred by a dining room table which was on its side.

'Samira?'

Nothing. Jess pushed harder. Once the gap was wide enough she twisted into the drawing room and stepped around the tipped-over table to find Samira on her knees, but slowly sitting up, holding her head with her hands. Jess saw blood coming from a wound in her skull, lots of it, from a deep cut.

Samira looked at her, dazed and not quite compos mentis, but managed to say, 'Sorry, sarge, sorry . . .'

Mags had gone.

TWENTY-ONE

In every police headquarters throughout the country there is what is known ominously as the corridor of power, along which can be found the offices of all the high-ranking officers in that particular force, such as the chief constable, the deputy and assistant chiefs plus civilian heads of departments such as HR and all their attendant staff, secretaries, PAs and other bag carriers and lackeys. It's a little world of its own, with its own culture, rules and foibles. Usually the corridors are sombre, subdued, dimly lit affairs, far away from the realities of day-to-day policing, but where key decisions are made about strategic and operational matters, discipline and, occasionally, firing officers.

And Lancashire Constabulary was no exception, the first-floor corridor in the HQ building at Hutton Hall to the south of Preston being its corridor of power.

These were the types of corridors that PS Jess Raker tried to mostly avoid during her career, corridors she had no aspiration to visit or become part of – although they did seem to draw her in too often these days. She wasn't a denizen of what was often called 'the dream factory' or other more derogatory terms used by officers at the sharp end of policing to describe the goings-on and thought processes at headquarters. Jess much preferred the hustle and bustle of response policing, loved a busy nick (although she had to admit she now had a very soft spot for her new home, Clitheroe, which even though pretty quiet, did have its moments) and a heaving, sweaty custody office. That was her world, but today she was at headquarters to face a further grilling, this time by the chief constable and her entourage, about events at Wolf Fell Hall, now over a month old.

She had walked along the corridor an hour earlier and was now sitting, waiting, in the outer office which was the buffer zone for both the chief constable's and the deputy chief's actual offices and in which sat three secretaries and the chief constable's bag carrier (personal assistant really), a supercilious chief inspector who continually looked sideways with a sneer on his face at Jess as she sat on a chair by the door, elbows on knees, head propped in her hands, pretty much staring at the carpet.

She was there to be asked questions. Lots of them. Hard ones, because since she and Samira had rocked up to the heist in progress at Wolf Fell Hall, got involved in a gunfight, found a few dead bodies and lost the majority of the offenders and others involved (even though this had been understandable in the circumstances), the whole force had been in ultra-drive as it faced huge pressure from many directions, including the prime minister's office, the Home Office, the royal family. And, of course, the media which, prior to the 'Killings on Wolf Fell' as the incident had now been colourfully termed, hadn't had any interest in the activities of two lowly members of the royal family, but now that the Armstrong-Bentley brothers had been murdered, every section of the media was fascinated by them and the whole, sordid tale of the goings-on at Wolf Fell Hall. Jess had had many a microphone, smartphone and camera shoved into her face as she emerged from Clitheroe nick and one intrepid reporter had even managed to follow her home and do the same on her doorstep. She'd had to rise above the rage she was feeling on that one and did not stick the mic where the sun didn't shine.

For the force it was a nightmare of epic proportions, particularly as – with the exception of Tommy Moss, who was very dead – none of the perpetrators had been arrested and the 'Killings on Wolf Fell' had become one of the biggest investigations and man – or woman – hunts mounted for many a year. Jess had not been coopted on to the investigation – she hadn't expected to be – which was being run by a plethora of self-important detectives from FMIT who had taken over Clitheroe nick as a satellite location for the main investigation which was being run from Blackburn.

Jess sighed as she looked down through her thighs. It was a nice carpet, she thought, if a bit old fashioned.

The heavy oak door of the chief's office finally opened and Samira Patel stepped out, looking exceptionally battle scarred. Jess knew Samira had been in there since about 10 a.m. and had undergone almost two hours of questioning by a review panel, and not for the first time.

It was the chief constable, a lady called Gail Newby, who had shown Samira out, thanking her with a rather wan smile. Jess saw the chief looked somewhat frayed around the edges these days as she dealt daily, hourly, minutely, with the heavy scrutiny the force was batting off from all sides. Newby had been crucial in sorting out Jess's move from the Met to Lancashire all those months ago, seemed like a lifetime now, and Jess wondered with everything that had happened since whether she was regretting it, because Jess seemed to have been nothing but trouble.

Samira nodded at Jess and whispered, 'Hindsight,' and rolled her eyes as she walked past and out. Jess had just enough time to whisper back, 'Canteen,' before Samira went out.

'Sergeant Raker?' Newby said. 'Jess? Come on inside.'

Steeling herself, Jess stood up and entered the office.

* * *

The review lasted so long that a running buffet was ordered for the office and the questioning did not even cease over tuna mayo or egg butties. Jess couldn't stomach anything other than to sip some tea, and even that went cold on her as she sat on her allocated seat across from the chief constable, who was the chair of the group flanked by the ACC Tactical Operations, ACC Crime, the detective superintendent in charge of FMIT and some high-ranking HR bod who sat there with blank eyes for most of the time, completely out of her depth.

It was an in-depth interview and questioned everything Jess had done, what her decision-making process had been right from the first incident at Wolf Fell Hall when responding to the treble-nine, to deciding to go and attempt to disrupt a robbery in progress with just a PCSO whilst technically off-duty and with no backup.

To be fair, even though the questions were in-depth, Jess had no great problem in answering them in equal depth, though she was now tiring of the process as this was the third formal panel she had faced since finding Samira with a cut on her head and then further finding the trussed-up duchess, two equally trussed-up security guards and two very dead members of the royal family. Plus, of course, the body of Tommy Moss on the gravel in the turning circle outside the hall.

On top of that lot there was the missing gang and their loot, no sign of Leanora Moss and definitely no sign of Maggie Horsefield. All had gone to ground, probably using well-prepared escape routes.

The fact that Lance Drake was also missing was just the cherry on the cake as far as Jess was concerned.

Almost two hours later, the grilling ebbed to a close and the chief announced that Jess could return to work and that the investigation would continue in order to try and apprehend the criminals who were now on a most-wanted list.

The chief herself showed Jess out and accompanied her into the corridor of power. Closing the door to the outer office the chief said, 'Jess, no worries about any of this,' reassuringly. 'As far as I'm concerned you did your job above and beyond the call of duty, which is what I would have expected from what I know of you. You're a one-hundred-and-ten per cent person, and by putting yourself in danger to keep others safe you continue to uphold the proud traditions of this force in protecting the community we serve. I will be telling that lot in there exactly that, and then the crime commissioner.'

'Thank you, ma'am, that's very kind.'

'My words also extend to PCSO Patel also and I will be speaking to her.'

'Thanks again.'

The chief then looked through narrowed eyes at Jess as though assessing her, then said, 'I'd just like to tell you something in confidence, and I know I can trust you.'

Jess nodded, intrigued. 'Yes, you can, boss.'

The chief sort of hustled Jess towards the other side of the corridor of power and stood quite close to her. Jess became even more intrigued.

'I had a phone call,' the chief said.

'Ma'am?' Jess said, wondering where this was going.

'From a very high-ranking member of the royal family.'

'OK.' Jess didn't know whether or not to be impressed.

'The king.'

'Ooooh!' Now she was impressed. 'As in *King Charles*?'

'That's the one. Confidential, obviously, but something you should know: he apologized for the behaviour of the Armstrong-Bentley brothers, neither of whom he knew at all well but acknowledged his distant family connection to them. He knew they were out of control.'

'Certainly were.'

'And something else that is not well known at the moment but came to light during interviews with Carolynne, the Duchess of Dunsop and Newton. She did something she was not legally entitled to do under the terms of her ownership of Wolf Fell Hall and her husband's will.' The chief gave Jess a conspiratorial nod. 'She sold most of the valuable paintings that adorned the walls of the hall years ago . . .'

Jess blinked. 'She what?'

'They were all replaced by fakes. Good fakes. The best fakes, but, nevertheless . . .'

'Fakes,' Jess said in disbelief.

'Apparently she sold them under their market value because she was struggling for cash. She made a lot of money but not the true value of the paintings, and commissioned a well-known forger to do copies so she wouldn't be rumbled.'

'Fakes?' Jess said again, shocked.

The chief nodded, smirking.

'So they robbed a whole load of fakes? A big, proper heist for fake artwork?'

Newby nodded again, grinning. 'It's something FMIT are keeping under wraps for the time being because that knowledge might just come in useful when flushing out the buyers and also the sellers.'

'You mean, and I'm guessing here, it's possible some very influential people have forked out big bad money for paintings they believed were genuine, now have them up on private display in their fortified castles in the hills of Albania or wherever, and pull up a chair, with a glass of fancy wine and a cigar and sit there looking smugly at their ill-gotten loot, thinking they're looking at the business. And they're not! When that truth emerges, I would guess that some very nasty individuals are going to be mightily brassed off, paying for fakes.'

'Which is what FMIT also think,' the Chief said. 'It's a bit of a trump card at the moment, so don't tell anyone,' she warned Jess again.

Samira was still waiting for Jess in the HQ dining room because they'd both come in the same car. Samira had killed a bit of time by going for a stroll on the surrounding roads around the campus, some three miles, but other than that she'd drunk tea and water and waited for her sergeant to reappear from the interrogation.

Jess had recovered some of her appetite since the ordeal and was now eating a sandwich with a brew, with a smirk on her face at the information she was not allowed to share. She even chuckled to herself a couple of times.

'So c'mon, sarge, where is she, where are they?' Samira asked, reviving the fantasy discussion she, Jess, Dougie and Vinnie had had between themselves numerous times since the shootings. So far they'd guessed at the Philippines, the Caribbean, Spain, the Far East or maybe just Anglesey.

Jess chewed thoughtfully on her cheese-and-onion butty, which she loved but knew would give her heartburn later. 'I can't speak for Leanora,' she said, 'but I think sooner, rather than later, Mags will be back in our clutches because she made one very big mistake when she disappeared, two if you include hitting you over the head.'

'What's that?' Samira asked, instinctively touching her scalp, which had required six stitches to repair after Mags had smashed her over the head with a broken chair arm.

'Her daughter.'

'But she took Caitlin with her.'

'Exactly.' Jess stood up. 'She'll be back – but in the meantime, Samira, let's do some policing, look after the community and at the same time hunt down some criminals, which may or may not include a dodgy cop or two.'

'Gotcha,' Samira said.

'Steve, Steve! Will you bloody well re-dress this . . . please?' Mags twisted her arm and looked disgustedly down at the bandage wrapped around the deep but now-stitched gouge made by Leanora's bullet across her bicep. Blood still seeped out of the wound, just tiny spots, even a month down the line and she was terrified of it becoming infected. So far, Steve had managed to keep it clean, having even removed the initial six stitches and replaced them with butterfly ones.

Mags looked over to the other side of the swimming pool at Steve who, affected by the heat of the Spanish sun, was sitting on a lounger in the shade underneath a wide parasol, in shorts and a sweaty T-shirt. He looked up from the fat, dog-eared novel he was trying to read. Mags beckoned him over, pointing at her arm.

'Bleeding again.'

He nodded, put the book down, took another sip of water from his glass – he had never drunk so much water in his life, as the heat dehydrated him constantly – and reluctantly stepped into the baking sunshine. He squatted next to her and gently peeled off the dressing. The doctor they had paid handsomely to stitch the wound had done a decent job, but because Mags had been on the move for three weeks after the gone-wrong heist at Wolf Fell Hall she had messed with it continuously and not allowed it to heal properly.

Now they were holed up in a hilltop villa in the small town of Los Urrutias on the Mar Menor, the saltwater lagoon on the coast of Murcia in Spain, and had been there about a week. It was a property Mags had owned for over a dozen years but rarely used; however, even that being so, she knew if she was going to stay out of police hands she needed to move even further. Fortunately she owned two more Spanish properties and also a villa on Gozo, Malta's sister island, which is where she was ultimately headed, although the prospect of spending a long time in such a barren place did distress her somewhat.

Steve was gentle with her. He inspected the stitches, dabbed them with a tissue. It looked clean and uninfected and was definitely healing, so maybe a week at rest here would do the trick.

'It's all OK,' he said and re-dressed it.

'Thank you, Steve,' Mags said and added genuinely, 'I appreciate what you've done for me.'

'Not a problem, though it's a bit hot for an older guy like me.'

'Once I'm sorted, you do what you have to do,' she promised him. He nodded and stepped back into the shade. 'Oh, where has Caitlin got to?'

'Gone for a walk on the beach, I think.'

'Will you go find her? Don't like it when I haven't seen her for over ten minutes.'

'She's with Lance and the dogs, so she'll be OK,' Steve assured her. 'But I'll go check.'

'Thanks, love.'

Mags lay back on the lounger which was fully in the sun. She was wearing a tiny bikini leaving little to the imagination, loved the heat on her skin. She tilted her head back to expose her throat and, not for the first time, ran through the images in her mind of that night at Wolf Fell Hall and the days and weeks that followed, but it was only now, after weeks on the road, having to constantly placate Caitlin, who moaned like *FUCK*, that she could spend just a little bit of time grieving for Tommy.

It had been an intense period.

There had been no way, even after being shot, that Mags was going to stay put and wait for the return of Jess Raker to the drawing room, or, God forbid, Leanora, so whilst the PCSO was busy heaving a broken table to barricade the door, and in spite of her wound, blood loss and weakening state, a determined Mags, who had no intention of ending up behind bars, selected a nice, chunky, broken piece of a chair arm and whacked the poor girl across the head as hard as possible, then managed to squirm out of the door and pull it shut behind her.

She knew Wolf Fell Hall well, having been there on too many occasions, so, clutching her wounded arm, she headed to the steps leading down to the kitchen in the basement, then out through the back door into the grounds and across the lawn towards the trees, at the same time managing to call Steve on her mobile phone.

'Get the Rolls, get the Rolls!' she implored him. 'It's all gone to rats!'

Somehow – and more by luck than judgement – they coordinated a meeting point, mainly because Steve remained cool and calm, unhurried, and as Mags stumbled out on to the lane just below Burnslack Fell, Steve was doing a tight, six-point turn in the Rolls-Royce on the narrow lane.

He helped her into the back of the car and she threw herself across the back seat, noticing that Steve had acquired a front seat passenger, namely Lance Drake.

'Hell's he doing here?' Mags demanded.

'Long story,' Steve muttered as he gunned the big car back down the lane as Mags sank into the leather and passed out.

From then it was just a series of images.

The tame doctor, a local GP from Clitheroe, was woken from his slumber by Steve and dragged from his bed to perform a clean-up and surgery on Mags' wound and supply good painkillers for which he was paid very well and told to keep very quiet. Then across to Primrose Breakers where the Rolls-Royce was abandoned and Steve's old BMW Alpina was taken into service. The hidden box under the desk was emptied of its contents, but not the gun which was left in there. The two XL bullies, Spike and Bullseye, were bundled into the back seat of the BMW alongside a very hazy Mags (and much to Lance's terror) and after more raids on other pre-prepared 'run' boxes filled with cash, pre-paid bank cards and passports, and another change of vehicle, Steve drove to Mags' house in Hurst Green and added Caitlin to the entourage.

There then followed a long, difficult journey, all sorted by Steve, and involving more vehicle changes, ferry journeys, sitting inside containers on goods vehicles and long hours along long roads in the night until finally the last leg down the coast in Murcia and the mothballed villa near Los Urrutias where Mags holed up whilst planning the next stage of her journey – and life.

As she lay on the sun lounger she could not stop thinking about Tommy Moss and the possibility of their future together which had been shattered by bullets and a mad Leanora.

A woman Mags was not yet finished with.

At first it was terrifying but exciting for Caitlin. She wasn't thick and knew exactly what her mother was involved in, the drug dealing and the rest, and as long as it didn't impact her she didn't care too much. Having so much wealth was nice, to be honest, but her secret ambition was to eventually get away from home when she was old enough and the first part of that was to do well at school, then university and then up sticks to New York or somewhere equally fab and leave Mags behind. It was a long-term plan and she was happy to bide her time, work diligently and keep out of trouble.

The last thing she expected was the middle of the night disruption by Steve, her mother, Lance and two dogs, being forced to pack quickly and have her phone taken from her and smashed to pieces, and then the long, arduous journey through England and Spain, which was like an ever-changing nightmare, until they arrived in Murcia with hardly any conversation between any of them, just a gritted teeth, stressed-out marathon.

But now she had had enough. She wanted to contact her friends and then go home, neither of which was something that Mags or Steve would allow. And to cap it all, Lance Drake, who Caitlin found well creepy, unofficially became her bodyguard, keeping watch on her. Not a nice experience. The only plus point was that he was terrified of the XLs and they knew it.

In turn, Lance could not believe his luck. He thought that Steve was going to finish him off whilst he was attached to the lamppost, completing the job that Dimbo's killers had begun. Instead he used a pair of bolt cutters from the boot of the Rolls to cut him free but then threw him into the car when his phone went berserk and suddenly everything became urgent, and Lance, being Lance, saw an opportunity to save his own neck again by becoming useful to Mags.

And life wasn't that bad for him, even though he wasn't all that comfortable watching over Caitlin because he could see she was highly amused by his fear of the two dogs, which responded to her every instruction but always looked at him as if they were going to savage him. She took every opportunity to make him look after them. *Little cow*, he thought.

And that morning Caitlin had decided to go for a walk down to the beach by the Mar Menor with the dogs which meant Lance had to go with her and hold their leads. It tickled her to watch him try to control the two muzzled dogs, but she also had an ulterior motive for going out. She had found a shop in the village that sold SIM-only mobile phones and her plan was to use the dogs to distract Lance so she could sneakily nip into the shop, buy a phone and make secret contact with some of her friends, despite her mother's and Steve's dire warnings not to.

Sod them, she thought as she walked along the beach, looking into the shallow water in which thousands of huge, fried-egg-like jellyfish proliferated despite the use of anti-jellyfish nets.

She looked around at Lance who was holding the leads of the dogs like reins, trying to control them and also stop them from attacking him. They were getting used to him but it was still funny.

But Caitlin stopped and turned, frowning, as she saw two men come up behind Lance who seemed out of place on a beach, wearing black joggers and tops and approaching quickly. Then Caitlin saw the guns at their sides and she screamed.

Mags stirred on hearing the noise of a door closing and a scraping noise of some sort, but she didn't open her eyes as, really, all she wanted to do was sleep and get back her strength. She assumed Caitlin, Steve and Lance were all back, but found it slightly strange she didn't hear their voices, nor the sound of the dogs' claws as they ran out to the pool area.

Then she heard the scraping sound of the empty sun lounger next to her being moved. Still not opening her eyes, she said, 'Good walk, Caitlin?'

There was no response and this time she did open her eyes, but all she could see, filling her vision, were the two muzzles of a side-by-side double barrelled shotgun just inches away from her face. Then she focused on the person holding the weapon.

'Hello, Mags,' said Leanora.